PENGUIN MODERN CLASSICS

# THE GRAND BABYLON HOTEL

Arnold Bennett was born in 1867 in the 'Potteries' – the region of England about which almost all his best novels were written. After studying art for a time, he began to prepare for his father's profession, that of solicitor; and at twenty-one he left Staffordshire to work in the office of a London firm.

He wrote a novel called *A Man from the North*, having meanwhile become assistant editor of a woman's weekly. Later he edited this paper, and noticed that the serial stories which were offered to him by a literary syndicate were not as good as they should be. He wrote a serial and sold it to the syndicate for £75. This sale encouraged him to write another, which became famous. It was *The Grand Babylon Hotel*.

He also wrote much serious criticism, and a serious novel, *Anna of the Five Towns*; and at last decided to give up his editorship and devote himself wholly to writing. This decision took him to Paris, where in the course of the next eight years he wrote a number of novels, several plays, and, at length, *The Old Wives' Tale*, which was an immediate success throughout the English-speaking world.

Subsequently Bennett wrote many other books, ranging from the farce of *The Card* to the elaborate documentation of *Imperial Palace*, and when he died in 1931 he was one of the best-loved figures in literary London, as well as being famous abroad.

# THE GRAND
# BABYLON HOTEL

*A Fantasia on Modern Themes*

ARNOLD BENNETT

PENGUIN BOOKS

Penguin Books Ltd, Harmondsworth, Middlesex, England
Viking Penguin Inc., 40 West 23rd Street, New York, New York 10010, U.S.A.
Penguin Books Australia Ltd, Ringwood, Victoria, Australia
Penguin Books Canada Ltd, 2801 John Street, Markham, Ontario, Canada L3R 1B4
Penguin Books (N.Z.) Ltd, 182–190 Wairau Road, Auckland 10, New Zealand

—

First published 1902
Published in Penguin Books 1938
Reprinted 1939, 1954, 1972, 1976, 1985

—

—

Printed and bound in Great Britain by
Cox & Wyman Ltd, Reading
Set in Intertype Plantin

# CONTENTS

# CONTENTS

# INTRODUCTION

WHEN Arnold Bennett was a boy in the Potteries, two of his favourite authors were Eugène Sue, who wrote *The Mysteries of Paris,* and Ouida, who pictured in some of her books the richly coloured doings of an imaginary high society. These works, for Bennett, were the equivalent of another boy's 'penny dreadfuls'; and if the term had been known in the early eighteen-eighties they would have been described as 'escapes' from the humdrum of the Five Towns.

They were not escapes; they answered a sedate boy's need for sweets or spices. Arnold Bennett liked sweets. There is a story that when on one occasion he was dining with Hugh Walpole the host had provided no pudding. Bennett said 'I must have my sweet'; and calmly proceeded with the privilege of an old friend to leave Walpole's flat, walk along to the Ritz or the Royal Thames Yacht Club, and have one. He then, in complete good humour, resumed his place at Walpole's table. In the same way, when he had written a grave book, he liked to follow it with what he called 'a lark'.

Long after he had left the Potteries at the age of twenty-one, and when he had for some time consorted with various young painters and musicians, he discovered with surprise that his friends expected him to make a reputation as a writer. 'Their belief in what I could do,' he wrote, 'kept me awake at nights.' It had the effect of causing him to begin a very serious novel indeed.

It was published, when he was thirty, under the title of *A Man from the North;* and as chance and influence by that time had made him first assistant editor and then editor of a weekly journal called *Woman,* he found himself committed to a literary career. Part of his work for *Woman* involved the purchase of stories for the paper; and as was common at that time he derived them from a great newspaper syndicate. The syndicate bought all rights from the authors; leased serial rights to editors all over the world; and in time sold the book rights to publishers. In this way such then famous popular novelists as S. Baring-Gould, William le Queux, and L. T. Meade made a regular living; and were sometimes inconvenienced when what they had forgotten having written turned up among a season's publications.

One day Bennett felt extremely dissatisfied with what was offered to him by this syndicate. Having come from the Potteries, he was given to sudden romantic ideas, and to abrupt and humorous boasts, all of which came from the heart. Turning dissatisfaction in his mind, therefore, he received from his romantic sense the notion that he, and no other, could do something better. He had published, besides *A Man from the North,* two other books, *Journalism for Women* and a small collection of what he called *Polite Farces;* he had reached the age of thirty; and he was instinctively seeking a new outlet for a lively talent. When next the syndicate's representative called upon him, accordingly, he said (no doubt stammering, as was incurably his habit from childhood): 'Why should all the buying be on one side? You know I'm an author.'

The syndicate's representative was uncooperative. He replied that he never bought serials from editors. Evidently, thought Bennett, this situation had arisen before; and it must be handled as only a man from the north could handle it. He did not insist. He remarked that there were other syndicates, that he was writing a serial, and that the serial would be a good one. He then gave the representative an order for other men's serials.

This, in a sense, was the first chapter in a long story. The truth was that Bennett had no plan for his serial. It was his way, as long as he lived, to make bold and boyish assertions of this kind; and he was forced by self-respect, having made them, to keep his promises. Having heard the boasts, men of smaller genius believed that he lived according to calculation, whereas he was as simple as that 'simple soul' Arthur Kipps. If you read *The Card,* which was about a fellow-townsman, H. K. Hales, and bear in mind that everything in that book is intended to be fantastic, you will understand how typical a lad from the Potteries Arnold Bennett was, and how he united to the strictest integrity an impulsive trick of pretending to have schemed something the possibility of which had just entered his head.

It was so with this first serial, which was called *For Love and Life*. He had told the syndicate's representative that it was being written; therefore it must be written. He called upon his brain to invent a story; and as he had noticed, in buying serials, that most of them lacked any powerful central theme, he determined that what he wrote must surpass all other serials by the grandeur of its invention. Memories of Ouida, of Wilkie Collins, of Eugène Sue crowded to his mind. He did not forget the aplomb with which Dumas handled a dazzlingly tall story. And soon he was fired by a splendid idea.

*For Love and Life* was written in twenty-four half-days; and the copyright was sold for seventy-five pounds. When the book was finished, Arnold Bennett saw all the possibilities he had missed through ignorance and inexperience. I am quite sure he told nobody about the misses; instead, he resolved, having taken that particular tide, that his next serial should be 'absolutely sublime in those qualities that should characterize a sensational serial . . .

I imagined a serial decked with the profuse ornament of an Eastern princess, a serial at once grandiose and witty, at once modern and transcendental, a serial of which the interest should gradually close on the reader like a vice until it became intolerable. I saw the whole of London preoccupied with this serial instead of with cricket and politics. I heard the dandiacal City youths discussing in first-class compartments on the Underground what would happen next in it. I witnessed a riot in Fleet Street because I had, accidentally on purpose, delayed my copy for twenty-four hours. . . . I did not realize my dream, but I was inspired by it.

He was inspired by it. The plot which came to him was less fine, he thought, than the previous one; but it began 'with a scene quite unique in the annals of syndicates.' It was the scene – you will find it here in hardly more than a couple of pages – where Theodore Racksole orders an Angel Kiss at the Grand Babylon Hotel, and in spite of the insolence of Jules, head waiter at that fabulously select establishment, obtains it. What follows is equally surprising, although it must be pointed out at once that when *The Grand Babylon Hotel* was written Edgar Wallace was still a journalist, and may easily have read and forgotten *The Grand Babylon Hotel* before, five years after its serialization, he invented *The Four Just Men*. Edgar Wallace had the cool, steady inventiveness of an instinctive gambler: to Arnold Bennett invention was a lark.

'I tried,' said he, 'to feel as much like Dumas *père* as I could. But when I had done I felt, physically, rather more like the fragile Shelley or some wan curate than Dumas.' He wrote the fifteen instalments in fifteen days. He sold the story for a hundred pounds. The syndicate sold first serial rights in it to *The Golden Penny,* which advertised tumultuously week after week on 800 railway stations and lavished magnificent illustrations upon every instalment. The paper described *The Grand Babylon Hotel* as the most original, amusing, and thrilling serial written in a decade, and the best thing of the sort since *The Mystery of a Hansom Cab*. Bennett's modest, astounded comment, made in his Journal for 18 January 1901, was 'Fancy writing a story as good as *The Mystery of a Hansom Cab!*'

*The Grand Babylon Hotel* was sold as a book to Messrs Chatto & Windus, who published it, with comparable enthusiasm, in the same year as Bennett's extremely ambitious serious novel, *Anna of the Five Towns*. They also bought, from the same syndicate, not only *For Love and Life,* which was re-titled *The Ghost,* but his other serials and 'fantasias'; and the author was afterwards to regret the impossibility of preventing their publication in book form. He did not regret *The Grand Babylon Hotel,* which until he wrote *The Old Wives' Tale* was the most famous of his works.

It led to a general assumption among superior persons that he was seriously enraptured by the splendours of luxury hotels. He was called a vulgarian whose eye was perpetually upon money and meretricious display. But readers of *The Grand Babylon Hotel* will observe that, in accordance with the practice of the greatest writers, Bennett refrained from particularizing the ornaments of his scene: he merely said they were magnificent. What interested him were the wonders of an immense microcosm. Theodore Racksole's discovery of the laundry system, of the wine cellars, of the kitchens testifies to this interest. 'It's strange how facts like those,' remarks a character in the book, 'unimportant in themselves, appeal to the imagination.' They appealed to Bennett's imagination. Just as he was struck one day in the Forest of Fontainbleau by a thought of the myriads of insects and small animals which must be all around him, so the sense of hundreds of human lives grouped about and dominated by a single industry stirred him deeply. He never escaped from it.

As for the sensational story of what Theodore Racksole discovered after buying the Grand Babylon as a multi-millionaire's whim, it is before you. The book is more than half a century old; the discomfitures of the leading actors, and their escapes from strange predicaments, were conditioned by the need to make each instalment conclude with a thrill; more sophisticated romances have accustomed us to themes and discussions of greater complexity. But the book has already had a lengthy life; and if a comparison with *The Mystery of a Hansom Cab* no longer excites us, as it did the author, that is because *The Grand Babylon Hotel* set a new standard for such books. It should be read as what Arnold Bennett intended it to be, a lark.

*1953*                                        FRANK SWINNERTON

## Chapter One

# THE MILLIONAIRE AND THE WAITER

'YES, sir?'

Jules, the celebrated head waiter of the Grand Babylon, was bending formally towards the alert, middle-aged man who had just entered the smoking-room and dropped into a basket-chair in the corner by the conservatory. It was 7.45 on a particularly sultry June night, and dinner was about to be served at the Grand Babylon. Men of all sizes, ages, and nationalities, but every one alike arrayed in faultless evening dress, were dotted about the large, dim apartment. A faint odour of flowers came from the conservatory, and the tinkle of a fountain. The waiters, commanded by Jules, moved softly across the thick Oriental rugs, balancing their trays with the dexterity of jugglers, and receiving and executing orders with that air of profound importance of which only really first-class waiters have the secret. The atmosphere was an atmosphere of serenity and repose, characteristic of the Grand Babylon. It seemed impossible that anything could occur to mar the peaceful, aristocratic monotony of existence in that perfectly-managed establishment. Yet on that night was to happen the mightiest upheaval that the Grand Babylon had ever known.

'Yes, sir?' repeated Jules, and this time there was a shade of august disapproval in his voice: it was not usual for him to have to address a customer twice.

'Oh!' said the alert, middle-aged man, looking up at length. Beautifully ignorant of the identity of the great Jules, he allowed his grey eyes to twinkle as he caught sight of the expression on the waiter's face. 'Bring me an Angel Kiss.'

'Pardon, sir?'

'Bring me an Angel Kiss, and be good enough to lose no time.'

'If it's an American drink, I fear we don't keep it, sir.' The voice of Jules fell icily distinct, and several men glanced round uneasily, as if to deprecate the slightest disturbance of their calm.

The appearance of the person to whom Jules was speaking, how-ever, reassured them somewhat, for he had all the look of that expert, the travelled Englishman, who can differentiate between one hotel and another by instinct, and who knows at once where he may make a fuss with propriety, and where it is advisable to behave exactly as at the club. The Grand Babylon was a hotel in whose smoking-room one behaved as though one was at one's club.

'I didn't suppose you did keep it, but you can mix it, I guess, even in this hotel.'

'This isn't an American hotel, sir.' The calculated insolence of the words was cleverly masked beneath an accent of humble submission.

The alert, middle-aged man sat up straight, and gazed placidly at Jules, who was pulling his famous red side-whiskers.

'Get a liqueur glass,' he said, half curtly and half with good-humoured tolerance, 'pour into it equal quantities of maraschino, cream, and crème de menthe. Don't stir it; don't shake it. Bring it to me. And, I say, tell the bar-tender —'

'Bar-tender, sir?'

'Tell the bar-tender to make a note of the recipe, as I shall probably want an Angel Kiss every evening before dinner so long as this weather lasts.'

'I will send the drink to you, sir,' said Jules distantly. That was his parting shot, by which he indicated that he was not as other waiters are, and that any person who treated him with disrespect did so at his own peril.

A few minutes later, while the alert, middle-aged man was tasting the Angel Kiss, Jules sat in conclave with Miss Spencer, who had charge of the bureau of the Grand Babylon. This bureau was a fairly large chamber, with two sliding glass partitions which overlooked the entrance-hall and the smoking-room. Only a small portion of the clerical work of the great hotel was performed there. The place served chiefly as the lair of Miss Spencer, who was as well known and as important as Jules himself. Most modern hotels have a male clerk to superintend the bureau. But the Grand Babylon went its own way. Miss Spencer had been bureau clerk almost since the Grand Babylon had first raised its massive chimneys to heaven, and she remained in her place despite the vagaries of other hotels. Always admirably dressed in plain black silk, with a small diamond brooch, immaculate wristbands, and frizzed yellow hair, she looked now just as she had looked an indefinite number of years ago. Her age – none knew it, save herself and perhaps one other, and none cared. The gracious and alluring contours of her figure were irreproachable; and in the evenings she was a useful ornament of which any hotel might be innocently proud. Her knowledge of Bradshaw, of steamship services, and the programmes of theatres and musichalls was unrivalled; yet she never travelled, she never went to a theatre or a music-hall. She seemed to spend the whole of her life in that official lair of hers, imparting information to guests, telephoning to the various departments, or engaged in intimate conversations with her special friends on the staff, as at present.

'Who's Number 107?' Jules asked this black-robed lady.

Miss Spencer examined her ledgers.

'Mr Theodore Racksole, New York.'

'I thought he must be a New Yorker,' said Jules, after a brief, significant pause, 'but he talks as good English as you or me. Says he wants an "Angel Kiss" – maraschino and cream, if you please – every night. I'll see he doesn't stop here too long.'

Miss Spencer smiled grimly in response. The notion of referring to Theodore Racksole as a 'New Yorker' appealed to her sense of humour, a sense in which she was not entirely deficient. She knew, of course, and she knew that Jules knew, that this Theodore Racksole must be the unique and only Theodore Racksole, the third richest man in the United States, and therefore probably in the world. Nevertheless she ranged herself at once on the side of Jules. Just as there was only one Racksole, so there was only one Jules, and Miss Spencer instinctively shared the latter's indignation at the spectacle of any person whatsoever, millionaire or Emperor, presuming to demand an 'Angel Kiss', that unrespectable concoction of maraschino and cream, within the precincts of the Grand Babylon. In the world of hotels it was currently stated that, next to the proprietor, there were three gods at the Grand Babylon – Jules, the head waiter, Miss Spencer, and, most powerful of all, Rocco, the renowned chef, who earned two thousand a year, and had a chalet on the Lake of Lucerne. All the great hotels in Northumberland Avenue and on the Thames Embankment had tried to get Rocco away from the Grand Babylon, but without success. Rocco was well aware that even he could rise no higher than the *maître hôtel* of the Grand Babylon, which, though it never advertised itself, and didn't belong to a limited company, stood an easy first among the hotels of Europe – first in expensiveness, first in exclusiveness, first in that mysterious quality known as 'style'.

Situated on the Embankment, the Grand Babylon, despite its noble proportions, was somewhat dwarfed by several colossal neighbours. It had but three hundred and fifty rooms, whereas there are two hotels within a quarter of a mile with six hundred and four hundred rooms respectively. On the other hand, the Grand Babylon was the only hotel in London with a genuine separate entrance for Royal visitors constantly in use. The Grand Babylon counted that day wasted on which it did not entertain, at the lowest, a German prince or the Maharajah of some Indian State. When Félix Babylon – after whom, and not with any reference to London's nickname, the hotel was christened – when Félix Babylon founded the hotel in 1869 he had set himself to cater for Royalty, and that was the secret of his triumphant eminence. The son of a rich Swiss hotel proprietor and financier, he had contrived to established a connection with the officials of several European Courts, and he had not spared money in that respect. Sundry kings and not a few princesses called him Félix, and spoke familiarly of the hotel as 'Félix's'; and Félix had found that this was very good for trade. The Grand Babylon was managed accordingly. The 'note' of its policy was discretion, always discretion, and quietude, simplicity, remoteness. The place was like a palace incognito. There was no gold sign over the roof, not even an explanatory word at the entrance. You walked down a small side street off the Strand, you saw a plain brown building in front of you, with two mahogany swing doors, and an official behind each; the doors opened noiselessly; you entered;

you were in Félix's. If you meant to be a guest, you, or your courier, gave your card to Miss Spencer. Upon no consideration did you ask for the tariff. It was not good form to mention prices at the Grand Babylon; the prices were enormous, but you never mentioned them. At the conclusion of your stay a bill was presented, brief and void of dry details, and you paid it without a word. You met with a stately civility, that was all. No one had originally asked you to come; no one expressed the hope that you would come again. The Grand Babylon was far above such manoeuvres; it defied competition by ignoring it; and consequently was nearly always full during the season.

If there was one thing more than another that annoyed the Grand Babylon – put its back up, so to speak – it was to be compared with, or to be mistaken for, an American hotel. The Grand Babylon was resolutely opposed to American methods of eating, drinking, and lodging – but especially American methods of drinking. The resentment of Jules, on being requested to supply Mr Theodore Racksole with an Angel Kiss, will therefore be appreciated.

'Anybody with Mr Theodore Racksole?' asked Jules, continuing his conversation with Miss Spencer. He put a scornful stress on every syllable of the guest's name.

'Miss Racksole – she's in No. 111.'

Jules paused, and stroked his left whisker as it lay on his gleaming white collar.

'She's where?' he queried, with a peculiar emphasis.

'No. 111. I couldn't help it. There was no other room with a bathroom and dressing-room on that floor.' Miss Spencer's voice had an appealing tone of excuse.

'Why didn't you tell Mr Theodore Racksole and Miss Racksole that we were unable to accommodate them?'

'Because Babs was within hearing.'

Only three people in the wide world ever dreamt of applying to Mr Félix Babylon the playful but mean abbreviation – Babs: those three were Jules, Miss Spencer, and Rocco. Jules had invented it. No one but he would have had either the wit or the audacity to do so.

'You'd better see that Miss Racksole changes her room to-night,' Jules said after another pause. 'Leave it to me: I'll fix it. Au revoir! It's three minutes to eight. I shall take charge of the dining-room myself to-night.' And Jules departed, rubbing his fine white hands slowly and meditatively. It was a trick of his, to rub his hands with a strange, roundabout motion, and the action denoted that some unusual excitement was in the air.

At eight o'clock precisely dinner was served in the immense salle à manger, that chaste yet splendid apartment of white and gold. At a small table near one of the windows a young lady sat alone. Her frocks said Paris, but her face unmistakably said New York. It was a self-possessed and bewitching face, the face of a woman thoroughly accustomed to doing exactly what she liked, when she liked, how she liked: the face of a woman who had taught hundreds of gilded young men the true art of fetching and carrying, and who, by twenty years or so of parental spoiling, had come to regard herself as the feminine equivalent of the Tsar of All the Russias. Such women are only made in America, and they only come to their full bloom in Europe, which they imagine to be a continent created by Providence for their diversion.

The young lady by the window glanced disapprovingly at the menu card. Then she looked round the dining-room, and, while admiring the diners, decided that the room itself was rather small and plain. Then she gazed through the open window, and told herself that though the Thames by twilight was passable enough, it was by no means level with the Hudson, on whose shores her father had a hundred thousand dollar country cottage. Then she returned to the menu, and with a pursing of lovely lips said that there appeared to be nothing to eat.

'Sorry to keep you waiting, Nella.' It was Mr Racksole, the intrepid millionaire who had dared to order an Angel Kiss in the smoke-room of the Grand Babylon. Nella – her proper name was Helen – smiled at her parent cautiously, reserving to herself the right to scold if she should feel so inclined.

'You always are late, father,' she said.

'Only on a holiday,' he added. 'What is there to eat?'

'Nothing.'

'Then let's have it. I'm hungry. I'm never so hungry as when I'm being seriously idle.'

'*Consommé Britannia*,' she began to read out from the menu, '*Saumon d'Ecosse, Sauce Génoise, Aspics de Homard*. Oh, heavens! Who wants these horrid messes on a night like this?'

'But, Nella, this is the best cooking in Europe,' he protested.

'Say, father,' she said, with seeming irrelevance, 'had you forgotten it's my birthday to-morrow?'

'Have I ever forgotten your birthday, O most costly daughter?'

'On the whole you've been a most satisfactory dad,' she answered sweetly, 'and to reward you I'll be content this year with the cheapest birthday treat you ever gave me. Only I'll have it to-night.'

'Well,' he said, with the long-suffering patience, the readiness for any surprise, of a parent whom Nella had thoroughly trained, 'what is it?'

'It's this. Let's have filleted steak and a bottle of Bass for dinner to-night. It will be simply exquisite. I shall love it.'

'But my dear Nella,' he exclaimed, 'steak and beer at Félix's! It's impossible! Moreover, young women still under twenty-three cannot be permitted to drink Bass.'

'I said steak and Bass, and as for being twenty-three, shall be going in twenty-four to-morrow.'

Miss Racksole set her small white teeth.

There was a gentle cough. Jules stood over them. It must have been out of a pure spirit of adventure that he had selected this table for his own services. Usually Jules did not personally wait at dinner. He merely hovered observant, like a captain on the bridge during the mate's watch. Regular frequenters of the hotel felt themselves honoured when Jules attached himself to their tables.

Theodore Racksole hesitated one second, and then issued the order with a fine air of carelessness:

'Filleted steak for two, and a bottle of Bass.' It was the bravest act of Theodore Racksole's life, and yet at more than one previous crisis a high courage had not been lacking to him.

'It's not in the menu, sir,' said Jules the imperturbable.

'Never mind. Get it. We want it.'

'Very good, sir.'

Jules walked to the service-door, and, merely affecting to look behind, came immediately back again.

'Mr Rocco's compliments, sir, and he regrets to be unable to serve steak and Bass to-night, sir.'

'Mr Rocco?' questioned Racksole lightly.

'Mr Rocco,' repeated Jules with firmness.

'And who is Mr Rocco?'

'Mr Rocco is our chef, sir.' Jules had the expression of a man who is asked to explain who Shakespeare was.

The two men looked at each other. It seemed incredible that Theodore Racksole, the ineffable Racksole, who owned a thousand miles of railway, several towns, and sixty votes in Congress, should be defied by a waiter, or even by a whole hotel. Yet so it was. When Europe's effete back is against the wall not a regiment of millionaires can turn its flank. Jules had the calm expression of a strong man sure of victory. His face said: 'You beat me once, but not this time, my New York friend!'

As for Nella, knowing her father, she foresaw interesting events, and waited confidently for the steak. She did not feel hungry, and she could afford to wait.

'Excuse me a moment, Nella,' said Theodore Racksole quietly, 'I shall be back in about two seconds,' and he strode out of the salle à manger. No one in the room recognized the millionaire, for he was unknown to London, this being his first visit to Europe for over twenty years. Had anyone done so, and caught the expression on his face, that man might have trembled for an explosion which should have blown the entire Grand Babylon into the Thames. Jules retired strategically to a corner. He had fired; it was the antagonist's turn. A long and varied experience had taught Jules that a guest who embarks on the subjugation of a waiter is almost always lost; the waiter has so many advantages in such a contest.

## Chapter Two

# HOW MR RACKSOLE OBTAINED HIS DINNER

NEVERTHELESS, there are men with a confirmed habit of getting their own way, even as guests in an exclusive hotel: and Theodore Racksole had long since fallen into that useful practice – except when his only daughter Helen, motherless but high-spirited girl, chose to think that his way crossed hers, in which case Theodore capitulated and fell back. But when Theodore and his daughter happened to be going one and the same road, which was pretty often, then Heaven alone might help any obstacle that was so ill-advised as to stand in their path. Jules, great and observant man though he was, had not noticed the terrible projecting chins of both father and daughter, otherwise it is possible he would have reconsidered the question of the steak and Bass.

Theodore Racksole went direct to the entrance-hall of the hotel, and entered Miss Spencer's sanctum.

'I want to see Mr Babylon,' he said, 'without the delay of an instant.'

Miss Spencer leisurely raised her flaxen head.

'I am afraid – ,' she began the usual formula. It was part of her daily duty to discourage guests who desired to see Mr Babylon.

'No, no,' said Racksole quickly, 'I don't want any "I'm afraids." This is business. If you had been the ordinary hotel clerk I should have slipped you a couple of sovereigns into your hand, and the thing would have been done. As you are not – as you are obviously above bribes – I merely say to you, I must see Mr Babylon at once on an affair of the utmost urgency. My name is Racksole – Theodore Racksole.'

'Of New York?' questioned a voice at the door, with a slight foreign accent.

The millionaire turned sharply, and saw a rather short, French-looking man, with a bald head, a grey beard, a long and perfectly-built frock coat, eye-glasses attached to a minute silver chain, and blue eyes that seemed to have the transparent innocence of a maid's.

'There is only one,' said Theodore Racksole succinctly.

'You wish to see me?' the new-comer suggested.

'You are Mr Félix Babylon?'

The man bowed.

'At this moment I wish to see you more than anyone else in the world,' said Racksole. 'I am consumed and burnt up with a desire to see you, Mr Babylon. I only want a few minutes' quiet chat. I fancy I can settle my business in that time.'

With a gesture Mr Babylon invited the millionaire down a side corridor, at the end of which was Mr Babylon's private room, a miracle of Louis XV furniture and tapestry: like most unmarried men with large incomes, Mr Babylon had 'tastes' of a highly expensive sort.

The landlord and his guest sat down opposite each other. Theodore Racksole had met with the usual millionaire's luck in this adventure, for Mr Babylon made a practice of not allowing himself to be interviewed by his guests, however distinguished, however wealthy, however pertinacious. If he had not chanced to enter Miss Spencer's office at that precise moment, and if he had not been impressed in a somewhat peculiar way by the physiognomy of the millionaire, not all Mr Racksole's American energy and ingenuity would have availed for a confabulation with the owner of the Grand Babylon Hotel that night. Theodore Racksole, however, was ignorant that a mere accident had served him. He took all the credit to himself.

'I read in the New York papers some months ago,' Theodore started, without even a clearing of the throat, 'that this hotel of yours, Mr Babylon, was to be sold to a limited company, but it appears that the sale was not carried out.'

'It was not,' answered Mr Babylon frankly, 'and the reason was that the middle-men between the proposed company and myself wished to make a large secret profit, and I declined to be a party to such a profit. They were firm; I was firm; and so the affair came to nothing.'

'The agreed price was satisfactory?'

'Quite.'

'May I ask what the price was?'

'Are you a buyer, Mr Racksole?'

'Are you a seller, Mr Babylon?'

'I am,' said Babylon, 'on terms. The price was four hundred thousand pounds, including the leasehold and goodwill. But I sell only on the condition that the buyer does not transfer the property to a limited company at a higher figure.'

'I will put one question to you, Mr Babylon,' said the millionaire. 'What have your profits averaged during the last four years?'

'Thirty-four thousand pounds per annum.'

'I buy,' said Theodore Racksole, smiling contentedly; 'and we will, if you please, exchange contract-letters on the spot.'

'You come quickly to a resolution, Mr Racksole. But perhaps you have been considering this question for a long time?'

'On the contrary,' Racksole looked at his watch, 'I have been considering it for just six minutes.'

Félix Babylon bowed, as one thoroughly accustomed to eccentricity of wealth.

'The beauty of being well-known,' Racksole continued, 'is that you needn't trouble about preliminary explanations. You, Mr Babylon, probably know all about me. I know a good deal about you. We can take each other for granted without reference. Really, it is as simple to buy an hotel or a railroad as it is to buy a watch, provided one is equal to the transaction.'

'Precisely,' agreed Mr Babylon smiling. 'Shall we draw up the little informal contract? There are details to be thought of. But it occurs to me that you cannot have dined yet, and might prefer to deal with minor questions after dinner.'

'I have not dined,' said the millionaire, with emphasis, 'and in that connexion will you do me a favour? Will you send for Mr Rocco?'

'You wish to see him, naturally.'

'I do,' said the millionaire, and added, 'about my dinner.'

'Rocco is a great man,' murmured Mr Babylon as he touched the bell, ignoring the last words. 'My compliments to Mr Rocco,' he said to the page who answered his summons, 'and if it is quite convenient I should be glad to see him here for a moment.'

'What do you give Rocco?' Racksole inquired.

'Two thousand a year and the treatment of an Ambassador.'

'I shall give him the treatment of an Ambassador and three thousand.'

'You will be wise,' said Félix Babylon.

At that moment Rocco came into the room, very softly – a man of forty, thin, with long, thin hands, and an inordinately long brown silky moustache.

'Rocco,' said Félix Babylon, 'let me introduce Mr Theodore Racksole, of New York.'

'Sharmed,' said Rocco, bowing. 'Ze – ze, vat you call it, millionaire?'

'Exactly,' Racksole put in, and continued quickly: 'Mr Rocco, I wish to acquaint you before any other person with the fact that I have purchased the Grand Babylon Hotel. If you think well to afford me the privilege of retaining your services I shall be happy to offer you a remuneration of three thousand a year.'

'Tree, you said?'

'Three.'

'Sharmed.'

'And now, Mr Rocco, will you oblige me very much by ordering a plain beefsteak and a bottle of Bass to be served by Jules – I particularly desire Jules – at table No. 17 in the dining-room in ten minutes from now? And will you do me the honour of lunching with me to-morrow?'

Mr Rocco gasped, bowed, muttered something in French, and departed.

Five minutes later the buyer and seller of the Grand Babylon Hotel had each signed a curt document, scribbled out on the hotel note-paper. Félix Babylon asked no questions, and it was this heroic absence of curiosity, of surprise on his part, that more than anything else impressed Theodore Racksole. How many hotel proprietors in the world, Racksole asked himself, would have let that beef-steak and Bass go by without a word of comment.

'From what date do you wish the purchase to take effect?' asked Babylon.

'Oh,' said Racksole lightly, 'it doesn't matter. Shall we say from to-night?'

'As you will. I have long wished to retire. And now that the moment has come – and so dramatically – I am ready. I shall return to Switzerland. One cannot spend much money there, but it is my native land. I shall be the richest man in Switzerland.' He smiled with a kind of sad amusement.

'I suppose you *are* fairly well off?' said Racksole, in that easy familiar style of his, as though the idea had just occurred to him.

'Besides what I shall receive from you, I have half a million invested.'

'Then you will be nearly a millionaire?'

Félix Babylon nodded.

'I congratulate you, my dear sir,' said Racksole, in the tone of a judge addressing a newly-admitted barrister. 'Nine hundred thousand pounds, expressed in francs, will sound very nice – in Switzerland.'

'Of course to you, Mr Racksole, such a sum would be poverty. Now if one might guess at your own wealth?' Félix Babylon was imitating the other's freedom.

'I do not know, to five millions or so, what I am worth,' said Racksole, with sincerity, his tone indicating that he would have been glad to give the information if it were in his power.

'You have had anxieties, Mr Racksole?'

'Still have them. I am now holiday-making in London with my daughter in order to get rid of them for a time.'

'Is the purchase of hotels your notion of relaxation, then?'

Racksole shrugged his shoulders. 'It is a change from rail-roads,' he laughed.

'Ah, my friend, you little know what you have bought.'

'Oh! yes I do,' returned Racksole; 'I have bought just the first hotel in the world.'

'That is true, that is true,' Babylon admitted, gazing meditatively at the antique Persian carpet. 'There is nothing, anywhere, like my hotel. But you will regret the purchase, Mr Racksole. It is no business of mine, of course, but I cannot help repeating that you will regret the purchase.'

'I never regret.'

'Then you will begin very soon – perhaps to-night.'

'Why do you say that?'

'Because the Grand Babylon is the Grand Babylon. You think because you control a railroad, or an iron-works, or a line of steamers, therefore you can control anything. But no. Not the Grand Babylon. There is something about the Grand Babylon –' He threw up his hands.

'Servants rob you, of course.'

'Of course. I suppose I lose a hundred pounds a week in that way. But it is not that I mean. It is the guests. The guests are too – too distinguished. The great Ambassadors, the great financiers, the great nobles, all the men that move the world, put up under my roof. London is the centre of everything, and my hotel – your hotel – is the centre of London. Once I had a King and a Dowager Empress staying here at the same time. Imagine that!'

'A great honour, Mr Babylon. But wherein lies the difficulty?'

'Mr Racksole,' was the grim reply, 'what has become of your shrewdness – that shrewdness which has made your fortune so immense that even you cannot calculate it? Do you not perceive that the roof which habitually shelters all the force, all the authority of the world, must necessarily also shelter nameless and numberless plotters, schemers, evil-doers, and workers of mischief? The thing is as clear as day – and as dark as night. Mr Racksole, I never know by whom I am surrounded. I never know what is going forward. Only sometimes I get hints, glimpses of strange acts and strange secrets. You mentioned my servants. They are almost all good servants, skilled, competent. But what are they besides? For anything I know my fourth sub-chef may be an agent of some European Government. For anything I know my invaluable Miss Spencer may be in the pay of a court dress-maker or a Frankfort banker. Even Rocco may be someone else in addition to Rocco.'

'That makes it all the more interesting,' remarked Theodore Racksole.

*

'What a long time you have been, Father,' said Nella, when he returned to table No. 17 in the salle à manger.

'Only twenty minutes, my dove.'

'But you said two seconds. There is a difference.'

'Well, you see, I had to wait for the steak to cook.'

'Did you have much trouble in getting my birthday treat?'

'No trouble. But it didn't come quite as cheap as you said.'

'What do you mean, Father?'

'Only that I've bought the entire hotel. But don't split.'

'Father, you always were a delicious parent. Shall you give me the hotel for a birthday present?'

'No. I shall run it – as an amusement. By the way, who is that chair for?' He noticed that a third cover had been laid at the table.

'That is for a friend of mine who came in about five minutes ago. Of course I told him he must share our steak. He'll be here in a moment.'

'May I respectfully inquire his name?'

'Dimmock – Christian name Reginald; profession, English companion to Prince Aribert of Posen. I met him when I was in St Petersburg with cousin Hetty last fall. Oh; here he is. Mr Dimmock, this is my dear father. He has succeeded with the steak.'

Theodore Racksole found himself confronted by a very young man, with deep black eyes, and a fresh, boyish expression. They began to talk.

Jules approached with the steak. Racksole tried to catch the waiter's eye, but could not. The dinner proceeded.

'Oh, Father!' cried Nella, 'what a lot of mustard you have taken!'

'Have I?' he said, and then he happened to glance into a mirror on his left hand between two windows. He saw the reflection of Jules, who stood behind his chair, and he saw Jules

give a slow, significant, ominous wink to Mr Dimmock –
Christian name, Reginald.

He examined his mustard in silence. He thought that perhaps
he had helped himself rather plenteously to mustard.

## Chapter Three

## AT THREE A.M.

MR REGINALD DIMMOCK proved himself, despite his extreme youth, to be a man of the world and of experiences, and a practised talker. Conversation between him and Nella Racksole seemed never to flag. They chattered about St Petersburg, and the ice on the Neva, and the tenor at the opera who had been exiled to Siberia, and the quality of Russian tea, and the sweetness of Russian champagne, and various other aspects of Muscovite existence. Russia exhausted, Nella lightly outlined her own doings since she had met the young man in the Tsar's capital, and this recital brought the topic round to London, where it stayed till the final piece of steak was eaten. Theodore Racksole noticed that Mr Dimmock gave very meagre information about his own movements, either past or future. He regarded the youth as a typical hanger-on of Courts, and wondered how he had obtained his post of companion to Prince Aribert of Posen, and who Prince Aribert of Posen might be. The millionaire thought he had once heard of Posen, but he wasn't sure; he rather fancied it was one of those small nondescript German States of which five-sixths of the subjects are Palace officials, and the rest charcoal-burners or innkeepers. Until the meal was nearly over, Racksole said little – perhaps his thoughts were too busy with Jules' wink to Mr Dimmock, but when ices had been followed by coffee, he decided that it might be as well, in the interests of the hotel, to discover something about his daughter's friend. He never for an instant questioned her right to possess her own friends; he had always left her in the most amazing liberty, relying on her inherited good sense to keep her out of mischief; but, quite apart from the wink, he was struck by Nella's attitude towards Mr Dimmock, an attitude in which an amiable scorn was blended with an evident desire to propitiate and please.

'Nella tells me, Mr Dimmock, that you hold a confidential

position with Prince Aribert of Posen,' said Racksole. 'You will pardon an American's ignorance, but is Prince Aribert a reigning Prince — what, I believe, you call in Europe, a Prince Regnant?'

'His Highness is not a reigning Prince, nor ever likely to be,' answered Dimmock. 'The Grand Ducal Throne of Posen is occupied by his Highness's nephew, the Grand Duke Eugen.'

'Nephew?' cried Nella with astonishment.

'Why not, dear lady?'

'But Prince Aribert is surely very young?'

'The Prince, by one of those vagaries of chance which occur sometimes in the history of families, is precisely the same age as the Grand Duke. The late Grand Duke's father was twice married. Hence this youthfulness on the part of an uncle.'

'How delicious to be the uncle of someone as old as yourself! But I suppose it is no fun for Prince Aribert. I suppose he has to be frightfully respectful and obedient, and all that, to his nephew?'

'The Grand Duke and my Serene master are like brothers. At present, of course, Prince Aribert is nominally heir to the throne, but as no doubt you are aware, the Grand Duke will shortly marry a near relative of the Emperor's, and should there be a family — ' Mr Dimmock stopped and shrugged his straight shoulders. 'The Grand Duke,' he went on, without finishing the last sentence, 'would much prefer Prince Aribert to be his successor. He really doesn't want to marry. Between ourselves, strictly between ourselves, he regards marriage as rather a bore. But, of course, being a German Grand Duke, he is bound to marry. He owes it to his country, to Posen.'

'How large is Posen?' asked Racksole bluntly.

'Father,' Nella interposed laughing, 'you shouldn't ask such inconvenient questions. You ought to have guessed that it isn't etiquette to inquire about the size of a German Dukedom.'

'I am sure,' said Dimmock, with a polite smile, 'that the Grand Duke is as much amused as anyone at the size of his territory. I forget the exact acreage, but I remember that once Prince Aribert and myself walked across it and back again in a single day.'

'Then the Grand Duke cannot travel very far within his own dominions? You may say that the sun does set on his empire?'

'It does,' said Dimmock.

'Unless the weather is cloudy,' Nella put in. 'Is the Grand Duke content always to stay at home?'

'On the contrary, he is a great traveller, much more so than Prince Aribert. I may tell you, what no one knows at present, outside this hotel, that his Royal Highness the Grand Duke, with a small suite, will be here to-morrow.'

'In London?' asked Nella.

'Yes.'

'In this hotel?'

'Yes.'

'Oh! How lovely!'

'That is why your humble servant is here to-night – a sort of advance guard.'

'But I understood,' Racksole said, 'that you were – er – attached to Prince Aribert, the uncle.'

'I am. Prince Aribert will also be here. The Grand Duke and the Prince have business about important investments connected with the Grand Duke's marriage settlement. . . . In the highest quarters, you understand.'

'For so discreet a person,' thought Racksole, 'you are fairly communicative.' Then he said aloud: 'Shall we go out on the terrace?'

As they crossed the dining-room Jules stopped Mr Dimmock and handed him a letter. 'Just come, sir, by messenger,' said Jules.

Nella dropped behind for a second with her father.

'Leave me alone with this boy a little – there's a dear parent,' she whispered in his ear.

'I am a mere cypher, an obedient nobody,' Racksole replied, pinching her arm surreptitiously. 'Treat me as such. Use me as you like. I will go and look after my hotel.' And soon afterwards he disappeared.

Nella and Mr Dimmock sat together on the terrace, sipping iced drinks. They made a handsome couple, bowered amid

plants which blossomed at the command of a Chelsea wholesale
florist. People who passed by remarked privately that from the
look of things there was the beginning of a romance in that
conversation. Perhaps there was, but a more intimate acquaintance with the character of Nella Racksole would have been
necessary in order to predict what precise form that romance
would take.

Jules himself served the liquids, and at ten o'clock he brought
another note. Entreating a thousand pardons, Reginald Dimmock, after he had glanced at the note, excused himself on the
plea of urgent business for his Serene master, uncle of the Grand
Duke of Posen. He asked if he might fetch Mr Racksole, or
escort Miss Racksole to her father. But Miss Racksole said gaily
that she felt no need of an escort, and should go to bed. She
added that her father and herself always endeavoured to be
independent of each other.

Just then Theodore Racksole had found his way once more
into Mr Babylon's private room. Before arriving there, however,
he had discovered that in some mysterious manner the news of
the change of proprietorship had worked its way down to the
lowest strata of the hotel's cosmos. The corridors hummed with
it, and even under-servants were to be seen discussing the thing,
just as though it mattered to them.

'Have a cigar, Mr Racksole,' said the urbane Mr Babylon,
'and a mouthful of the oldest cognac in all Europe.'

In a few minutes these two were talking eagerly, rapidly. Félix
Babylon was astonished at Racksole's capacity for absorbing the
details of hotel management. And as for Racksole he soon
realized that Félix Babylon must be a prince of hotel managers.
It had never occurred to Racksole before that to manage an
hotel, even a large hotel, could be a specially interesting affair,
or that it could make any excessive demands upon the brains of
the manager; but he came to see that he had underrated the possibilities of an hotel. The business of the Grand Babylon was
enormous. It took Racksole, with all his genius for organization,
exactly half an hour to master the details of the hotel laundry-
work. And the laundry-work was but one branch of activity

amid scores, and not a very large one at that. The machinery of
checking supplies, and of establishing a mean ratio between
the raw stuff received in the kitchen and the number of meals
served in the salle à manger and the private rooms, was very
complicated and delicate. When Racksole had grasped it, he at
once suggested some improvements, and this led to a long
theoretical discussion, and the discussion led to digressions, and
then Félix Babylon, in a moment of absent-mindedness, yawned.

Racksole looked at the gilt clock on the high mantelpiece.

'Great Scott!' he said. 'It's three o'clock. Mr Babylon, accept
my apologies for having kept you up to such an absurd hour.'

'I have not spent so pleasant an evening for many years. You
have let me ride my hobby to my heart's content. It is I who
should apologize.'

Racksole rose.

'I should like to ask you one question,' said Babylon. 'Have
you ever had anything to do with hotels before?'

'Never,' said Racksole.

'Then you have missed your vocation. You could have been
the greatest of all hotel-managers. You would have been greater
than me, and I am unequalled, though I keep only one hotel,
and some men have half a dozen. Mr Racksole, why have you
never run an hotel?'

'Heaven knows,' he laughed, 'but you flatter me, Mr Babylon.'

'I? Flatter? You do not know me. I flatter no one, except,
perhaps, now and then an exceptionally distinguished guest. In
which case I give suitable instructions as to the bill.'

'Speaking of distinguished guests, I am told that a couple of
German princes are coming here to-morrow.'

'That is so.'

'Does one do anything? Does one receive them formally –
stand bowing in the entrance-hall, or anything of that sort?'

'Not necessarily. Not unless one wishes. The modern hotel
proprietor is not like an innkeeper of the Middle Ages, and even
princes do not expect to see him unless something should happen
to go wrong. As a matter of fact, though the Grand Duke of
Posen and Prince Aribert have both honoured me by staying

here before, I have never even set eyes on them. You will find all arrangements have been made.'

They talked a little longer, and then Racksole said good night.

'Let me see you to your room. The lifts will be closed and the place will be deserted. As for myself, I sleep here,' and Mr Babylon pointed to an inner door.

'No, thanks,' said Racksole; 'let me explore my own hotel unaccompanied. I believe I can discover my room.'

When he got fairly into the passages, Racksale was not so sure that he could discover his own room. The number was 107, but he had forgotten whether it was on the first or second floor. Travelling in a lift, one is unconscious of floors. He passed several lift-doorways, but he could see no glint of a staircase; in all self-respecting hotels staircases have gone out of fashion, and though hotel architects still continue, for old sakes' sake, to build staircases, they are tucked away in remote corners where their presence is not likely to offend the eye of a spoiled and cosmopolitan public.

The hotel seemed vast, uncanny, deserted. An electric light glowed here and there at long intervals. On the thick carpets, Racksole's thinly-shod feet made no sound, and he wandered at ease to and fro, rather amused, rather struck by the peculiar senses of night and mystery which had suddenly come over him. He fancied he could hear a thousand snores peacefully descending from the upper realms. At length he found a staircase, a very dark and narrow one, and presently he was on the first floor. He soon discovered that the numbers of the rooms on this floor did not get beyond seventy. He encountered another staircase and ascended to the second floor. By the decoration of the walls he recognized this floor as his proper home, and as he strolled through the long corridor he whistled a low, meditative whistle of satisfaction. He thought he heard a step in the transverse corridor, and instinctively he obliterated himself in a recess which held a service-cabinet and a chair. He did hear a step. Peeping cautiously out, he perceived, what he had not perceived previously, that a piece of white ribbon had been tied round the handle of the door of one of the bedrooms. Then a man came round the corner of the transverse corridor, and Racksole drew back. It was Jules – Jules with his hands in his pockets and a slouch hat over his eyes, but in other respects attired as usual.

Racksole, at that instant, remembered with a special vividness what Félix Babylon had said to him at their first interview. He wished he had brought his revolver. He didn't know why he should feel the desirability of a revolver in a London hotel of the most unimpeachable fair fame, but he did feel the desirability of such an instrument of attack and defence. He privately decided that if Jules went past his recess he would take him by the throat and in that attitude put a few plain questions to this highly dubious waiter. But Jules had stopped. The millionaire made another cautious observation. Jules, with infinite gentleness, was turning the handle of the door to which the white ribbon was attached. The door slowly yielded and Jules disappeared within the room. After a brief interval, the night-prowling Jules reappeared, closed the door as softly as he had opened it, removed the ribbon, returned upon his steps, and vanished down the transverse corridor.

'This is quaint,' said Racksole; 'quaint to a degree!'

It occurred to him to look at the number of the room, and he stole towards it.

'Well, I'm d – d!' he murmured wonderingly.

The number was 111, his daughter's room! He tried to open it, but the door was locked. Rushing to his own room, No. 107, he seized one of a pair of revolvers (the kind that are made for millionaires) and followed after Jules down the transverse corridor. At the end of this corridor was a window; the window was open; and Jules was innocently gazing out of the window. Ten silent strides, and Theodore Racksole was upon him.

'One word, my friend,' the millionaire began, carelessly waving the revolver in the air. Jules was indubitably startled, but by an admirable exercise of self-control he recovered possession of his faculties in a second.

'Sir?' said Jules.

'I just want to be informed, what the deuce you were doing in No. 111 a moment ago.'

'I had been requested to go there,' was the calm response.

'You are a liar, and not a very clever one. That is my daughter's room. Now – out with it, before I decide whether to shoot you or throw you into the street.'

'Excuse me, sir, No. 111 is occupied by a gentleman.'

'I advise you that it is a serious error of judgement to contradict me, my friend. Don't do it again. We will go to the room together, and you shall prove that the occupant is a gentleman, and not my daughter.'

'Impossible, sir,' said Jules.

'Scarcely that,' said Racksole, and he took Jules by the sleeve. The millionaire knew for a certainty that Nella occupied No. 111, for he had examined the room with her, and himself seen that her trunks and her maid and herself had arrived there in safety. 'Now open the door,' whispered Racksole, when they reached No. 111.

'I must knock.'

'That is just what you mustn't do. Open it. No doubt you have your pass-key.'

Confronted by the revolver, Jules readily obeyed, yet with a deprecatory gesture, as though he would not be responsible for this outrage against the decorum of hotel life. Racksole entered. The room was brilliantly lighted.

'A visitor, who insists on seeing you, sir,' said Jules, and fled.

Mr Reginald Dimmock, still in evening dress, and smoking a cigarette, rose hurriedly from a table.

'Hello, my dear Mr Racksole, this is an unexpected – ah – pleasure.'

'Where is my daughter? This is her room.'

'Did I catch what you said, Mr Racksole?'

'I venture to remark that this is Miss Racksole's room.'

'My good sir,' answered Dimmock, 'you must be mad to dream of such a thing. Only my respect for your daughter prevents me from expelling you forcibly, for such an extraordinary suggestion.'

A small spot half-way down the bridge of the millionaire's nose turned suddenly white.

'With your permission,' he said in a low calm voice, 'I will examine the dressing-room and the bath-room.'

'Just listen to me a moment,' Dimmock urged, in a milder tone.

'I'll listen to you afterwards, my young friend,' said Racksole, and he proceeded to search the bath-room, and the dressing-room, without any result whatever. 'Lest my attitude might be open to misconstruction, Mr Dimmock, I may as well tell you that I have the most perfect confidence in my daughter, who is as well able to take care of herself as any woman I ever met, but since you entered it there have been one or two rather mysterious occurrences in this hotel. That is all.' Feeling a draught of air on his shoulder, Racksole turned to the window. 'For instance,' he added, 'I perceive that this window is broken, badly broken, and from the outside. Now, how could that have occurred?'

'If you will kindly hear reason, Mr Racksole,' said Dimmock in his best diplomatic manner, 'I will endeavour to explain things to you. I regarded your first question to me when you entered my room as being offensively put, but I now see that you had some justification.' He smiled politely. 'I was passing along this corridor about eleven o'clock, when I found Miss Racksole in a difficulty with the hotel servants. Miss Racksole was retiring to rest in this room when a large stone, which must have been thrown from the Embankment, broke the window, as you see. Apart from the discomfort of the broken window, she did not care to remain in the room. She argued that where one stone had come another might follow. She therefore insisted on her room being changed. The servants said that there was no other room available with a dressing-room and bath-room attached, and your daughter made a point of these matters. I at once offered to exchange apartments with her. She did me the honour to accept my offer. Our respective belongings were moved – and that is all. Miss Racksole is at this moment, I trust, asleep in No. 124.'

Theodore Racksole looked at the young man for a few seconds in silence.

There was a faint knock at the door.

'Come in,' said Racksole loudly.

Someone pushed open the door, but remained standing on the mat. It was Nella's maid, in a dressing-gown.

'Miss Racksole's compliments, and a thousand excuses, but a book of hers was left on the mantelshelf in this room. She cannot sleep, and wishes to read.'

'Mr Dimmock, I tender my apologies – my formal apologies,' said Racksole, when the girl had gone away with the book. 'Good night.'

'Pray don't mention it,' said Dimmock suavely – and bowed him out.

## Chapter Four

## ENTRANCE OF THE PRINCE

NEVERTHELESS, sundry small things weighed on Racksole's mind. First there was Jules' wink. Then there was the ribbon on the door-handle and Jules' visit to No. 111, and the broken window – broken from the outside. Racksole did not forget that the time was 3 a.m. He slept but little that night, but he was glad that he had bought the Grand Babylon Hotel. It was an acquisition which seemed to promise fun and diversion.

The next morning he came across Mr Babylon early.

'I have emptied my private room of all personal papers,' said Babylon, 'and it is now at your disposal. I purpose, if agreeable to yourself, to stay on in the hotel as a guest for the present. We have much to settle with regard to the completion of the purchase, and also there are things which you might want to ask me. Also, to tell the truth, I am not anxious to leave the old place with too much suddenness. It will be a wrench to me.'

'I shall be delighted if you will stay,' said the millionaire, 'but it must be as my guest, not as the guest of the hotel.'

'You are very kind.'

'As for wishing to consult you, no doubt I shall have need to do so, but I must say that the show seems to run itself.'

'Ah!' said Babylon thoughtfully. 'I have heard of hotels that run themselves. If they do, you may be sure that they obey the laws of gravity and run downwards. You will have your hands full. For example, have you yet heard about Miss Spencer?'

'No,' said Racksole. 'What of her?'

'She has mysteriously vanished during the night, and nobody appears to be able to throw any light on the affair. Her room is empty, her boxes gone. You will want someone to take her place, and that someone will not be very easy to get.'

'H'm!' Racksole said, after a pause. 'Hers is not the only post that falls vacant to-day.'

A little later, the millionaire installed himself in the late owner's private room and rang the bell.

'I want Jules,' he said to the page.

While waiting for Jules, Racksole considered the question of Miss Spencer's disappearance.

'Good morning, Jules,' was his cheerful greeting, when the imperturbable waiter arrived.

'Good morning, sir.'

'Take a chair.'

'Thank you, sir.'

'We have met before this morning, Jules.'

'Yes, sir, at 3 a.m.'

'Rather strange about Miss Spencer's departure, is it not?' suggested Racksole.

'It is remarkable, sir.'

'You are aware, of course, that Mr Babylon has transferred all his interests in this hotel to me?'

'I have been informed to that effect, sir.'

'I suppose you know everything that goes on in the hotel, Jules?'

'As the head waiter, sir, it is my business to keep a general eye on things.'

'You speak very good English for a foreigner, Jules.'

'For a foreigner, sir! I am an Englishman, a Hertfordshire man born and bred. Perhaps my name has misled you, sir. I am only called Jules because the head waiter of any really high-class hotel must have either a French or an Italian name.'

'I see,' said Racksole. 'I think you must be rather a clever person, Jules.'

'That is not for me to say, sir.'

'How long has the hotel enjoyed the advantage of your services?'

'A little over twenty years.'

'That is a long time to be in one place. Don't you think it's time you got out of the rut? You are still young, and might make a reputation for yourself in another and wider sphere.'

Racksole looked at the man steadily, and his glance was steadily returned.

'You aren't satisfied with me, sir?'

'To be frank, Jules, I think – I think you – er – wink too much. And I think that it is regrettable when a head waiter falls into a habit of taking white ribbons from the handles of bedroom doors at three in the morning.'

Jules started slightly.

'I see how it is, sir. You wish me to go, and one pretext, if I may use the term, is as good as another. Very well, I can't say that I'm surprised. It sometimes happens that there is incompatibility of temper between a hotel proprietor and his head waiter, and then, unless one of them goes, the hotel is likely to suffer. I will go, Mr Racksole. In fact, I had already thought of giving notice.'

The millionaire smiled appreciatively.

'What wages do you require in lieu of notice? It is my intention that you leave the hotel within an hour.'

'I require no wages in lieu of notice, sir. I would scorn to accept anything. And I will leave the hotel in fifteen minutes.'

'Good-day, then. You have my good wishes and my admiration, so long as you keep out of my hotel.'

Racksole got up.

'Good-day, sir. And thank you.'

'By the way, Jules, it will be useless for you to apply to any other first-rate European hotel for a post, because I shall take measures which will ensure the rejection of any such application.'

'Without discussing the question whether or not there aren't at least half a dozen hotels in London alone that would jump for joy at the chance of getting me,' answered Jules, 'I may tell you, sir, that I shall retire from my profession.'

'Really! You will turn your brains to a different channel.'

'No, sir. I shall take rooms in Albemarle Street or Jermyn Street, and just be content to be a man-about-town. I have saved some twenty thousand pounds – a mere trifle, but sufficient for my needs, and I shall now proceed to enjoy it. Pardon me for troubling you with my personal affairs. And good-day again.'

That afternoon Racksole went with Félix Babylon first to a firm of solicitors in the City, and then to a stockbroker, in order to carry out the practical details of the purchase of the hotel.

'I mean to settle in England,' said Racksole, as they were coming back. 'It is the only country – ' and he stopped.

'The only country?'

'The only country where you can invest money and spend money with a feeling of security. In the United States there is nothing worth spending money on, nothing to buy. In France or Italy, there is no real security.'

'But surely you are a true American?' questioned Babylon.

'I am a true American,' said Racksole, 'but my father, who began by being a bedmaker at an Oxford college, and ultimately made ten million dollars out of iron in Pittsburg – my father took the wise precaution of having me educated in England. I had my three years at Oxford, like any son of the upper middle class! It did me good. It has been worth more to me than many successful speculations. It taught me that the English language is different from, and better than, the American language, and that there is something – I haven't yet found out exactly what – in English life that Americans will never get. Why,' he added, 'in the United States we still bribe our judges and our newspapers. And we talk of the eighteenth century as though it was the beginning of the world. Yes, I shall transfer my securities to London. I shall build a house in Park Lane, and I shall buy some immemorial country seat with a history as long as the A.T. and S. railroad, and I shall calmly and gradually settle down. D'you know – I am rather a good-natured man for a millionaire, and of a social disposition, and yet I haven't six real friends in the whole of New York City. Think of that!'

'And I,' said Babylon, 'have no friends except the friends of my boyhood in Lausanne. I have spent thirty years in England, and gained nothing but a perfect knowledge of the English language and as much gold coin as would fill a rather large box.'

These two plutocrats breathed a simultaneous sigh.

'Talking of gold coin,' said Racksole, 'how much money should you think Jules has contrived to amass while he has been with you?'

'Oh!' Babylon smiled. 'I should not like to guess. He has had unique opportunities – unique opportunities.'

'Should you consider twenty thousand an extraordinary sum under the circumstances?'

'Not at all. Has he been confiding in you?'

'Somewhat. I have dismissed him.'

'You have dismissed him?'

'Why not?'

'There is no reason why not. But I have felt inclined to dismiss him for the past ten years, and never found courage to do it.'

'It was a perfectly simple proceeding, I assure you. Before I had done with him, I rather liked the fellow.'

'Miss Spencer and Jules – both gone in one day!' mused Félix Babylon.

'And no one to take their places,' said Racksole. 'And yet the hotel continues its way!'

But when Racksole reached the Grand Babylon he found that Miss Spencer's chair in the bureau was occupied by a stately and imperious girl, dressed becomingly in black.

'Heavens, Nella!' he cried, going to the bureau. 'What are you doing here?'

'I am taking Mis Spencer's place. I want to help you with your hotel, Dad. I fancy I shall make an excellent hotel clerk. I have arranged with a Miss Selina Smith, one of the typists in the office, to put me up to all the tips and tricks, and I shall do very well.'

'But look here, Helen Racksole. We shall have the whole of London talking about this thing – the greatest of all American heiresses a hotel clerk! And I came here for quiet and rest!'

'I suppose it was for the sake of quiet and rest that you bought the hotel, Papa?'

'You would insist on the steak,' he retorted. 'Get out of this, on the instant.'

'Here I am, here to stay,' said Nella, and deliberately laughed at her parent.

Just then the face of a fair-haired man of about thirty years appeared at the bureau window. He was very well-dressed, very aristocratic in his pose, and he seemed rather angry.

He looked fixedly at Nella and started back.

'Ach!' he exclaimed. 'You!'

'Yes, your Highness, it is indeed I. Father, this is his Serene Highness Prince Aribert of Posen – one of our most esteemed customers.'

'You know my name, Fräulein?' the new-comer murmured in German.

'Certainly, Prince,' Nella replied sweetly. 'You were plain Count Steenbock last spring in Paris – doubtless travelling incognito –'

'Silence,' he entreated, with a wave of the hand, and his forehead went as white as paper.

## Chapter Five

# WHAT OCCURRED TO REGINALD DIMMOCK

IN another moment they were all three talking quite nicely, and with at any rate an appearance of being natural. Prince Aribert became suave, even deferential to Nella, and more friendly towards Nella's father than their respective positions demanded. The latter amused himself by studying this sprig of royalty, the first with whom he had ever come into contact. He decided that the young fellow was personable enough, 'had no frills on him,' and would make an exceptionally good commercial traveller for a first-class firm. Such was Theodore Racksole's preliminary estimate of the man who might one day be the reigning Grand Duke of Posen.

It occurred to Nella, and she smiled at the idea, that the bureau of the hotel was scarcely the correct place in which to receive this august young man. There he stood, with his head half-way through the bureau window, negligently leaning against the woodwork, just as though he were a stockbroker or the manager of a New York burlesque company.

'Is your Highness travelling quite alone?' she asked.

'By a series of accidents I am,' he said. 'My equerry was to have met me at Charing Cross, but he failed to do so – I cannot imagine why.'

'Mr Dimmock?' questioned Racksole.

'Yes, Dimmock. I do not remember that he ever missed an appointment before. You know him? He has been here?'

'He dined with us last night,' said Racksole – 'on Nella's invitation,' he added maliciously; 'but to-day we have seen nothing of him. I know, however, that he has engaged the State apartments, and also a suite adjoining the State apartments – No. 55. That is so, isn't it, Nella?'

'Yes, Papa,' she said, having first demurely examined a ledger. 'Your Highness would doubtless like to be conducted to your room – apartments I mean.' Then Nella laughed deliberately

at the Prince, and said, 'I don't know who is the proper person
to conduct you, and that's a fact. The truth is that Papa and I
are rather raw yet in the hotel line. You see, we only bought the
place last night.'

'You have bought the hotel!' exclaimed the Prince.

'That's so,' said Racksole.

'And Félix Babylon has gone?'

'He is going, if he has not already gone.'

'Ah! I see,' said the Prince; 'this is one of your American
"strokes". You have bought to sell again, is that not it? You are
on your holidays, but you cannot resist making a few thousands
by way of relaxation. I have heard of such things.'

'We sha'n't sell again, Prince, until we are tired of our bargain. Sometimes we tire very quickly, and sometimes we don't.
It depends – eh? What?' Racksole broke off suddenly to attend
to a servant in livery who had quietly entered the bureau and was
making urgent mysterious signs to him.

'If you please, sir,' the man by frantic gestures implored Mr
Theodore Racksole to come out.

'Pray don't let me detain you, Mr Racksole,' said the Prince,
and therefore the proprietor of the Grand Babylon departed
after the servant, with a queer, curt little bow to Prince
Aribert.

'Mayn't I come inside?' said the Prince to Nella immediately
the millionaire had gone.

'Impossible, Prince,' Nella laughed. 'The rule against visitors
entering this bureau is frightfully strict.'

'How do you know the rule is so strict if you only came into
possession last night?'

'I know because I made the rule myself this morning, your
Highness.'

'But seriously, Miss Racksole, I want to talk to you.'

'Do you want to talk to me as Prince Aribert or as the friend
– the acquaintance – whom I knew in Paris last year?'

'As the friend, dear lady, if I may use the term.'

'And you are sure that you would not like first to be conducted
to your apartments?'

'Not yet. I will wait till Dimmock comes; he cannot fail to be here soon.'

'Then we will have tea served in father's private room – the proprietor's private room, you know.'

'Good!' he said.

Nella talked through a telephone, and rang several bells, and behaved generally in a manner calculated to prove to Princes and to whomever it might concern that she was a young woman of business instincts and training, and then she stepped down from her chair of office, emerged from the bureau, and, preceded by two menials, led Prince Aribert to the Louis XV chamber in which her father and Félix Babylon had had their long confabulation on the previous evening.

'What do you want to talk to me about?' she asked her companion, as she poured out for him a second cup of tea. The Prince looked at her for a moment as he took the proffered cup, and being a young man of sane, healthy, instincts, he could think of nothing for the moment except her loveliness. Nella was indeed beautiful that afternoon. The beauty of even the most beautiful woman ebbs and flows from hour to hour. Nella's this afternoon was at the flood. Vivacious, alert, imperious, and yet ineffably sweet, she seemed to radiate the very joy and exuberance of life.

'I have forgotten,' he said.

'You have forgotten! That is surely very wrong of you? You gave me to understand that it was something terribly important. But of course I knew it couldn't be, because no man, and especially no Prince, ever discussed anything really important with a woman.'

'Recollect, Miss Racksole, that this afternoon, here, I am not the Prince.'

'You are Count Steenbock, is that it?'

He started. 'For you only,' he said, unconsciously lowering his voice. 'Miss Racksole, I particularly wish that no one here should know that I was in Paris last spring.'

'An affair of State?' she smiled.

'An affair of State,' he replied soberly. 'Even Dimmock doesn't

47

know. It was strange that we should be fellow guests at that quiet out-of-the-way hotel – strange but delightful. I shall never forget that rainy afternoon that we spent together in the Museum of the Trocadéro. Let us talk about that.'

'About the rain, or the museum?'

'I shall never forget that afternoon,' he repeated, ignoring the lightness of her question.

'Nor I,' she murmured corresponding to his mood.

'You, too enjoyed it?' he said eagerly.

'The sculptures were magnificent,' she replied, hastily glancing at the ceiling.

'Ah! So they were! Tell me, Miss Racksole, how did you discover my identity.'

'I must not say,' she answered. 'That is my secret. Do not seek to penetrate it. Who knows what horrors you might discover if you probed too far?' She laughed, but she laughed alone. The Prince remained pensive – as it were brooding.

'I never hoped to see you again,' he said.

'Why not?'

'One never sees again those whom one wishes to see.'

'As for me, I was perfectly convinced that we should meet again.'

'Why?'

'Because I always get what I want.'

'Then you wanted to see me again?'

'Certainly. You interested me extremely. I have never met another man who could talk so well about sculpture as the Count Steenbock.'

'Do you really always get what you want, Miss Racksole?'

'Of course.'

'That is because your father is so rich, I suppose?'

'Oh, no, it isn't!' she said. 'It's simply because I always do get what I want. It's got nothing to do with Father at all.'

'But Mr Racksole is extremely wealthy?'

'Wealthy isn't the word, Count. There is no word. It's positively awful the amount of dollars poor Papa makes. And the worst of it is he can't help it. He told me once that when a man had made ten millions no power on earth could stop those ten millions from growing into twenty. And so it continues. I spend what I can, but I can't come near coping with it; and of course Papa is no use whatever at spending.'

'And you have no mother?'

'Who told you I had no mother?' she asked quietly.

'I – er – inquired about you,' he said, with equal candour and humility.

'In spite of the fact that you never hoped to see me again?'

'Yes, in spite of that.'

'How funny!' she said, and lapsed into a meditative silence.

'Yours must be a wonderful existence,' said the Prince. 'I envy you.'

'You envy me – what? My father's wealth?'

'No,' he said; 'your freedom and your responsibilities.'

'I have no responsibilities,' she remarked.

'Pardon me,' he said; 'you have, and the time is coming when you will feel them.'

'I'm only a girl,' she murmured with sudden simplicity. 'As for you, Count, surely you have sufficient responsibilities of your own?'

'I?' he said sadly. 'I have no responsibilties. I am a nobody – a Serene Highness who has to pretend to be very important, always taking immense care never to do anything that a Serene Highness ought not to do. Bah!'

'But if your nephew, Prince Eugen, were to die, would you not come to the throne, and would you not then have these responsibilities which you so much desire?'

'Eugen die?' said Prince Aribert, in a curious tone. 'Impossible. He is the perfection of health. In three months he will be married. No, I shall never be anything but a Serene Highness, the most despicable of God's creatures.'

'But what about the State secret which you mentioned? Is not that a responsibility?'

'Ah!' he said. 'That is over. That belongs to the past. It was an accident in my dull career. I shall never be Count Steenbock again.'

'Who knows?' she said. 'By the way, is not Prince Eugen coming here to-day? Mr Dimmock told us so.'

'See!' answered the Prince, standing up and bending over her. 'I am going to confide in you. I don't know why, but I am.'

'Don't betray State secrets,' she warned him, smiling into his face.

But just then the door of the room was unceremoniously opened.

'Go right in,' said a voice sharply. It was Theodore Racksole's.

Two men entered, bearing a prone form on a stretcher, and Racksole followed them. Nella sprang up. Racksole stared to see his daughter.

'I didn't know you were in here, Nell. Here,' to the two men, 'out again.'

'Why!' exclaimed Nella, gazing fearfully at the form on the stretcher, 'it's Mr Dimmock!'

'It is,' her father acquiesced. 'He's dead,' he added laconically. 'I'd have broken it to you more gently had I known. Your pardon, Prince.' There was a pause.

'Dimmock dead!' Prince Aribert whispered under his breath, and he kneeled down by the side of the stretcher. 'What does this mean?'

'The poor fellow was just walking across the quadrangle towards the portico when he fell down. A commissionaire who saw him says he was walking very quickly. At first I thought it was sunstroke, but it couldn't have been, though the weather certainly is rather warm. It must be heart disease. But anyhow, he's dead. We did what we could. I've sent for a doctor, and for the police. I suppose there'll have to be an inquest.'

Theodore Racksole stopped, and in an awkward solemn silence they all gazed at the dead youth. His features were slightly drawn, and his eyes closed; that was all. He might have been asleep.

'My poor Dimmock!' exclaimed the Prince, his voice broken. 'And I was angry because the lad did not meet me at Charing Cross!'

'Are you sure he is dead, Father?' Nella said.

'You'd better go away, Nella,' was Racksole's only reply; but the girl stood still, and began to sob quietly. On the previous night she had secretly made fun of Reginald Dimmock. She had deliberately set herself to get information from him on a topic in which she happened to be specially interested and she had got it, laughing the while at his youthful crudities – his vanity, his transparent cunning, his absurd airs. She had not liked him; she had even distrusted him, and decided that he was not 'nice'. But now, as he lay on the stretcher, these things were forgotten. She went so far as to reproach herself for them. Such is the strange commanding power of death.

'Oblige me by taking the poor fellow to my apartments,' said the Prince, with a gesture to the attendants. 'Surely it is time the doctor came.' Racksole felt suddenly at that moment he was nothing but a mere hotel proprietor with an awkward affair on his hands. For a fraction of a second he wished he had never bought the Grand Babylon.

A quarter of an hour later Prince Aribert, Theodore Racksole, a doctor, and an inspector of police were in the Prince's reception-room. They had just come from an ante-chamber, in which lay the mortal remains of Reginald Dimmock.

'Well?' said Racksole, glancing at the doctor.

The doctor was a big, boyish-looking man, with keen, quizzical eyes.

'It is not heart disease,' said the doctor.

'Not heart disease?'

'No.'

'Then what is it?' asked the Prince.

'I may be able to answer that question after the post-mortem,' said the doctor. 'I certainly can't answer it now. The symptoms are unusual to a degree.'

The inspector of police began to write in a note-book.

*Chapter Six*

## IN THE GOLD ROOM

AT the Grand Babylon a great ball was given that night in the Gold Room, a huge saloon attached to the hotel, though scarcely part of it, and certainly less exclusive than the hotel itself. Theodore Racksole knew nothing of the affair, except that it was an entertainment offered by a Mr and Mrs Sampson Levi to their friends. Who Mr and Mrs Sampson Levi were he did not know, nor could anyone tell him anything about them except that Mr Sampson Levi was a prominent member of that part of the Stock Exchange familiarly called the Kaffir Circus, and that his wife was a stout lady with an aquiline nose and many diamonds, and that they were very rich and very hospitable. Theodore Racksole did not want a ball in his hotel that evening, and just before dinner he had almost a mind to issue a decree that the Gold Room was to be closed and the ball forbidden, and Mr and Mrs Sampson Levi might name the amount of damages suffered by them. His reasons for such a course were threefold – first, he felt depressed and uneasy; second, he didn't like the name of Sampson Levi; and, third, he had a desire to show these so-called plutocrats that their wealth was nothing to him, that they could not do what they chose with Theodore Racksole, and that for two pins Theodore Racksole would buy them up, and the whole Kaffir Circus to boot. But something warned him that though such a high-handed proceeding might be tolerated in America, that land of freedom, it would never be tolerated in England. He felt instinctively that in England there are things you can't do, and that this particular thing was one of them. So the ball went forward, and neither Mr nor Mrs Sampson Levi had ever the least suspicion what a narrow escape they had had of looking very foolish in the eyes of the thousand or so guests invited by them to the Gold Room of the Grand Babylon that evening.

The Gold Room of the Grand Babylon was built for a ball-room. A balcony, supported by arches faced with gilt and lapis-lazulo, ran around it, and from this vantage men and maidens and chaperons who could not or would not dance might survey the scene. Everyone knew this, and most people took advantage of it. What everyone did not know – what no one knew – was that higher up than the balcony there was a little barred window in the end wall from which the hotel authorities might keep a watchful eye, not only on the dancers, but on the occupants of the balcony itself.

It may seem incredible to the uninitiated that the guests at any social gathering held in so gorgeous and renowned an apartment as the Gold Room of the Grand Babylon should need the observation of a watchful eye. Yet so it was. Strange matters and un-expected faces had been descried from the little window, and more than one European detective had kept vigil there with the most eminently satisfactory results.

At eleven o'clock Theodore Racksole, afflicted by vexation of spirit, found himself gazing idly through the little barred window. Nella was with him. Together they had been wandering about the corridors of the hotel, still strange to them both, and it was quite by accident that they had lighted upon the small room which had a surreptitious view of Mr and Mrs Sampson Levi's ball. Except for the light of the chandelier of the ball-room the little cubicle was in darkness. Nella was looking through the window; her father stood behind.

'I wonder which is Mrs Sampson Levi?' Nella said, 'and whether she matches her name. Wouldn't you love to have a name like that, Father – something that people could take hold of – instead of Racksole?'

The sound of violins and a confused murmur of voices rose gently up to them.

'Umph!' said Theodore. 'Curse those evening papers!' he added, inconsequently but with sincerity.

'Father, you're very horrid to-night. What have the evening papers been doing?'

'Well, my young madame, they've got me in for one, and you for another; and they're manufacturing mysteries like fun. It's young Dimmock's death that has started 'em.'

'Well, Father, you surely didn't expect to keep yourself out of the papers. Besides, as regards newspapers, you ought to be glad you aren't in New York. Just fancy what the dear old *Herald* would have made out of a little transaction like yours of last night.'

'That's true,' assented Racksole. 'But it'll be all over New York to-morrow morning, all the same. The worst of it is that Babylon has gone off to Switzerland.'

'Why?'

'Don't know. Sudden fancy, I guess, for his native heath.'

'What difference does it make to you?'

'None. Only I feel sort of lonesome. I feel I want someone to lean up against in running this hotel.'

'Father, if you have that feeling you must be getting ill.'

'Yes,' he sighed, 'I admit it's unusual with me. But perhaps you haven't grasped the fact, Nella, that we're in the middle of a rather queer business.'

'You mean about poor Mr Dimmock?'

'Partly Dimmock and partly other things. First of all, that Miss Spencer, or whatever her wretched name is, mysteriously disappears. Then there was the stone thrown into your bedroom. Then I caught that rascal Jules conspiring with Dimmock at three o'clock in the morning. Then your precious Prince Aribert arrives without any suite – which I believe is a most peculiar and wicked thing for a Prince to do – and moreover I find my daughter on very intimate terms with the said Prince. Then young Dimmock goes and dies, and there is to be an inquest; then Prince Eugen and his suite, who were expected here for dinner, fail to turn up at all – '

'Prince Eugen has not come?'

'He has not; and Uncle Aribert is in a deuce of a stew about him, and telegraphing all over Europe. Altogether, things are working up pretty lively.'

'Do you really think, Dad, there was anything between Jules and poor Mr Dimmock?'

'Think! I know! I tell you I saw that scamp give Dimmock a wink last night at dinner that might have meant – well!'

'So you caught that wink, did you, Dad?'

'Why, did you?'

'Of course, Dad. I was going to tell you about it.'

The millionaire grunted.

'Look here, Father,' Nella whispered suddenly, and pointed to the balcony immediately below them. 'Who's that?' She indicated a man with a bald patch on the back of his head, who was propping himself up against the railing of the balcony and gazing immovable into the ball-room.

'Well, who is it?'

'Isn't it Jules?'

'Gemini! By the beard of the prophet, it is!'

'Perhaps Mr Jules is a guest of Mrs Sampson Levi.'

'Guest or no guest, he goes out of this hotel, even if I have to throw him out myself.'

Theodore Racksole disappeared without another word, and Nella followed him. But when the millionaire arrived on the balcony floor he could see nothing of Jules, neither there nor in the ball-room itself. Saying no word aloud, but quietly whispering wicked expletives, he searched everywhere in vain, and then, at last, by tortuous stairways and corridors returned to his original post of observation, that he might survey the place anew from the vantage ground. To his surprise he found a man in the dark little room, watching the scene of the ball as intently as he himself had been doing a few minutes before. Hearing footsteps, the man turned with a start.

It was Jules.

The two exchanged glances in the half light for a second.

'Good evening, Mr Racksole,' said Jules calmly. 'I must apologize for being here.'

'Force of habit, I suppose,' said Theodore Racksole drily.

'Just so, sir.'

'I fancied I had forbidden you to re-enter this hotel?'

'I thought your order applied only to my professional capacity. I am here to-night as the guest of Mr and Mrs Sampson Levi.'

'In your new rôle of man-about-town, eh?'

'Exactly.'

'But I don't allow men-about-town up here, my friend.'

'For being up here I have already apologized.'

'Then, having apologized, you had better depart; that is my disinterested advice to you.'

'Good night, sir.'

'And, I say, Mr Jules, if Mr and Mrs Sampson Levi, or any other Hebrews or Christians, should again invite you to my hotel you will oblige me by declining the invitation. You'll find that will be the safest course for you.'

'Good night, sir.'

Before midnight struck Theodore Racksole had ascertained that the invitation-list of Mr and Mrs Sampson Levi, though a somewhat lengthy one, contained no reference to any such person as Jules.

He sat up very late. To be precise, he sat up all night. He was a man who, by dint of training, could comfortably dispense with sleep when he felt so inclined, or when circumstances made such a course advisable. He walked to and fro in his room, and cogitated as few people beside Theodore Racksole could cogitate. At 6 a.m. he took a stroll round the business part of his premises, and watched the supplies come in from Covent Garden, from Smithfield, from Billingsgate, and from other strange places. He found the proceedings of the kitchen department quite interesting, and made mental notes of things that he would have altered, of men whose wages he would increase and men whose wages he would reduce. At 7 a.m. he happened to be standing near the luggage lift, and witnessed the descent of vast quantities of luggage, and its disappearance into a Carter Paterson van.

'Whose luggage is that?' he inquired peremptorily.

The luggage clerk, with an aggrieved expression, explained to him that it was the luggage of nobody in particular, that it belonged to various guests, and was bound for various destinations; that it was, in fact, 'expressed' luggage despatched in advance, and that a similar quantity of it left the hotel every morning about that hour.

Theodore Racksole walked away, and breakfasted upon one cup of tea and half a slice of toast.

At ten o'clock he was informed that the inspector of police desired to see him. The inspector had come, he said, to superintend the removal of the body of Reginald Dimmock to the mortuary adjoining the place of inquest, and a suitable vehicle waited at the back entrance of the hotel.

The inspector had also brought subpoenas for himself and Prince Aribert of Posen and the commissionaire to attend the inquest.

'I thought Mr Dimmock's remains were removed last night,' said Racksole wearily.

'No, sir. The fact is the van was engaged on another job.'

The inspector gave the least hint of a professional smile, and Racksole, disgusted, told him curtly to go and perform his duties.

In a few minutes a message came from the inspector requesting Mr Racksole to be good enough to come to him on the first floor. Racksole went. In the ante-room, where the body of Reginald Dimmock had originally been placed, were the inspector and Prince Aribert, and two policemen.

'Well?' said Racksole, after he and the Prince had exchanged bows. Then he saw a coffin laid across two chairs. 'I see a coffin has been obtained,' he remarked. 'Quite right.' He approached it. 'It's empty,' he observed unthinkingly.

'Just so,' said the inspector. 'The body of the deceased has disappeared. And his Serene Highness Prince Aribert informs me that though he has occupied a room immediately opposite, on the other side of the corridor, he can throw no light on the affair.'

'Indeed, I cannot!' said the Prince, and though he spoke with sufficient calmness and dignity, you could see that he was deeply pained, even distressed.

'Well, I'm –' murmured Racksole, and stopped.

## Chapter Seven

## NELLA AND THE PRINCE

IT appeared impossible to Theodore Racksole that so cumbrous an article as a corpse could be removed out of his hotel, with no trace, no hint, no clue as to the time or the manner of the performance of the deed. After the first feeling of surprise, Racksole grew coldly and severely angry. He had a mind to dismiss the entire staff of the hotel. He personally examined the night-watchman, the chambermaids and all other persons who by chance might or ought to know something of the affair; but without avail. The corpse of Reginald Dimmock had vanished utterly – disappeared like a fleshless spirit. Of course there were the police. But Theodore Racksole held the police in sorry esteem. He acquainted them with the facts, answered their queries with a patient weariness, and expected nothing whatever from that quarter. He also had several interviews with Prince Aribert of Posen, but though the Prince was suavity itself and beyond doubt genuinely concerned about the fate of his dead attendant, yet it seemed to Racksole that he was keeping something back, that he hesitated to say all he knew. Racksole, with characteristic insight, decided that the death of Reginald Dimmock was only a minor event, which had occurred, as it were, on the fringe of some far more profound mystery. And, therefore, he decided to wait, with his eyes very wide open, until something else happened that would throw light on the business. At the moment he took only one measure – he arranged that the theft of Dimmock's body should not appear in the newspapers. It is astonishing how well a secret can be kept, when the possessors of the secret are handled with the proper mixture of firmness and persuasion. Racksole managed this very neatly. It was a complicated job, and his success in it rather pleased him.

At the same time he was conscious of being temporarily worsted by an unknown group of schemers, in which he felt convinced that Jules was an important item. He could scarcely look Nella in the eyes. The girl had evidently expected him to unmask this conspiracy at once, with a single stroke of the millionaire's magic wand. She was thoroughly accustomed, in the land of her birth, to seeing him achieve impossible feats. Over there he was a 'boss'; men trembled before his name; when he wished a thing to happen – well, it happened; if he desired to know a thing, he just knew it. But here, in London, Theodore Racksole was not quite the same Theodore Racksole. He dominated New York; but London, for the most part, seemed not to take much interest in him; and there were certainly various persons in London who were capable of snapping their fingers at him – at Theodore Racksole. Neither he nor his daughter could get used to that fact.

As for Nella, she concerned herself for a little with the ordinary business of the bureau, and watched the incomings and outgoings of Prince Aribert with a kindly interest. She perceived, what her father had failed to perceive, that His Highness had assumed an attitude of reserve merely to hide the secret distraction and dismay which consumed him. She saw that the poor fellow had no settled plan in his head, and that he was troubled by something which, so far, he had confided to nobody. It came to her knowledge that each morning he walked to and fro on the Victoria Embankment, alone, and apparently with no object. On the third morning she decided that driving exercise on the Embankment would be good for her health, and thereupon ordered a carriage and issued forth, arrayed in a miraculous putty-coloured gown. Near Blackfriars Bridge she met the Prince, and the carriage was drawn up by the pavement.

'Good morning, Prince,' she greeted him. 'Are you mistaking this for Hyde Park?'

He bowed and smiled.

'I usually walk here in the mornings,' he said.

'You surprise me,' she returned. 'I thought I was the only person in London who preferred the Embankment, with this view of the river, to the dustiness of Hyde Park. I can't imagine how it is that London will never take exercise anywhere except in that ridiculous Park. Now, if they had Central Park – '

'I think the Embankment is the finest spot in all London,' he said.

She leaned a little out of the landau, bringing her face nearer to his.

'I do believe we are kindred spirits, you and I,' she murmured; and then, 'Au revoir, Prince!'

'One moment, Miss Racksole.' His quick tones had a note of entreaty.

'I am in a hurry,' she fibbed; 'I am not merely taking exercise this morning. You have no idea how busy we are.'

'Ah! then I will not trouble you. But I leave the Grand Babylon to-night.'

'Do you?' she said. 'Then will your Highness do me the honour of lunching with me today in Father's room? Father will be out – he is having a day in the City with some stockbroking persons.'

'I shall be charmed,' said the Prince, and his face showed that he meant it.

Nella drove off.

If the lunch was a success that result was due partly to Rocco, and partly to Nella. The Prince said little beyond what the ordinary rules of the conversational game demanded. His hostess talked much and talked well, but she failed to rouse her guest. When they had had coffee he took a rather formal leave of her.

'Good-bye, Prince,' she said, 'but I thought – that is, no I didn't. Good-bye.'

'You thought I wished to discuss something with you. I did; but I have decided that I have no right to burden your mind with my affairs.'

'But suppose – suppose I wish to be burdened?'

'That is your good nature.'

'Sit down,' she said abruptly, 'and tell me everything; mind, everything. I adore secrets.'

Almost before he knew it he was talking to her, rapidly, eagerly.

'Why should I weary you with my confidences?' he said. 'I don't know, I cannot tell; but I feel that I must. I feel that you will understand me better than anyone else in the world. And yet why should you understand me? Again, I don't know. Miss Racksole, I will disclose to you the whole trouble in a word. Prince Eugen, the hereditary Grand Duke of Posen, has disappeared. Four days ago I was to have met him at Ostend. He had affairs in London. He wished me to come with him. I sent Dimmock on in front, and waited for Eugen. He did not arrive. I telegraphed back to Cologne, his last stopping-place, and I learned that he had left there in accordance with his programme; I learned also that he had passed through Brussels. It must have been between Brussels and the railway station at Ostend Quay that he disappeared. He was travelling with a single equerry, and the equerry, too, has vanished. I need not explain to you, Miss Racksole, that when a person of the importance of my nephew contrives to get lost one must proceed cautiously. One cannot advertise for him in the London *Times*. Such a disappearance must be kept secret. The people at Posen and at Berlin believe that Eugen is in London, here, at this hotel; or, rather, they did so believe. But this morning I received a cypher telegram from – from His Majesty the Emperor, a very peculiar telegram, asking when Eugen might be expected to return to Posen, and requesting that he should go first to Berlin. That telegram was addressed to myself. Now, if the Emperor thought that Eugen was here, why should he have caused the telegram to be addressed to me? I have hesitated for three days, but I can hesitate no longer. I must myself go to the Emperor and acquaint him with the facts.'

'I suppose you've just got to keep straight with him?' Nella was on the point of saying, but she checked herself and substituted, 'The Emperor is your chief, is he not? "First among equals", you call him.'

'His Majesty is our over-lord,' said Aribert quietly.

'Why do you not take immediate steps to inquire as to the whereabouts of your Royal nephew?' she asked simply. The affair seemed to her just then so plain and straightforward.

'Because one of two things may have happened. Either Eugen may have been, in plain language, abducted, or he may have had his own reasons for changing his programme and keeping in the background – out of reach of telegraph and post and railways.'

'What sort of reasons?'

'Do not ask me. In the history of every family there are passages – ' He stopped.

'And what was Prince Eugen's object in coming to London?'

Aribert hesitated.

'Money,' he said at length. 'As a family we are very poor – poorer than anyone in Berlin suspects.'

'Prince Aribert,' Nella said, 'shall I tell you what I think?'

She leaned back in her chair, and looked at him out of half-closed eyes. His pale, thin, distinguished face held her gaze as if by some fascination. There could be no mistaking this man for anything else but a Prince.

'If you will,' he said.

'Prince Eugen is the victim of a plot.'

'You think so?'

'I am perfectly convinced of it.'

'But why? What can be the object of a plot against him?'

'That is a point of which you should know more than me,' she remarked drily.

'Ah! Perhaps, perhaps,' he said. 'But, dear Miss Racksole, why are you so sure?'

'There are several reasons, and they are connected with Mr Dimmock. Did you ever suspect, your Highness, that that poor young man was not entirely loyal to you?'

'He was absolutely loyal,' said the Prince, with all the earnestness of conviction.

'A thousand pardons, but he was not.'

'Miss Racksole, if any other than yourself made that assertion, I would – I would – '

'Consign them to the deepest dungeon in Posen?' she laughed lightly. 'Listen.' And she told him of the incidents which had occurred in the night preceding his arrival in the hotel.

'Do you mean, Miss Racksole, that there was an understanding between poor Dimmock and this fellow Jules?'

'There was an understanding.'

'Impossible!'

'Your Highness, the man who wishes to probe a mystery to

its root never uses the word "impossible". But I will say this for young Mr Dimmock. I think he repented, and I think that it was because he repented that he – er – died so suddenly, and that his body was spirited away.'

'Why has no one told me these things before?' Aribert exclaimed.

'Princes seldom hear the truth,' she said.

He was astonished at her coolness, her firmness of assertion, her air of complete acquaintance with the world.

'Miss Racksole,' he said, 'if you will permit me to say it, I have never in my life met a woman like you. May I rely on your sympathy – your support?'

'My support, Prince? But how?'

'I do not know,' he replied. 'But you could help me if you would. A woman, when she has brain, always has more brain than a man.'

'Ah!' she said ruefully, 'I have no brains, but I do believe I could help you.'

What prompted her to make that assertion she could not have explained, even to herself. But she made it, and she had a suspicion – a prescience – that it would be justified, though by what means, through what good fortune, was still a mystery to her.

'Go to Berlin,' she said. 'I see that you must do that; you have no alternative. As for the rest, we shall see. Something will occur. I shall be here. My father will be here. You must count us as your friends.'

He kissed her hand when he left, and afterwards, when she was alone, she kissed the spot his lips had touched again and again. Now, thinking the matter out in the calmness of solitude, all seemed strange, unreal, uncertain to her. Were conspiracies actually possible nowadays? Did queer things actually happen in Europe? And did they actually happen in London hotels? She dined with her father that night.

'I hear Prince Aribert has left,' said Theodore Racksole.

'Yes,' she assented. She said not a word about their interview.

## Chapter Eight

## ARRIVAL AND DEPARTURE OF THE BARONESS

ON the following morning, just before lunch, a lady, accompanied by a maid and a considerable quantity of luggage, came to the Grand Babylon Hotel. She was a plump, little old lady, with white hair and an old-fashioned bonnet, and she had a quaint, simple smile of surprise at everything in general. Nevertheless, she gave the impression of belonging to some aristocracy, though not the English aristocracy. Her tone to her maid, whom she addressed in broken English – the girl being apparently English – was distinctly insolent, with the calm, unconscious insolence peculiar to a certain type of Continental nobility. The name on the lady's card ran thus: 'Baroness Zerlinski'. She desired rooms on the third floor. It happened that Nella was in the bureau.

'On the third floor, madam?' questioned Nella, in her best clerkly manner.

'I did say on de tird floor,' said the plump little old lady.

'We have accommodation on the second floor.'

'I wish to be high up, out of de dust and in de light,' explained the Baroness.

'We have no suites on the third floor, madam.'

'Never mind, no mattaire! Have you not two rooms that communicate?'

Nella consulted her books, rather awkwardly.

'Numbers 122 and 123 communicate.'

'Or is it 121 and 122?' the little old lady remarked quickly, and then bit her lip.

'I beg your pardon. I should have said 121 and 122.'

At the moment Nella regarded the Baroness's correction of her figures as a curious chance, but afterwards, when the Baroness had ascended in the lift, the thing struck her as somewhat strange. Perhaps the Baroness Zerlinski had stayed at the hotel before. For the sake of convenience an index of visitors to the hotel was kept and the index extended back for thirty years. Nella examined it, but it did not contain the name of Zerlinski. Then it was that Nella began to imagine, what had swiftly crossed her mind when first the Baroness presented herself at the bureau, that the features of the Baroness were remotely familiar to her. She thought, not that she had seen the old lady's face before, but that she had seen somewhere, some time, a face of a similar cast. It occurred to Nella to look at the 'Almanach de Gotha' – that record of all the mazes of Continental blue blood; but the 'Almanach de Gotha' made no reference to any barony of Zerlinski. Nella inquired where the Baroness meant to take lunch, and was informed that a table had been reserved for her in the dining-room, and she at once decided to lunch in the dining-room herself. Seated in a corner, half-hidden by a pillar, she could survey all the guests, and watch each group as it entered or left. Presently the Baroness appeared, dressed in black, with a tiny lace shawl, despite the June warmth; very stately, very quaint, and gently smiling. Nella observed her intently. The lady ate heartily, working without haste and without delay through the elaborate menu of the luncheon. Nella noticed that she had beautiful white teeth. Then a remarkable thing happened. A cream puff was served to the Baroness by way of sweets, and Nella was astonished to see the little lady remove the top, and with a spoon quietly take something from the interior which looked like a piece of folded paper. No one who had not been watching with the eye of a lynx would have noticed anything extraordinary in the action; indeed, the chances were nine hundred and ninety-nine to one that it would pass unheeded. But, unfortunately for the Baroness, it was the thousandth chance that happened. Nella jumped up, and walking over to the Baroness, said to her:

'I'm afraid that the tart is not quite nice, your ladyship.'

'Thanks, it is delightful,' said the Baroness coldly; her smile had vanished. 'Who are you? I thought you were de bureau clerk.'

'My father is the owner of this hotel. I thought there was something in the tart which ought not to have been there.'

Nella looked the Baroness full in the face. The piece of folded paper, to which a little cream had attached itself, lay under the edge of a plate.

'No, thanks.' The Baroness smiled her simple smile.

Nella departed. She had noticed one trifling thing besides the paper – namely, that the Baroness could pronounce the English 'th' sound if she chose.

That afternoon, in her own room, Nella sat meditating at the window for a long time, and then she suddenly sprang up, her eyes brightening.

'I know,' she exclaimed, clapping her hands. 'It's Miss Spencer, disguised! Why didn't I think of that before?' Her thoughts ran instantly to Prince Aribert. 'Perhaps I can help him,' she said to herself, and gave a little sigh. She went down to the office and inquired whether the Baroness had given any instructions about dinner. She felt that some plan must be formulated. She wanted to get hold of Rocco, and put him in the rack. She knew now that Rocco, the unequalled, was also concerned in this mysterious affair.

'The Baroness Zerlinski has left, about a quarter of an hour ago,' said the attendant.

'But she only arrived this morning.'

'The Baroness's maid said that her mistress had received a telegram and must leave at once. The Baroness paid the bill, and went away in a four-wheeler.'

'Where to?'

'The trunks were labelled for Ostend.'

Perhaps it was instinct, perhaps it was the mere spirit of adventure; but that evening Nella was to be seen of all men on the steamer for Ostend which leaves Dover at 11 p.m. She told no one of her intentions – not even her father, who was not in the hotel when she left. She had scribbled a brief note to him to expect her back in a day or two, and had posted this at Dover. The steamer was the *Marie Henriette*, a large and luxurious boat, whose state-rooms on deck vie with the glories of the

Cunard and White Star liners. One of these state-rooms, the best, was evidently occupied, for every curtain of its windows was carefully drawn. Nella did not hope that the Baroness was on board; it was quite possible for the Baroness to have caught the eight o'clock steamer, and it was also possible for the Baroness not to have gone to Ostend at all, but to some other place in an entirely different direction. Nevertheless, Nella had a faint hope that the lady who called herself Zerlinski might be in that curtained stateroom, and throughout the smooth moonlit voyage she never once relaxed her observation of its doors and its windows.

The *Maria Henriette* arrived in Ostend Harbour punctually at 2 a.m. in the morning. There was the usual heterogeneous, gesticulating crowd on the quay. Nella kept her post near the door of the state-room, and at length she was rewarded by seeing it open. Four middle-aged Englishmen issued from it. From a glimpse of the interior Nella saw that they had spent the voyage in card-playing.

It would not be too much to say that she was distinctly annoyed. She pretended to be annoyed with circumstances, but really she was annoyed with Nella Racksole. At two in the morning, without luggage, without any companionship, and without a plan of campaign, she found herself in a strange foreign port – a port of evil repute, possessing some of the worst-managed hotels in Europe. She strolled on the quay for a few minutes, and then she saw the smoke of another steamer in the offing. She inquired from an official what that steamer might be, and was told that it was the eight o'clock from Dover, which had broken down, put into Calais for some slight necessary repairs, and was arriving at its destination nearly four hours late. Her mercurial spirits rose again. A minute ago she was regarding herself as no better than a ninny engaged in a wild-goose chase. Now she felt that after all she had been very sagacious and cunning. She was morally sure that she would find the Zerlinski woman on this second steamer, and she took all the credit to herself in advance. Such is human nature.

The steamer seemed interminably slow in coming into harbour. Nella walked on the Digue for a few minutes to watch it the better. The town was silent and almost deserted. It had a false and sinister aspect. She remembered tales which she had heard of this glittering resort, which in the season holds more scoundrels than any place in Europe, save only Monte Carlo. She remembered that the gilded adventures of every nation under the sun forgathered there either for business or pleasure, and that some of the most wonderful crimes of the latter half of the century had been schemed and matured in that haunt of cosmopolitan iniquity.

When the second steamer arrived Nella stood at the end of the gangway, close to the ticket-collector. The first person to step on shore was – not the Baroness Zerlinski, but Miss Spencer herself! Nella turned aside instantly, hiding her face, and Miss Spencer, carrying a small bag, hurried with assured footsteps to the Custom House. It seemed as if she knew the port of Ostend fairly well. The moon shone like day, and Nella had full opportunity to observe her quarry. She could see now quite plainly that the Baroness Zerlinski had been only Miss Spencer in disguise. There was the same gait, the same movement of the head and of the hips; the white hair was easily to be accounted for by a wig, and the wrinkles by a paint brush and some grease paints. Miss Spencer, whose hair was now its old accustomed yellow, got through the Custom House without difficulty, and Nella saw her call a closed carriage and say something to the driver. The vehicle drove off. Nella jumped into the next carriage – an open one – that came up.

'Follow that carriage,' she said succinctly to the driver in French.

'Bien, madame!' The driver whipped up his horse, and the animal shot forward with a terrific clatter over the cobbles. It appeared that this driver was quite accustomed to following other carriages.

'Now I am fairly in for it!' said Nella to herself. She laughed unsteadily, but her heart was beating with an extraordinary thump.

For some time the pursued vehicle kept well in front. It crossed the town nearly from end to end, and plunged into a maze of small streets far on the south side of the Kursaal. Then gradually Nella's equipage began to overtake it. The first carriage stopped with a jerk before a tall dark house, and Miss Spencer emerged. Nella called to her driver to stop, but he, determined to be in at the death, was engaged in whipping his horse, and he completely ignored her commands. He drew up triumphantly at the tall dark house just at the moment when Miss Spencer disappeared into it. The other carriage drove away. Nella, uncertain what to do, stepped down from her carriage and gave the driver some money. At the same moment a man reopened the door of the house, which had closed on Miss Spencer.

'I want to see Miss Spencer,' said Nella impulsively. She couldn't think of anything else to say.

'Miss Spencer?'

'Yes; she's just arrived.'

'It's O. K., I suppose,' said the man.

'I guess so,' said Nella, and she walked past him into the house. She was astonished at her own audacity.

Miss Spencer was just going into a room off the narrow hall. Nella followed her into the apartment, which was shabbily furnished in the Belgian lodging-house style.

'Well, Miss Spencer,' she greeted the former Baroness Zerlinski, 'I guess you didn't expect to see me. You left our hotel very suddenly this afternoon, and you left it very suddenly a few days ago; and so I've just called to make a few inquiries.'

To do the lady justice, Miss Spencer bore the surprising ordeal very well. She did not flinch; she betrayed no emotion. The sole sign of perturbation was in her hurried breathing.

'You have ceased to be the Baroness Zerlinski,' Nella continued. 'May I sit down?'

'Certainly, sit down,' said Miss Spencer, copying the girl's tone. 'You are a fairly smart young woman, that I will say. What do you want? Weren't my books all straight?'

'Your books were all straight. I haven't come about your books. I have come about the murder of Reginald Dimmock, the disappearance of his corpse, and the disappearance of Prince Eugen of Posen. I thought you might be able to help me in some investigations which I am making.'

Miss Spencer's eyes gleamed, and she stood up and moved swiftly to the mantelpiece.

'You may be a Yankee, but you're a fool,' she said.

She took hold of the bell-rope.

'Don't ring that bell if you value your life,' said Nella.

'If what?' Miss Spencer remarked.

'If you value your life,' said Nella calmly, and with the words she pulled from her pocket a very neat and dainty little revolver.

## Chapter Nine

## TWO WOMEN AND THE REVOLVER

'You – you're only doing that to frighten me,' stammered Miss Spencer, in a low, quavering voice.

'Am I?' Nella replied, as firmly as she could, though her hand shook violently with excitement, could Miss Spencer but have observed it. 'Am I? You said just now that I might be a Yankee girl, but I was a fool. Well, I am a Yankee girl, as you call it; and in my country, if they don't teach revolver-shooting in boarding-schools, there are at least a lot of girls who can handle a revolver. I happen to be one of them. I tell you that if you ring that bell you will suffer.'

Most of this was simple bluff on Nella's part, and she trembled lest Miss Spencer should perceive that it was simple bluff. Happily for her, Miss Spencer belonged to that order of women who have every sort of courage except physical courage. Miss Spencer could have withstood successfully any moral trial, but persuade her that her skin was in danger, and she would succumb. Nella at once divined this useful fact, and proceeded accordingly, hiding the strangeness of her own sensations as well as she could.

'You had better sit down now,' said Nella, 'and I will ask you a few questions.'

And Miss Spencer obediently sat down, rather white, and trying to screw her lips into a formal smile.

'Why did you leave the Grand Babylon that night?' Nella began her examination, putting on a stern, barrister-like expression.

'I had orders to, Miss Racksole.'

'Whose orders?'

'Well, I'm – I'm – the fact is, I'm a married woman, and it was my husband's orders.'

'Who is your husband?'

'Tom Jackson – Jules, you know, head waiter at the Grand Babylon.'

'So Jules's real name is Tom Jackson? Why did he want you to leave without giving notice?'

'I'm sure I don't know, Miss Racksole. I swear I don't know. He's my husband, and, of course, I do what he tells me, as you will some day do what your husband tells you. Please heaven you'll get a better husband than mine!'

Miss Spencer showed a sign of tears.

Nella fingered the revolver, and put it at full cock. 'Well,' she repeated, 'why did he want you to leave?' She was tremendously surprised at her own coolness, and somewhat pleased with it, too.

'I can't tell you, I can't tell you.'

'You've just got to,' Nella said, in a terrible, remorseless tone.

'He – he wished me to come over here to Ostend. Something had gone wrong. Oh! he's a fearful man, is Tom. If I told you, he'd – '

'Had something gone wrong in the hotel, or over here?'

'Both.'

'Was it about Prince Eugen of Posen?'

'I don't know – that is, yes, I think so.'

'What has your husband to do with Prince Eugen?'

'I believe he has some – some sort of business with him, some money business.'

'And was Mr Dimmock in this business?'

'I fancy so, Miss Racksole. I'm telling you all I know, that I swear.'

'Did your husband and Mr Dimmock have a quarrel that night in Room 111?'

'They had some difficulty.'

'And the result of that was that you came to Ostend instantly?'

'Yes; I suppose so.'

'And what were you to do in Ostend? What were your instructions from this husband of yours?'

Miss Spencer's head dropped on her arms on the table which separated her from Nella, and she appeared to sob violently.

'Have pity on me,' she murmured, 'I can't tell you any more.'

'Why?'

'He'd kill me if he knew.'

'You're wandering from the subject,' observed Nella coldly. 'This is the last time I shall warn you. Let me tell you plainly I've got the best reasons for being desperate, and if anything happens to you I shall say I did it in self-defence. Now, what were you to do in Ostend?'

'I shall die for this anyhow,' whined Miss Spencer, and then, with a sort of fierce despair, 'I had to keep watch on Prince Eugen.'

'Where? In this house?'

Miss Spencer nodded, and, looking up, Nella could see the traces of tears in her face.

'Then Prince Eugen was a prisoner? Some one had captured him at the instigation of Jules?'

'Yes, if you must have it.'

'Why was it necessary for you specially to come to Ostend?'

'Oh! Tom trusts me. You see, I know Ostend. Before I took that place at the Grand Babylon I had travelled over Europe, and Tom knew that I knew a thing or two.'

'Why did you take the place at the Grand Babylon?'

'Because Tom told me to. He said I should be useful to him there.'

'Is your husband an Anarchist, or something of that kind, Miss Spencer?'

'I don't know. I'd tell you in a minute if I knew. But he's one of those that keep themselves to themselves.'

'Do you know if he has ever committed a murder?'

'Never!' said Miss Spencer, with righteous repudiation of the mere idea.

'But Mr Dimmock was murdered. He was poisoned. If he had not been poisoned why was his body stolen? It must have been stolen to prevent inquiry, to hide traces. Tell me about that.'

'I take my dying oath,' said Miss Spencer, standing up a little way from the table, 'I take my dying oath I didn't know Mr Dimmock was dead till I saw it in the newspaper.'

'You swear you had no suspicion of it?'

'I swear I hadn't.'

Nella was inclined to believe the statement. The woman and the girl looked at each other in the tawdry, frowsy, lamp-lit room. Miss Spencer nervously patted her yellow hair into shape, as if gradually recovering her composure and equanimity. The whole affair seemed like a dream to Nella, a disturbing, sinister nightmare. She was a little uncertain what to say. She felt that she had not yet got hold of any very definite information. 'Where is Prince Eugen now?' she asked at length.

'I don't know, miss.'

'He isn't in this house?'

'No, miss.'

'Ah! We will see presently.'

'They took him away, Miss Racksole.'

'Who took him away? Some of your husband's friends?'

'Some of his – acquaintances.'

'Then there is a gang of you?'

'A gang of us – a gang! I don't know what you mean,' Miss Spencer quavered.

'Oh, but you must know,' smiled Nella calmly. 'You can't possibly be so innocent as all that, Mrs Tom Jackson. You can't play games with me. You've just got to remember that I'm what you call a Yankee girl. There's one thing that I mean to find out, within the next five minutes, and that is – how your charming husband kidnapped Prince Eugen, and why he kidnapped him. Let us begin with the second question. You have evaded it once.'

Miss Spencer looked into Nella's face, and then her eyes dropped, and her fingers worked nervously with the table-cloth.

'How can I tell you,' she said, 'when I don't know? You've got the whip-hand of me, and you're tormenting me for your own pleasure.' She wore an expression of persecuted innocence.

'Did Mr Tom Jackson want to get some money out of Prince Eugen?'

'Money! Not he! Tom's never short of money.'

'But I mean a lot of money – tens of thousands, hundreds of thousands?'

'Tom never wanted money from anyone,' said Miss Spencer doggedly.

'Then had he some reason for wishing to prevent Prince Eugen from coming to London?'

'Perhaps he had. I don't know. If you kill me, I don't know.'

Nella stopped to reflect. Then she raised the revolver. It was a mechanical, unintentional sort of action, and certainly she had no intention of using the weapon, but, strange to say, Miss Spencer again cowered before it. Even at that moment Nella wondered that a woman like Miss Spencer could be so simple as to think the revolver would actually be used. Having absolutely no physical cowardice herself, Nella had the greatest difficulty in imagining that other people could be at the mercy of a bodily fear. Still, she saw her advantage, and used it relentlessly, and with as much theatrical gesture as she could command. She raised the revolver till it was level with Miss Spencer's face, and suddenly a new, queer feeling took hold of her. She knew that she would indeed use that revolver now, if the miserable woman before her drove her too far. She felt afraid – afraid of herself; she was in the grasp of a savage, primeval instinct. In a flash she saw Miss Spencer dead at her feet – the police – a court of justice – the scaffold. It was horrible.

'Speak,' she said hoarsely, and Miss Spencer's face went whiter.

'Tom did say,' the woman whispered rapidly, awesomely, 'that if Prince Eugen got to London it would upset his scheme.'

'What scheme? What scheme? Answer me.'

'Heaven help me, I don't know.' Miss Spencer sank into a chair. 'He said Mr Dimmock had turned tail, and he should have to settle him and then Rocco –'

'Rocco! What about Rocco?' Nella could scarcely hear herself. Her grip of the revolver tightened.

Miss Spencer's eyes opened wider; she gazed at Nella with a glassy stare.

'Don't ask me. It's death!' Her eyes were fixed as if in horror.

'It is,' said Nella, and the sound of her voice seemed to her to issue from the lips of some third person.

75

'It's death,' repeated Miss Spencer, and gradually her head and shoulders sank back, and hung loosely over the chair. Nella was conscious of a sudden revulsion. The woman had surely fainted. Dropping the revolver she ran round the table. She was herself again – feminine, sympathetic, the old Nella. She felt immensely relieved that this had happened. But at the same instant Miss Spencer sprang up from the chair like a cat, seized the revolver, and with a wild movement of the arm flung it against the window. It crashed through the glass, exploding as it went, and there was a tense silence.

'I told you that you were a fool,' remarked Miss Spencer slowly, 'coming here like a sort of female Jack Sheppard, and trying to get the best of me. We are on equal terms now. You frightened me, but I knew I was a cleverer woman than you, and that in the end, if I kept on long enough, I should win. Now it will be my turn.'

Dumbfounded, and overcome with a miserable sense of the truth of Miss Spencer's words, Nella stood still. The idea of her colossal foolishness swept through her like a flood. She felt almost ashamed. But even at this juncture she had no fear. She faced the woman bravely, her mind leaping about in search of some plan. She could think of nothing but a bribe – an enormous bribe.

'I admit you've won,' she said, 'but I've not finished yet. Just listen.'

Miss Spencer folded her arms, and glanced at the door, smiling bitterly.

'You know my father is a millionaire; perhaps you know that he is one of the richest men in the world. If I give you my word of honour not to reveal anything that you've told me, what will you take to let me go free?'

'What sum do you suggest?' asked Miss Spencer carelessly.

'Twenty thousand pounds,' said Nella promptly. She had begun to regard the affair as a business operation.

Miss Spencer's lip curled.

'A hundred thousand.'

Again Miss Spencer's lip curled.

'Well, say a million. I can rely on my father, and so may you.'

'You think you are worth a million to him?'

'I do,' said Nella.

'And you think we could trust you to see that it was paid?'

'Of course you could.'

'And we should not suffer afterwards in any way?'

'I would give you my word, and my father's word.'

'Bah!' exclaimed Miss Spencer: 'how do you know I wouldn't let you go free for nothing? You are only a rash, silly girl.'

'I know you wouldn't. I can read your face too well.'

'You are right,' Miss Spencer replied slowly. 'I wouldn't. I wouldn't let you go for all the dollars in America.'

Nella felt cold down the spine, and sat down again in her chair. A draught of air from the broken window blew on her cheek. Steps sounded in the passage; the door opened, but Nella did not turn round. She could not move her eyes from Miss Spencer's. There was a noise of rushing water in her ears. She lost consciousness, and slipped limply to the ground.

# Chapter Ten

## AT SEA

IT seemed to Nella that she was being rocked gently in a vast cradle, which swayed to and fro with a motion at once slow and incredibly gentle. This sensation continued for some time, and there was added to it the sound of a quick, quiet, muffled beat. Soft, exhilarating breezes wafted her forward in spite of herself, and yet she remained in a delicious calm. She wondered if her mother was kneeling by her side, whispering some lullaby in her childish ears. Then strange colours swam before her eyes, her eyelids wavered, and at last she awoke. For a few moments her gaze travelled to and fro in a vain search for some clue to her surroundings. She was aware of nothing except a sense of repose and a feeling of relief that some mighty and fatal struggle was over; she cared not whether she had conquered or suffered defeat in the struggle of her soul with some other soul; it was finished, done with, and the consciousness of its conclusion satisfied and contented her. Gradually her brain, recovering from its obsession, began to grasp the phenomena of her surroundings, and she saw that she was on a yacht, and that the yacht was moving. The motion of the cradle was the smooth rolling of the vessel; the beat was the beat of its screw; the strange colours were the cloud tints thrown by the sun as it rose over a distant and receding shore in the wake of the yacht; her mother's lullaby was the crooned song of the man at the wheel. Nella all through her life had had many experiences of yachting. From the waters of the River Hudson to those bluer tides of the Mediterranean Sea, she had yachted in all seasons and all weathers. She loved the water, and now it seemed deliciously right and proper that she should be on the water again. She raised her head to look round, and then let it sink back: she was fatigued, enervated; she desired only solitude and calm; she had no care, no anxiety, no responsibility: a hundred years might have passed since her meeting with Miss Spencer, and the memory of that meeting appeared to have faded into the remotest background of her mind.

It was a small yacht, and her practised eye at once told that it belonged to the highest aristocracy of pleasure craft. As she reclined in the deck-chair (it did not occur to her at that moment to speculate as to the identity of the person who had led her therein) she examined all visible details of the vessel. The deck was as white and smooth as her own hand, and the seams ran along its length like blue veins. All the brass-work, from the band round the slender funnel to the concave surface of the binnacle, shone like gold. The tapered masts stretched upwards at a rakish angle, and the rigging seemed like spun silk. No sails were set; the yacht was under steam, and doing about seven or eight knots. She judged that it was a boat of a hundred tons or so, probably Clyde-built, and not more than two or three years old. No one was to be seen on deck except the man at the wheel: this man wore a blue jersey; but there was neither name nor initial on the jersey, nor was there a name on the white life-buoys lashed to the main rigging, nor on the polished dinghy which hung on the starboard davits. She called to the man, and called again, in a feeble voice, but the steerer took no notice of her, and continued his quiet song as though nothing else existed in the universe save the yacht, the sea, the sun, and himself.

Then her eyes swept the outline of the land from which they were hastening, and she could just distinguish a lighthouse and a great white irregular dome, which she recognized as the Kursaal at Ostend, that gorgeous rival of the gaming palace at Monte Carlo. So she was leaving Ostend. The rays of the sun fell on her caressingly, like a restorative. All around the water was changing from wonderful greys and dark blues to still more wonderful pinks and translucent unearthly greens; the magic kaleidoscope of dawn was going forward in its accustomed way, regardless of the vicissitudes of mortals. Here and there in the distance she descried a sail – the brown sail of some Ostend fishing-boat returning home after a night's trawling. Then the beat of paddles caught her ear, and a steamer blundered past, wallowing clumsily among the waves like a tortoise. It was the *Swallow* from London. She could see some of its passengers leaning curiously over the aft-rail. A girl in a mackintosh signalled to her, and mechanically she answered the salute with her arm. The officer of the bridge of the *Swallow* hailed the yacht, but the man at the wheel offered no reply. In another minute the *Swallow* was nothing but a blot in the distance.

Nella tried to sit straight in the deck-chair, but she found herself unable to do so. Throwing off the rug which covered her, she discovered that she had been tied to the chair by means of a piece of broad webbing. Instantly she was alert, awake, angry; she knew that her perils were not over; she felt that possibly they had scarcely yet begun. Her lazy contentment, her dreamy sense of peace and repose, vanished utterly, and she steeled herself to meet the dangers of a grave and difficult situation.

Just at that moment a man came up from below. He was a man of forty or so, clad in irreproachable blue, with a peaked yachting cap. He raised the cap politely.

'Good morning,' he said. 'Beautiful sunrise, isn't it?' The clever and calculated insolence of his tone cut her like a lash as she lay bound in the chair. Like all people who have lived easy and joyous lives in those fair regions where gold smoothes every crease and law keeps a tight hand on disorder, she found it hard to realize that there were other regions where gold was useless and law without power. Twenty-four hours ago she would have declared it impossible that such an experience as she had suffered could happen to anyone; she would have talked airily about civilization and the nineteenth century, and progress and the police. But her experience was teaching her that human nature remains always the same, and that beneath the thin crust of security on which we good citizens exist the dark and secret forces of crime continue to move, just as they did in the days when you couldn't go from Cheapside to Chelsea without being set upon by thieves. Her experience was in a fair way to teach her this lesson better than she could have learnt it even in the bureaux of the detective police of Paris, London, and St Petersburg.

'Good morning,' the man repeated, and she glanced at him with a sullen, angry gaze.

'You!' she exclaimed, 'You, Mr Thomas Jackson, if that is your name! Loose me from this chair, and I will talk to you.' Her eyes flashed as she spoke, and the contempt in them added mightily to her beauty. Mr Thomas Jackson, otherwise Jules, erstwhile head waiter at the Grand Babylon, considered himself a connoisseur in feminine loveliness, and the vision of Nella Racksole smote him like an exquisite blow.

'With pleasure,' he replied. 'I had forgotten that to prevent you from falling I had secured you to the chair'; and with a quick movement he unfastened the band. Nella stood up, quivering with fiery annoyance and scorn.

'Now,' she said, fronting him, 'what is the meaning of this?'

'You fainted,' he replied imperturbably. 'Perhaps you don't remember.'

The man offered her a deck-chair with a characteristic gesture. Nella was obliged to acknowledge, in spite of herself, that the fellow had distinction, an air of breeding. No one would have guessed that for twenty years he had been an hotel waiter. His long, lithe figure, and easy, careless carriage seemed to be the figure and carriage of an aristocrat, and his voice was quiet, restrained, and authoritative.

'That has nothing to do with my being carried off in this yacht of yours.'

'It is not my yacht,' he said, 'but that is a minor detail. As to the more important matter, forgive me that I remind you that only a few hours ago you were threatening a lady in my house with a revolver.'

'Then it was your house?'

'Why not? May I not possess a house?' He smiled.

'I must request you to put the yacht about at once, instantly, and take me back.' She tried to speak firmly.

'Ah!' he said, 'I am afraid that's impossible. I didn't put out to sea with the intention of returning at once, instantly.' In the last words he gave a faint imitation of her tone.

'When I do get back,' she said, 'when my father gets to know of this affair, it will be an exceedingly bad day for you, Mr Jackson.'

'But supposing your father doesn't hear of it –'

'What?'

'Supposing you never get back?'

'Do you mean, then, to have my murder on your conscience?'

'Talking of murder,' he said, 'you came very near to murdering my friend, Miss Spencer. At least, so she tells me.'

'Is Miss Spencer on board?' Nella asked, seeing perhaps a faint ray of hope in the possible presence of a woman.

'Miss Spencer is not on board. There is no one on board except you and myself and a small crew – a very discreet crew, I may add.'

'I will have nothing more to say to you. You must take your own course.'

'Thanks for the permission,' he said. 'I will send you up some breakfast.'

He went to the saloon stairs and whistled, and a Negro boy appeared with a tray of chocolate. Nella took it, and, without the slightest hesitation, threw it overboard. Mr Jackson walked away a few steps and then returned.

'You have spirit,' he said, 'and I admire spirit. It is a rare quality.'

She made no reply.

'Why did you mix yourself up in my affairs at all?' he went on.

Again she made no reply, but the question set her thinking: why had she mixed herself up in this mysterious business? It was quite at variance with the usual methods of her gay and butter-fly existence to meddle at all with serious things. Had she acted merely from a desire to see justice done and wickedness punished? Or was it the desire of adventure? Or was it, perhaps, the desire to be of service to His Serene Highness Prince Aribert?

'It is no fault of mine that you are in this fix,' Jules continued. 'I didn't bring you into it. You brought yourself into it. You and your father – you have been moving along at a pace which is rather too rapid.'

'That remains to be seen,' she put in coldly.

'It does,' he admitted. 'And I repeat that I can't help admiring you – that is, when you aren't interfering with my private affairs. That is a proceeding which I have never tolerated from anyone – not even from a millionaire, nor even from a beautiful woman.' He bowed. 'I will tell you what I propose to do. I propose to escort you to a place of safety, and to keep you there till my operations are concluded, and the possibility of interference entirely removed. You spoke just now of murder. What a crude notion that was of yours! It is only the amateur who practises murder – '

'What about Reginald Dimmock?' she interjected quickly.

He paused gravely.

'Reginald Dimmock,' he repeated. 'I had imagined his was a case of heart disease. Let me send you up some more chocolate. I'm sure you're hungry.'

'I will starve before I touch your food,' she said.

'Gallant creature!' he murmured, and his eyes roved over her face. Her superb, supercilious beauty overcame him. 'Ah!' he said, 'what a wife you would make!' He approached nearer to her. 'You and I, Miss Racksole, your beauty and wealth and my brains – we could conquer the world. Few men are worthy of you, but I am one of the few. Listen! You might do worse. Marry me. I am a great man; I shall be greater. I adore you. Marry me, and I will save your life. All shall be well. I will begin again. The past shall be as though there had been no past.'

'This is somewhat sudden – Jules,' she said with biting contempt.

'Did you expect me to be conventional?' he retorted. 'I love you.'

'Granted,' she said, for the sake of the argument. 'Then what will occur to your present wife?'

'My present wife?'

'Yes, Miss Spencer, as she is called.'

'She told you I was her husband?'

'Incidentally she did.'

'She isn't.'

'Perhaps she isn't. But, nevertheless, I think I won't marry you.' Nella stood like a statue of scorn before him.

He went still nearer to her. 'Give me a kiss, then; one kiss – I won't ask for more; one kiss from those lips, and you shall go free. Men have ruined themselves for a kiss. I will.'

'Coward!' she ejaculated.

'Coward!' he repeated. 'Coward, am I? Then I'll be a coward, and you shall kiss me whether you will or not.'

He put a hand on her shoulder. As she shrank back from his lustrous eyes, with an involuntary scream, a figure sprang out of the dinghy a few feet away. With a single blow, neatly directed to Mr Jackson's ear, Mr Jackson was stretched senseless on the deck. Prince Aribert of Posen stood over him with a revolver. It was probably the greatest surprise of Mr Jackson's whole life.

'Don't be alarmed,' said the Prince to Nella, 'my being here is the simplest thing in the world, and I will explain it as soon as I have finished with this fellow.'

Nella could think of nothing to say, but she noticed the revolver in the Prince's hand.

'Why,' she remarked, 'that's my revolver.'

'It is,' he said, 'and I will explain that, too.'

The man at the wheel gave no heed whatever to the scene.

## Chapter Eleven

## THE COURT PAWNBROKER

'MR SAMPSON LEVI wishes to see you, sir.'

These words, spoken by a servant to Theodore Racksole, aroused the millionaire from a reverie which had been the reverse of pleasant. The fact was, and it is necessary to insist on it, that Mr Racksole, owner of the Grand Babylon Hotel, was by no means in a state of self-satisfaction. A mystery had attached itself to his hotel, and with all his acumen and knowledge of things in general he was unable to solve that mystery. He laughed at the fruitless efforts of the police, but he could not honestly say that his own efforts had been less barren. The public was talking, for, after all, the disappearance of poor Dimmock's body had got noised abroad in an indirect sort of way, and Theodore Racksole did not like the idea of his impeccable hotel being the subject of sinister rumours. He wondered, grimly, what the public and the Sunday newspapers would say if they were aware of all the other phenomena, not yet common property: of Miss Spencer's disappearance, of Jules' strange visits, and of the non-arrival of Prince Eugen of Posen. Theodore Racksole had worried his brain without result. He had conducted an elaborate private investigation without result, and he had spent a certain amount of money without result. The police said that they had a clue; but Racksole remarked that it was always the business of the police to have a clue, that they seldom had more than a clue, and that a clue without some sequel to it was a pretty stupid business. The only sure thing in the whole affair was that a cloud rested over his hotel, his beautiful new toy, the finest of its kind. The cloud was not interfering with business, but, nevertheless, it was a cloud, and he fiercely resented its presence; perhaps it would be more correct to say that he fiercely resented his inability to dissipate it.

'Mr Sampson Levi wishes to see you, sir,' the servant repeated, having received no sign that his master had heard him.

'So I hear,' said Racksole. 'Does he want to see me, personally?'
'He asked for you, sir.'

'Perhaps it is Rocco he wants to see, about a menu or something of that kind?'

'I will inquire, sir,' and the servant made a move to withdraw.

'Stop,' Racksole commanded suddenly. 'Desire Mr Sampson Levi to step this way.'

The great stockbroker of the 'Kaffir Circus' entered with a simple unassuming air. He was a rather short, florid man, dressed like a typical Hebraic financier, with too much watch-chain and too little waistcoat. In his fat hand he held a gold-headed cane, and an absolutely new silk hat – for it was Friday, and Mr Levi purchased a new hat every Friday of his life, holiday times only excepted. He breathed heavily and sniffed through his nose a good deal, as though he had just performed some Herculean physical labour. He glanced at the American millionaire with an expression in which a slight embarrassment might have been detected, but at the same time his round, red face disclosed a certain frank admiration and good nature.

'Mr Racksole, I believe – Mr Theodore Racksole. Proud to meet you, sir.' Such were the first words of Mr Sampson Levi. In form they were the greeting of a third-rate chimney-sweep, but, strangely enough, Theodore Racksole liked their tone. He said to himself that here, precisely where no one would have expected to find one, was an honest man.

'Good day,' said Racksole briefly. 'To what do I owe the pleasure – '

'I expect your time is limited,' answered Sampson Levi. 'Anyhow, mine is, and so I'll come straight to the point, Mr Racksole. I'm a plain man. I don't pretend to be a gentleman or any nonsense of that kind. I'm a stockbroker, that's what I am, and I don't care who knows it. The other night I had a ball in this hotel. It cost me a couple of thousand and odd pounds, and, by the way, I wrote out a cheque for your bill this morning. I don't like balls, but they're useful to me, and my little wife likes 'em, and so we give 'em. Now, I've nothing to say against the hotel management as regards that ball: it was very decently done, very decently, but what I want to know is this – Why did you have a private detective among my guests?'

'A private detective?' exclaimed Racksole, somewhat surprised at this charge.

'Yes,' Mr Sampson Levi said firmly, fanning himself in his chair, and gazing at Theodore Racksole with the direct earnest expression of a man having a grievance. 'Yes; a private detective. It's a small matter, I know, and I dare say you think you've got a right, as proprietor of the show, to do what you like in that line; but I've just called to tell you that I object. I've called as a matter of principle. I'm not angry; it's the principle of the thing.'

'My dear Mr Levi,' said Racksole, 'I assure you that, having let the Gold Room to a private individual for a private entertainment, I should never dream of doing what you suggest.'

'Straight?' asked Mr Sampson Levi, using his own picturesque language.

'Straight,' said Racksole smiling.

'There was a gent present at my ball that I didn't ask. I've got a wonderful memory for faces, and I know. Several fellows asked me afterwards what he was doing there. I was told by someone that he was one of your waiters, but I didn't believe that. I know nothing of the Grand Babylon; it's not quite my style of tavern, but I don't think you'd send one of your own waiters to watch my guests – unless, of course, you sent him as a waiter; and this chap didn't do any waiting, though he did his share of drinking.'

'Perhaps I can throw some light on this mystery,' said Racksole. 'I may tell you that I was already aware that a man had attended your ball uninvited.'

'How did you get to know?'

'By pure chance, Mr Levi, and not by inquiry. That man was a former waiter at this hotel – the head waiter, in fact – Jules. No doubt you have heard of him.'

'Not I,' said Mr Levi positively.

'Ah!' said Racksole, 'I was informed that everyone knew Jules, but it appears not. Well, be that as it may, previously to the night of your ball, I had dismissed Jules. I had ordered him never to enter the Babylon again. But on that evening I encountered him here – not in the Gold Room, but in the hotel itself. I asked him to explain his presence, and he stated he was your guest. That is all I know of the matter, Mr Levi, and I am extremely sorry that you should have thought me capable of the enormity of placing a private detective among your guests.'

'This is perfectly satisfactory to me,' Mr Sampson Levi said, after a pause. 'I only wanted an explanation, and I've got it. I was told by some pals of mine in the City I might rely on Mr Theodore Racksole going straight to the point, and I'm glad they were right. Now as to that feller Jules, I shall make my own inquiries as to him. Might I ask you why you dismissed him?'

'I don't know why I dismissed him.'

'You don't know? Oh! come now! I'm only asking because I thought you might be able to give me a hint why he turned up uninvited at my ball. Sorry if I'm too inquisitive.'

'Not at all, Mr Levi; but I really don't know. I only sort of felt that he was a suspicious character. I dismissed him on instinct, as it were. See?'

Without answering this question Mr Levi asked another. 'If this Jules is such a well-known person,' he said, 'how could the feller hope to come to my ball without being recognized?'

'Give it up,' said Racksole promptly.

'Well, I'll be moving on,' was Mr Sampson Levi's next remark. 'Good day, and thank ye. I suppose you aren't doing anything in Kaffirs?'

Mr Racksole smiled a negative.

'I thought not,' said Levi. 'Well, I never touch American rails myself, and so I reckon we sha'n't come across each other. Good day.'

'Good day,' said Racksole politely, following Mr Sampson Levi to the door. With his hand on the handle of the door, Mr Levi stopped, and, gazing at Theodore Racksole with a shrewd, quizzical expression, remarked:

'Strange things been going on here lately, eh?'

The two men looked very hard at each other for several seconds.

'Yes,' Racksole assented. 'Know anything about them?'

'Well – no, not exactly,' said Mr Levi. 'But I had a fancy you and I might be useful to each other; I had a kind of fancy to that effect.'

'Come back and sit down again, Mr Levi,' Racksole said, attracted by the evident straightforwardness of the man's tone. 'Now, how can we be of service to each other? I flatter myself I'm something of a judge of character, especially financial character, and I tell you – if you'll put your cards on the table, I'll do ditto with mine.'

'Agreed,' said Mr Sampson Levi. 'I'll begin by explaining my interest in your hotel. I have been expecting to receive a summons from a certain Prince Eugen of Posen to attend him here, and that summons hasn't arrived. It appears that Prince Eugen hasn't come to London at all. Now, I could have taken my dying davy that he would have been here yesterday at the latest.'

'Why were you so sure?'

'Question for question,' said Levi. 'Let's clear the ground first, Mr Racksole. Why did you buy this hotel? That's a conundrum that's been puzzling a lot of our fellows in the City for some days past. Why did you buy the Grand Babylon? And what is the next move to be?'

'There is no next move,' answered Racksole candidly, 'and I will tell you why I bought the hotel; there need be no secret about it. I bought it because of a whim.' And then Theodore Racksole gave this little Jew, whom he had begun to respect, a faithful account of the transaction with Mr Félix Babylon. 'I suppose,' he added, 'you find a difficulty in appreciating my state of mind when I did the deal.'

'Not a bit,' said Mr Levi. 'I once bought an electric launch on the Thames in a very similar way, and it turned out to be one of the most satisfactory purchases I ever made. Then it's a simple accident that you own this hotel at the present moment?'

'A simple accident – all because of a beefsteak and a bottle of Bass.'

'Um!' grunted Mr Sampson Levi, stroking his triple chin.

'To return to Prince Eugen,' Racksole resumed. 'I was expecting His Highness here. The State apartments had been prepared for him. He was due on the very afternoon that young Dimmock died. But he never came, and I have not heard why he has failed to arrive; nor have I seen his name in the papers. What his business was in London, I don't know.'

'I will tell you,' said Mr Sampson Levi, 'he was coming to arrange a loan.'

'A State loan?'

'No – a private loan.'

'Whom from?'

'From me, Sampson Levi. You look surprised. If you'd lived in London a little longer, you'd know that I was just the person the Prince would come to. Perhaps you aren't aware that down Throgmorton Street way I'm called "The Court Pawnbroker", because I arrange loans for the minor, second-class Princes of Europe. I'm a stockbroker, but my real business is financing some of the little Courts of Europe. Now, I may tell you that the Hereditary Prince of Posen particularly wanted a million, and he wanted it by a certain date, and he knew that if the affair wasn't fixed up by a certain time here he wouldn't be able to get it by that certain date. That's why I'm surprised he isn't in London.'

'What did he need a million for?'

'Debts,' answered Sampson Levi laconically.

'His own?'

'Certainly.'

'But he isn't thirty years of age?'

'What of that? He isn't the only European Prince who has run up a million of debts in a dozen years. To a Prince the thing is as easy as eating a sandwich.'

'And why has he taken this sudden resolution to liquidate them?'

'Because the Emperor and the lady's parents won't let him marry till he has done so! And quite right, too! He's got to show a clean sheet, or the Princess Anna of Eckstein-Schwartzburg will never be Princess of Posen. Even now the Emperor has no idea how much Prince Eugen's debts amount to. If he had – !'

'But would not the Emperor know of this proposed loan?'

'Not necessarily at once. It could be so managed. Twig?' Mr Sampson Levi laughed. 'I've carried these little affairs through before. After marriage it might be allowed to leak out. And you know the Princess Anna's fortune is pretty big! Now, Mr Racksole,' he added, abruptly changing his tone, 'where do you suppose Prince Eugen has disappeared to? Because if he doesn't turn up to-day he can't have that million. To-day is the last day. To-morrow the money will be appropriated elsewhere. Of course, I'm not alone in this business, and my friends have something to say.'

'You ask me where I think Prince Eugen has disappeared to?'

'I do.'

'Then you think it's a disappearance?'

Sampson Levi nodded. 'Putting two and two together,' he said, 'I do. The Dimmock business is very peculiar – very peculiar, indeed. Dimmock was a left-handed relation of the Posen family. Twig? Scarcely anyone knows that. He was made secretary and companion to Prince Aribert, just to keep him in the domestic circle. His mother was an Irishwoman, whose misfortune was that she was too beautiful. Twig?' (Mr Sampson Levi always used this extraordinary word when he was in a communicative mood.) 'My belief is that Dimmock's death has something to do with the disappearance of Prince Eugen. The only thing that passes me is this: Why should anyone want to make Prince Eugen disappear? The poor little Prince hasn't an enemy in the world. If he's been "copped", as they say, why has he been "copped"? It won't do anyone any good.'

'Won't it?' repeated Racksole, with a sudden flash.

'What do you mean?' asked Mr Levi.

'I mean this: Suppose some other European pauper Prince was anxious to marry Princess Anna and her fortune, wouldn't that Prince have an interest in stopping this loan of yours to Prince Eugen? Wouldn't he have an interest in causing Prince Eugen to disappear – at any rate, for a time?'

Sampson Levi thought hard for a few moments.

'Mr Theodore Racksole,' he said at length, 'I do believe you have hit on something.'

## Chapter Twelve

### ROCCO AND ROOM NO. 111

ON the afternoon of the same day – the interview just described had occurred in the morning – Racksole was visited by another idea, and he said to himself that he ought to have thought of it before. The conversation with Mr Sampson Levi had continued for a considerable time, and the two men had exchanged various notions, and agreed to meet again, but the theory that Reginald Dimmock had probably been a traitor to his family – a traitor whose repentance had caused his death – had not been thoroughly discussed; the talk had tended rather to Continental politics, with a view to discovering what princely family might have an interest in the temporary disappearance of Prince Eugen. Now, as Racksole considered in detail the particular affair of Reginald Dimmock, deceased, he was struck by one point especially, to wit: Why had Dimmock and Jules manoeuvred to turn Nella Racksole out of Room No. 111 on that first night? That they had so manoeuvred, that the broken window-pane was not a mere accident, Racksole felt perfectly sure. He had felt perfectly sure all along; but the significance of the facts had not struck him. It was plain to him now that there must be something of extraordinary and peculiar importance about Room No. 111. After lunch he wandered quietly upstairs and looked at Room No. 111; that is to say, he looked at the outside of it; it happened to be occupied, but the guest was leaving that evening. The thought crossed his mind that there could be no object in gazing blankly at the outside of a room; yet he gazed; then he wandered quickly down again to the next floor, and in passing along the corridor of that floor he stopped, and with an involuntary gesture stamped his foot.

'Great Scott!' he said, 'I've got hold of something – No. 111 is exactly over the State apartments.'

He went to the bureau, and issued instructions that No. 111

was not to be re-let to anyone until further orders. At the bureau they gave him Nella's note, which ran thus:

Dearest Papa, – I am going away for a day or two on the trail of a clue. If I'm not back in three days, begin to inquire for me at Ostend. Till then leave me alone. – Your sagacious daughter,

NELL.

These few words, in Nella's large scrawling hand, filled one side of the paper. At the bottom was a P.T.O. He turned over, and read the sentence, underlined, 'P.S. – Keep an eye on Rocco.'

'I wonder what the little creature is up to?' he murmured, as he tore the letter into small fragments, and threw them into the waste-paper basket. Then, without any delay, he took the lift down to the basement, with the object of making a preliminary inspection of Rocco in his lair. He could scarcely bring himself to believe that this suave and stately gentleman, this enthusiast of gastronomy, was concerned in the machinations of Jules and other rascals unknown. Nevertheless, from habit, he obeyed his daughter, giving her credit for a certain amount of perspicuity and cleverness.

The kitchens of the Grand Babylon Hotel are one of the wonders of Europe. Only three years before the events now under narration Félix Babylon had had them newly installed with every device and patent that the ingenuity of two continents could supply. They covered nearly an acre of superficial space. They were walled and floored from end to end with tiles and marble, which enabled them to be washed down every morning like the deck of a man-of-war. Visitors were sometimes taken to see the potato-paring machine, the patent plate-dryer, the Babylon-spit (a contrivance of Félix Babylon's own), the silver-grill, the system of connected stock-pots, and other amazing phenomena of the department. Sometimes, if they were fortunate, they might also see the artist who sculptured ice into forms of men and beasts for table ornaments, or the first napkin-folder in London, or the man who daily invented fresh designs for pastry and blancmanges. Twelve chefs pursued their labours in those kitchens, helped by ninety assistant chefs, and a further army of unconsidered menials. Over all these was Rocco, supreme and unapproachable. Half-way along the suite of kitchens, Rocco had an apartment of his own, wherein he thought out those magnificent combinations, those marvellous feats of succulence and originality, which had given him his fame. Vistors never caught a glimpse of Rocco in the kitchens, though sometimes, on a special night, he would stroll nonchalantly through the dining-room, like the great man he was, to receive the compliments of the hotel habitués – people of insight who recognized his uniqueness.

Theodore Racksole's sudden and unusual appearance in the kitchen caused a little stir. He nodded to some of the chefs, but said nothing to anyone, merely wandering about amid the maze of copper utensils, and white-capped workers. At length he saw Rocco, surrounded by several admiring chefs. Rocco was bending over a freshly-roasted partridge which lay on a blue dish. He plunged a long fork into the back of the bird, and raised it in the air with his left hand. In his right he held a long glittering carving-knife. He was giving one of his world-famous exhibitions of carving. In four swift, unerring, delicate, perfect strokes he cleanly severed the limbs of the partridge. It was a wonderful achievement – how wondrous none but the really skilful carver can properly appreciate. The chefs emitted a hum of applause, and Rocco, long, lean, and graceful, retired to his own apartment. Racksole followed him. Rocco sat in a chair, one hand over his eyes; he had not noticed Theodore Racksole.

'What are you doing, M. Rocco?' the millionaire asked smiling.

'Ah!' exclaimed Rocco, starting up with an apology. 'Pardon! I was inventing a new mayonnaise, which I shall need for a certain menu next week.'

'Do you invent these things without materials, then?' questioned Racksole.

'Certainly. I do dem in my mind. I tink dem. Why should I want materials? I know all flavours. I tink, and tink, and tink, and it is done. I write down. I give the recipe to my best chef – dere you are. I need not even taste, I know how it will taste. It is like composing music. De great composers do not compose at de piano.'

'I see,' said Racksole.

'It is because I work like dat dat you pay me three thousand a year,' Rocco added gravely.

'Heard about Jules?' said Racksole abruptly.

'Jules?'

'Yes. He's been arrested in Ostend,' the millionaire continued, lying cleverly at a venture. 'They say that he and several others are implicated in a murder case – the murder of Reginald Dimmock.'

'Truly?' drawled Rocco, scarcely hiding a yawn. His indifference was so superb, so gorgeous, that Racksole instantly divined that it was assumed for the occasion.

'It seems that, after all, the police are good for something. But this is the first time I ever knew them to be worth their salt. There is to be a thorough and systematic search of the hotel to-morrow,' Racksole went on. 'I have mentioned it to you to warn you that so far as you are concerned the search is of course merely a matter of form. You will not object to the detectives looking through your rooms?'

'Certainly not,' and Rocco shrugged his shoulders.

'I shall ask you to say nothing about this to anyone,' said Racksole. 'The news of Jules' arrest is quite private to myself. The papers know nothing of it. You comprehend?'

Rocco smiled in his grand manner, and Rocco's master thereupon went away. Racksole was very well satisfied with the little conversation. It was perhaps dangerous to tell a series of mere lies to a clever fellow like Rocco, and Racksole wondered how he should ultimately explain them to this great master-chef if his and Nella's suspicions should be unfounded, and nothing came of them. Nevertheless, Rocco's manner, a strange elusive something in the man's eyes, had nearly convinced Racksole that he was somehow implicated in Jules' schemes – and probably in the death of Reginald Dimmock and the disappearance of Prince Eugen of Posen.

That night, or rather about half-past one the next morning,

when the last noises of the hotel's life had died down, Racksole made his way to Room 111 on the second floor. He locked the door on the inside, and proceeded to examine the place, square foot by square foot. Every now and then some creak or other sound startled him, and he listened intently for a few seconds. The bedroom was furnished in the ordinary splendid style of bedrooms at the Grand Babylon Hotel, and in that respect called for no remark. What most interested Racksole was the flooring. He pulled up the thick Oriental carpet, and peered along every plank, but could discover nothing unusual. Then he went to the dressing-room, and finally to the bathroom, both of which opened out of the main room. But in neither of these smaller chambers was he any more successful than in the bedroom itself. Finally he came to the bath, which was enclosed in a panelled casing of polished wood, after the manner of baths. Some baths have a cupboard beneath the taps, with a door at the side, but this one appeared to have none. He tapped the panels, but not a single one of them gave forth that 'curious hollow sound' which usually betokens a secret place. Idly he turned the cold-tap of the bath, and the water began to rush in. He turned off the cold-tap and turned on the waste-tap, and as he did so his knee, which was pressing against the panelling, slipped forward. The panelling had given way, and he saw that one large panel was hinged from the inside, and caught with a hasp, also on the inside. A large space within the casing of the end of the bath was thus revealed. Before doing anything else, Racksole tried to repeat the trick with the waste-tap, but he failed; it would not work again, nor could he in any way perceive that there was any connection between the rod of the waste-tap and the hasp of the panel. Racksole could not see into the cavity within the casing, and the electric light was fixed, and could not be moved about like a candle. He felt in his pockets, and fortunately discovered a box of matches. Aided by these, he looked into the cavity, and saw nothing; nothing except a rather large hole at the far end – some three feet from the casing. With some difficulty he squeezed himself through the open panel, and took a half-kneeling, half-sitting posture within. There he struck a match, and it was a most unfortunate thing that in striking, the box being half open, he set fire to all the matches, and was half smothered in the atrocious stink of phosphorus which resulted. One match burned clear on the floor of the cavity, and, rubbing his eyes, Racksole picked it up, and looked down the hole which he had previously descried. It was a hole apparently bottomless, and about eighteen inches square. The curious part about the hole was that a rope-ladder hung down it. When he saw that rope-ladder Racksole smiled the smile of a happy man.

The match went out.

Should he make a long journey, perhaps to some distant corner of the hotel, for a fresh box of matches, or should he attempt to descend that rope-ladder in the dark? He decided on the latter course, and he was the more strongly moved thereto as he could now distinguish a faint, a very faint tinge of light at the bottom of the hole.

With infinite care he compressed himself into the well-like hole, and descended the latter. At length he arrived on firm ground, perspiring, but quite safe and quite excited. He saw now that the tinge of light came through a small hole in the wood. He put his eye to the wood, and found that he had a fine view of the State bathroom, and through the door of the State bathroom into the State bedroom. At the massive marble-topped washstand in the State bedroom a man was visible, bending over some object which lay thereon.

The man was Rocco!

*Chapter Thirteen*

## IN THE STATE BEDROOM

It was of course plain to Racksole that the peculiar passage-way which he had, at great personal inconvenience, discovered between the bathroom of No. 111 and the State bathroom on the floor below must have been specially designed by some person or persons for the purpose of keeping a nefarious watch upon the occupants of the State suite of apartments. It was a means of communication at once simple and ingenious. At that moment he could not be sure of the precise method employed for it, but he surmised that the casing of the waterpipes had been used as a 'well', while space for the pipes themselves had been found in the thickness of the ample brick walls of the Grand Babylon. The eye-hole, through which he now had a view of the bedroom, was a very minute one, and probably would scarcely be noticed from the exterior. One thing he observed concerning it, namely, that it had been made for a man somewhat taller than himself; he was obliged to stand on tiptoe in order to get his eye in the correct position. He remembered that both Jules and Rocco were distinctly above the average height; also that they were both thin men, and could have descended the well with comparative ease. Theodore Racksole, though not stout, was a well-set man with large bones.

These things flashed through his mind as he gazed, spell-bound, at the mysterious movements of Rocco. The door between the bathroom and the bedroom was wide open, and his own situation was such that his view embraced a considerable portion of the bedroom, including the whole of the immense and gorgeously-upholstered bedstead, but not including the whole of the marble washstand. He could see only half of the washstand, and at intervals Rocco passed out of sight as his lithe hands moved over the object which lay on the marble. At first Theodore Racksole could not decide what this object was, but after a time, as his eyes grew accustomed to the position and the light, he made it out.

It was the body of a man. Or, rather, to be more exact, Racksole could discern the legs of a man on that half of the table which was visible to him. Involuntarily he shuddered, as the conviction forced itself upon him that Rocco had some unconscious human being helpless on that cold marble surface. The legs never moved. Therefore, the hapless creature was either asleep or under the influence of an anaesthetic – or (horrible thought!) dead.

Racksole wanted to call out, to stop by some means or other the dreadful midnight activity which was proceeding before his astonished eyes; but fortunately he restrained himself.

On the washstand he could see certain strangely-shaped utensils and instruments which Rocco used from time to time. The work seemed to Racksole to continue for interminable hours, and then at last Rocco ceased, gave a sign of satisfaction, whistled several bars from 'Cavalleria Rusticana', and came into the bathroom, where he took off his coat, and very quietly washed his hands. As he stood calmly and leisurely wiping those long fingers of his, he was less than four feet from Racksole, and the cooped-up millionaire trembled, holding his breath, lest Rocco should detect his presence behind the woodwork. But nothing happened, and Rocco returned unsuspectingly to the bedroom. Racksole saw him place some sort of white flannel garment over the prone form on the table, and then lift it bodily on to the great bed, where it lay awfully still. The hidden watcher was sure now that it was a corpse upon which Rocco had been exercising his mysterious and sinister functions. But whose corpse? And what functions?

Could this be a West End hotel, Racksole's own hotel, in the very heart of London, the best-policed city in the world? It seemed incredible, impossible; yet so it was. Once more he remembered what Félix Babylon had said to him and realized the truth of the saying anew. The proprietor of a vast and complicated establishment like the Grand Babylon could never know a tithe of the extraordinary and queer occurrences which happened daily under his very nose; the atmosphere of such a caravanserai must necessarily be an atmosphere of mystery and problems apparently inexplicable. Nevertheless, Racksole thought that Fate was carrying things with rather a high hand when she permitted his chef to spend the night hours over a man's corpse in his State bedroom, this sacred apartment which was supposed to be occupied only by individuals of Royal Blood. Racksole would not have objected to a certain amount of mystery, but he decidedly thought that there was a little too much mystery here for his taste. He thought that even Félix Babylon would have been surprised at this.

The electric chandelier in the centre of the ceiling was not lighted; only the two lights on either side of the washstand were switched on, and these did not sufficiently illuminate the features of the man on the bed to enable Racksole to see them clearly. In vain the millionaire strained his eyes; he could only make out that the corpse was probably that of a young man. Just as he was wondering what would be the best course of action to pursue, he saw Rocco with a square-shaped black box in his hand. Then the chef switched off the two electric lights, and the State bedroom was in darkness. In that swift darkness Racksole heard Rocco spring on to the bed. Another half-dozen moments of suspense, and there was a blinding flash of white, which endured for several seconds, and showed Rocco standing like an evil spirit over the corpse, the black box in one hand and a burning piece of aluminium wire in the other. The aluminium wire burnt out, and darkness followed blacker than before.

Rocco had photographed the corpse by flashlight.

But the dazzling flare which had disclosed the features of the dead man to the insensible lens of the camera had disclosed them also to Theodore Racksole. The dead man was Reginald Dimmock!

Stung into action by this discovery, Racksole tried to find the exit from his place of concealment. He felt sure that there existed some way out into the State bathroom, but he sought for it fruitlessly, groping with both hands and feet. Then he decided that he must ascend the rope-ladder, make haste for the first-floor corridor, and intercept Rocco when he left the State apartments. It was a painful and difficult business to ascend that thin and yielding ladder in such a confined space, but Racksole was managing it very nicely, and had nearly reached the top, when, by some untoward freak of chance, the ladder broke above his weight, and he slipped ignominiously down to the bottom of the wooden tube. Smothering an excusable curse, Racksole crouched, baffled. Then he saw that the force of his fall had somehow opened a trap-door at his feet. He squeezed through, pushed open another tiny door, and in another second stood in the State bathroom. He was dishevelled, perspiring, rather bewildered; but he was there. In the next second he had resumed absolute command of all his faculties.

Strange to say, he had moved so quietly that Rocco had apparently not heard him. He stepped noiselessly to the door between the bathroom and the bedroom, and stood there in silence. Rocco had switched on again the lights over the wash-stand and was busy with his utensils.

Racksole deliberately coughed.

## Chapter Fourteen

## ROCCO ANSWERS SOME QUESTIONS

Rocco turned round with the swiftness of a startled tiger, and gave Theodore Racksole one long piercing glance.

'D—n!' said Rocco, with as pure an Anglo-Saxon accent and intonation as Racksole himself could have accomplished.

The most extraordinary thing about the situation was that at this juncture Theodore Racksole did not know what to say. He was so dumbfounded by the affair, and especially by Rocco's absolute and sublime calm, that both speech and thought failed him.

'I give in,' said Rocco. 'From the moment you entered this cursed hotel I was afraid of you. I told Jules I was afraid of you. I knew there would be trouble with a man of your kidney, and I was right; confound it! I tell you I give in. I know when I'm beaten. I've got no revolver and no weapons of any kind. I surrender. Do what you like.'

And with that Rocco sat down on a chair. It was magnificently done. Only a truly great man could have done it. Rocco actually kept his dignity.

For answer, Racksole walked slowly into the vast apartment, seized a chair, and, dragging it up to Rocco's chair, sat down opposite to him. Thus they faced each other, their knees almost touching, both in evening dress. On Rocco's right hand was the bed, with the corpse of Reginald Dimmock. On Racksole's right hand, and a little behind him, was the marble washstand, still littered with Rocco's implements. The electric light shone on Rocco's left cheek, leaving the other side of his face in shadow. Racksole tapped him on the knee twice.

'So you're another Englishman masquerading as a foreigner in my hotel,' Racksole remarked, by way of commencing the interrogation.

'I'm not,' answered Rocco quietly. 'I'm a citizen of the United States.'

'The deuce you are!' Racksole exclaimed.

'Yes, I was born at West Orange, New Jersey, New York State. I call myself an Italian because it was in Italy that I first made a name as a chef – at Rome. It is better for a great chef like me to be a foreigner. Imagine a great chef named Elihu P. Rucker. You can't imagine it. I changed my nationality for the same reason that my friend and colleague, Jules, otherwise Mr Jackson, changed his.'

'So Jules is your friend and colleague, is he?'

'He was, but from this moment he is no longer. I began to disapprove of his methods no less than a week ago, and my disapproval will now take active form.'

'Will it?' said Racksole. 'I calculate it just won't, Mr Elihu P. Rucker, citizen of the United States. Before you are very much older you'll be in the kind hands of the police, and your activities, in no matter what direction, will come to an abrupt conclusion.'

'It is possible,' sighed Rocco.

'In the meantime, I'll ask you one or two questions for my own private satisfaction. You've acknowledged that the game is up, and you may as well answer them with as much candour as you feel yourself capable of. See?'

'I see,' replied Rocco calmly, 'but I guess I can't answer all questions. I'll do what I can.'

'Well,' said Racksole, clearing his throat, 'what's the scheme all about? Tell me in a word.'

'Not in a thousand words. It isn't my secret, you know.'

'Why was poor little Dimmock poisoned?' The millionaire's voice softened as he looked for an instant at the corpse of the unfortunate young man.

'I don't know,' said Rocco. 'I don't mind informing you that I objected to that part of the business. I wasn't made aware of it till after it was done, and then I tell you it got my dander up considerable.'

'You mean to say you don't know why Dimmock was done to death?'

'I mean to say I couldn't see the sense of it. Of course he – er – died, because he sort of cried off the scheme, having previously taken a share of it. I don't mind saying that much, because you probably guessed it for yourself. But I solemnly state that I have a conscientious objection to murder.'

'Then it was murder?'

'It was a kind of murder,' Rocco admitted.

'Who did it?'

'Unfair question,' said Rocco.

'Who else is in this precious scheme besides Jules and yourself?'

'Don't know, on my honour.'

'Well, then, tell me this. What have you been doing to Dimmock's body?'

'How long were you in that bathroom?' Rocco parried with sublime impudence.

'Don't question me, Mr Rucker,' said Theodore Racksole. 'I feel very much inclined to break your back across my knee. Therefore I advise you not to irritate me. What have you been doing to Dimmock's body?'

'I've been embalming it.'

'Em – balming it.'

'Certainly; Richardson's system of arterial fluid injection, as improved by myself. You weren't aware that I included the art of embalming among my accomplishments. Nevertheless, it is so.'

'But why?' asked Racksole, more mystified than ever. 'Why should you trouble to embalm the poor chap's corpse?'

'Can't you see? Doesn't it strike you? That corpse has to be taken care of. It contains, or rather, it did contain, very serious evidence against some person or persons unknown to the police. It may be necessary to move it about from place to place. A corpse can't be hidden for long; a corpse betrays itself. One couldn't throw it in the Thames, for it would have been found inside twelve hours. One couldn't bury it – it wasn't safe. The only thing was to keep it handy and movable, ready for emergencies. I needn't inform you that, without embalming, you can't keep a corpse handy and movable for more than four or five days. It's the kind of thing that won't keep. And so it was suggested that I should embalm it, and I did. Mind you, I still objected to

the murder, but I couldn't go back on a colleague, you understand. You do understand that, don't you? Well, here you are,
and here it is, and that's all.'

Rocco leaned back in his chair as though he had said everything
that ought to be said. He closed his eyes to indicate that so far as
he was concerned the conversation was also closed. Theodore
Racksole stood up.

'I hope,' said Rocco, suddenly opening his eyes, 'I hope you'll
call in the police without any delay. It's getting late, and I don't
like going without my night's rest.'

'Where do you suppose you'll get a night's rest?' Racksole
asked.

'In the cells, of course. Haven't I told you I know when I'm
beaten. I'm not so blind as not to be able to see that there's at
any rate a *prima facie* case against me. I expect I shall get off
with a year or two's imprisonment as accessory after the fact –
I think that's what they call it. Anyhow, I shall be in a position
to prove that I am not implicated in the murder of this unfortunate nincompoop.' He pointed, with a strange, scornful gesture
of his elbow, to the bed. 'And now, shall we go? Everyone is
asleep, but there will be a policeman within call of the watchman
in the portico. I am at your service. Let us go down together,
Mr Racksole. I give you my word to go quietly.'

'Stay a moment,' said Theodore Racksole curtly; 'there is no
hurry. It won't do you any harm to forego another hour's sleep,
especially as you will have no work to do tomorrow. I have one
or two more questions to put to you.'

'Well?' Rocco murmured, with an air of tired resignation, as
if to say, 'What must be must be.'

'Where has Dimmock's corpse been during the last three or
four days, since he – died?'

'Oh!' answered Rocco, apparently surprised at the simplicity
of the question. 'It's been in my room, and one night it was on
the roof; once it went out of the hotel as luggage, but it came
back the next day as a case of Demerara sugar. I forgot where
else it has been, but it's been kept perfectly safe and treated with
every consideration.'

'And who contrived all these manoeuvres?' asked Racksole as calmly as he could.

'I did. That is to say, I invented them and I saw that they were carried out. You see, the suspicions of your police obliged me to be particularly spry.'

'And who carried them out?'

'Ah! that would be telling tales. But I don't mind assuring you that my accomplices were innocent accomplices. It is absurdly easy for a man like me to impose on underlings – absurdly easy.'

'What did you intend to do with the corpse ultimately?' Racksole pursued his inquiry with immovable countenance.

'Who knows?' said Rocco, twisting his beautiful moustache. 'That would have depended on several things – on your police, for instance. But probably in the end we should have restored this mortal clay' – again he jerked his elbow – 'to the man's sorrowing relatives.'

'Do you know who the relatives are?'

'Certainly. Don't you? If you don't I need only hint that Dimmock had a Prince for his father.'

'It seems to me,' said Racksole, with cold sarcasm, 'that you behaved rather clumsily in choosing this bedroom as the scene of your operations.'

'Not at all,' said Rocco. 'There was no other apartment so suitable in the whole hotel. Who would have guessed that anything was going on here? It was the very place for me.'

'I guessed,' said Racksole succinctly.

'Yes, you guessed, Mr Racksole. But I had not counted on you. You are the only smart man in the business. You are an American citizen, and I hadn't reckoned to have to deal with that class of person.'

'Apparently I frightened you this afternoon?'

'Not in the least.'

'You were not afraid of a search?'

'I knew that no search was intended. I knew that you were trying to frighten me. You must really credit me with a little sagacity and insight, Mr Racksole. Immediately you began to talk to me in the kitchen this afternoon I felt you were on the track. But I was not frightened. I merely decided that there was no time to be lost – that I must act quickly. I did act quickly, but, it seems, not quickly enough. I grant that your rapidity exceeded mine. Let us go downstairs, I beg.'

Rocco rose and moved towards the door. With an instinctive action Racksole rushed forward and seized him by the shoulder.

'No tricks!' said Racksole. 'You're in my custody and don't forget it.'

Rocco turned on his employer a look of gentle, dignified scorn.

'Have I not informed you,' he said, 'that I have the intention of going quietly?'

Racksole felt almost ashamed for the moment. It flashed across him that a man can be great, even in crime.

'What an ineffable fool you were,' said Racksole, stopping him at the threshold, 'with your talents, your unique talents, to get yourself mixed up in an affair of this kind. You are ruined. And, by Jove! you were a great man in your own line.'

'Mr Racksole,' said Rocco very quickly, 'that is the truest word you have spoken this night. I was a great man in my own line. And I am an ineffable fool. Alas!' He brought his long arms to his sides with a thud.

'Why did you do it?'

'I was fascinated – fascinated by Jules. He, too, is a great man. We had great opportunities, here in the Grand Babylon. It was a great game. It was worth the candle. The prizes were enormous. You would admit these things if you knew the facts. Perhaps some day you will know them, for you are a fairly clever person at getting to the root of a matter. Yes, I was blinded, hypnotized.'

'And now you are ruined.'

'Not ruined, not ruined. Afterwards, in a few years, I shall come up again. A man of genius like me is never ruined till he is dead. Genius is always forgiven. I shall be forgiven. Suppose I am sent to prison. When I emerge I shall be no gaol-bird. I shall be Rocco – the great Rocco. And half the hotels in Europe will invite me to join them.'

'Let me tell you, as man to man, that you have achieved your own degradation. There is no excuse.'

'I know it,' said Rocco. 'Let us go.'

Racksole was distinctly and notably impressed by this man — by this master spirit to whom he was to have paid a salary at the rate of three thousand pounds a year. He even felt sorry for him. And so, side by side, the captor and the captured, they passed into the vast deserted corridor of the hotel. Rocco stopped at the grating of the first lift.

'It will be locked,' said Racksole. 'We must use the stairs to-night.'

'But I have a key. I always carry one,' said Rocco, and he pulled one out of his pocket, and, unfastening the iron screen, pushed it open. Racksole smiled at his readiness and aplomb.

'After you,' said Rocco, bowing in his finest manner, and Racksole stepped into the lift.

With the swiftness of lighting Rocco pushed forward the iron screen, which locked itself automatically. Theodore Racksole was hopelessly a prisoner within the lift, while Rocco stood free in the corridor.

'Good-bye, Mr Racksole,' he remarked suavely, bowing again, lower than before. 'Good-bye: I hate to take a mean advantage of you in this fashion, but really you must allow that you have been very simple. You are a clever man, as I have already said, up to a certain point. It is past that point that my own cleverness comes in. Again, good-bye. After all, I shall have no rest to-night, but perhaps even that will be better that sleeping in a police cell. If you make a great noise you may wake someone and ultimately get released from this lift. But I advise you to compose yourself, and wait till morning. It will be more dignified. For the third time, good-bye.'

And with that Rocco, without hastening, walked down the corridor and so out of sight.

Racksole said never a word. He was too disgusted with himself to speak. He clenched his fists, and put his teeth together, and held his breath. In the silence he could hear the dwindling sound of Rocco's footsteps on the thick carpet.

It was the greatest blow of Racksole's life.

The next morning the high-born guests of the Grand Babylon were aroused by a rumour that by some accident the millionaire proprietor of the hotel had remained all night locked
up in the lift. It was also stated that Rocco had quarrelled with
his new master and incontinently left the place. A duchess said
that Rocco's departure would mean the ruin of the hotel, whereupon her husband advised her not to talk nonsense.

As for Racksole, he sent a message for the detective in charge
of the Dimmock affair, and bravely told him the happenings of
the previous night. The narration was a decided ordeal to a man
of Racksole's temperament.

'A strange story!' commented Detective Marshall, and he could
not avoid a smile. 'The climax was unfortunate, but you have
certainly got some valuable facts.'

Racksole said nothing.

'I myself have a clue,' added the detective. 'When your message arrived I was just coming up to see you. I want you to
accompany me to a certain spot not far from here. Will you
come, now, at once?'

'With pleasure,' said Racksole.

At that moment a page entered with a telegram. Racksole
opened it read: 'Please come instantly. Nella. Hotel Wellington,
Ostend.'

He looked at his watch.

'I can't come,' he said to the detective. 'I'm going to Ostend.'

'To Ostend?'

'Yes, now.'

'But really, Mr Racksole,' protested the detective. 'My business is urgent.'

'So's mine,' said Racksole.

In ten minutes he was on his way to Victoria Station.

## Chapter Fifteen

## END OF THE YACHT ADVENTURE

WE must now return to Nella Racksole and Prince Aribert of Posen on board the yacht without a name. The Prince's first business was to make Jules, otherwise Mr Tom Jackson, perfectly secure by means of several pieces of rope. Although Mr Jackson had been stunned into a complete unconsciousness, and there was a contused wound under his ear, no one could say how soon he might not come to himself and get very violent. So the Prince, having tied his arms and legs, made him fast to a stanchion.

'I hope he won't die,' said Nella. 'He looks very white.'

'The Mr Jacksons of this world,' said Prince Aribert sententiously, 'never die till they are hung. By the way, I wonder how it is that no one has interfered with us. Perhaps they are discreetly afraid of my revolver — of your revolver, I mean.'

Both he and Nella glanced up at the imperturbable steersman, who kept the yacht's head straight out to sea. By this time they were about a couple of miles from the Belgian shore.

Addressing him in French, the Prince ordered the sailor to put the yacht about, and make again for Ostend Harbour, but the fellow took no notice whatever of the summons. The Prince raised the revolver, with the idea of frightening the steersman, and then the man began to talk rapidly in a mixture of French and Flemish. He said that he had received Jules' strict orders not to interfere in any way, no matter what might happen on the deck of the yacht. He was the captain of the yacht, and he had to make for a certain English port, the name of which he could not divulge: he was to keep the vessel at full steam ahead under any and all circumstances. He seemed to be a very big, a very strong, and a very determined man, and the Prince was at a loss what course of action to pursue. He asked several more questions, but the only effect of them was to render the man taciturn and ill-humoured. In vain Prince Aribert explained that Miss Nella Racksole, daughter of millionaire Racksole, had been abducted

by Mr Tom Jackson; in vain he flourished the revolver threaten-
ingly; the surly but courageous captain said merely that that had
nothing to do with him; he had instructions, and he should carry
them out. He sarcastically begged to remind his interlocutor that
he was the captain of the yacht.

'It won't do to shoot him, I suppose,' said the Prince to Nella.
'I might bore a hole into his leg, or something of that kind.'

'It's rather risky, and rather hard on the poor captain, with
his extraordinary sense of duty,' said Nella. 'And, besides, the
whole crew might turn on us. No, we must think of something
else.'

'I wonder where the crew is,' said the Prince.

Just then Mr Jackson, prone and bound on the deck, showed
signs of recovering from his swoon. His eyes opened, and he
gazed vacantly around. At length he caught sight of the Prince,
who approached him with the revolver well in view.

'It's you, is it?' he murmured faintly. 'What are you doing on
board? Who's tied me up like this?'

'See here!' replied the Prince, 'I don't want to have any argu-
ments, but this yacht must return to Ostend at once, where you
will be given up to the authorities.'

'Really!' snarled Mr Tom Jackson. 'Shall I!' Then he called
out in French to the man at the wheel, 'Hi André! let these two
be put off in the dinghy.'

It was a peculiar situation. Certain of nothing but the possession of Nella's revolver, the Prince scarcely knew whether to
carry the argument further, and with stronger measures, or to
accept the situation with as much dignity as the circumstances
would permit.

'Let us take the dinghy,' said Nella; 'we can row ashore in an
hour.'

He felt that she was right. To leave the yacht in such a manner
seemed somewhat ignominious, and it certainly involved the
escape of that profound villain, Mr Thomas Jackson. But what
else could be done? The Prince and Nella constituted one party
on the vessel; they knew their own strength, but they did not
know the strength of their opponents. They held the hostile

ringleader bound and captive, but this man had proved himself capable of giving orders, and even to gag him would not help them if the captain of the yacht persisted in his obstinate course. Moreover, there was a distinct objection to promiscuous shooting; the Prince felt that; there was no knowing how promiscuous shooting might end.

'We will take the dinghy,' said the Prince quickly, to the captain.

A bell rang below, and a sailor and the Negro boy appeared on deck. The pulsations of the screw grew less rapid. The yacht stopped. The dinghy was lowered. As the Prince and Nella prepared to descend into the little cock-boat Mr Tom Jackson addressed Nella, all bound as he lay.

'Good-bye,' he said, 'I shall see you again, never fear.'

In another moment they were in the dinghy, and the dinghy was adrift. The yacht's screw churned the water, and the beautiful vessel slipped away from them. As it receded a figure appeared at the stern. It was Mr Thomas Jackson. He had been released by his minions. He held a white handkerchief to his ear, and offered a calm, enigmatic smile to the two forlorn but victorious occupants of the dinghy. Jules had been defeated for once in his life; or perhaps it would be more just to say that he had been out-manoeuvred. Men like Jules are incapable of being defeated. It was characteristic of his luck that now, in the very hour when he had been caught red-handed in a serious crime against society, he should be effecting a leisurely escape – an escape which left no clue behind.

The sea was utterly calm and blue in the morning sun. The dinghy rocked itself lazily in the swell of the yacht's departure. As the mist cleared away the outline of the shore became more distinct, and it appeared as if Ostend was distant scarcely a cable's length. The white dome of the great Kursaal glittered in the pale turquoise sky, and the smoke of steamers in the harbour could be plainly distinguished. On the offing was a crowd of brown-sailed fishing luggers returning with the night's catch. The many-hued bathing-vans could be counted on the distant beach. Everything seemed perfectly normal. It was difficult for either Nella or her companion to realize that anything extraordinary had happened within the last hour. Yet there was the yacht, not a mile off, to prove to them that something very extraordinary had, in fact, happened. The yacht was no vision, nor was that sinister watching figure at its stern a vision, either.

'I suppose Jules was too surprised and too feeble to inquire how I came to be on board his yacht,' said the Prince, taking the oars.

'Oh! How did you?' asked Nella, her face lighting up. 'Really, I had almost forgotten that part of the affair.'

'I must begin at the beginning and it will take some time,' answered the Prince. 'Had we not better postpone the recital till we get ashore?'

'I will row and you shall talk,' said Nella. 'I want to know now.'

He smiled happily at her, but gently declined to yield up the oars.

'Is it not sufficient that I am here?' he said.

'It is sufficient, yes,' she replied, 'but I want to know.'

With a long, easy stroke he was pulling the dinghy shorewards. She sat in the stern-sheets.

'There is no rudder,' he remarked, 'so you must direct me. Keep the boat's head on the lighthouse. The tide seems to be running in strongly; that will help us. The people on shore will think that we have only been for a little early morning excursion.'

'Will you kindly tell me how it came about that you were able to save my life, Prince?' she said.

'Save your life, Miss Racksole? I didn't save your life; I merely knocked a man down.'

'You saved my life,' she repeated. 'That villain would have stopped at nothing. I saw it in his eye.'

'Then you were a brave woman, for you showed no fear of death.' His admiring gaze rested full on her. For a moment the oars ceased to move.

She gave a gesture of impatience.

'It happened that I saw you last night in your carriage,' he said. 'The fact is, I had not had the audacity to go to Berlin with my story. I stopped in Ostend to see whether I could do a little detective work on my own account. It was a piece of good luck that I saw you. I followed the carriage as quickly as I could, and I just caught a glimpse of you as you entered that awful house. I knew that Jules had something to do with that house. I guessed what you were doing. I was afraid for you. Fortunately I had surveyed the house pretty thoroughly. There is an entrance to it at the back, from a narrow lane. I made my way there. I got into the yard at the back, and I stood under the window of the room where you had the interview with Miss Spencer. I heard everything that was said. It was a courageous enterprise on your part to follow Miss Spencer from the Grand Babylon to Ostend. Well, I dared not force an entrance, lest I might precipitate matters too suddenly, and involve both of us in a difficulty. I merely kept watch. Ah, Miss Racksole! you were magnificent with Miss Spencer; as I say, I could hear every word, for the window was slightly open. I felt that you needed no assistance from me. And then she cheated you with a trick, and the revolver came flying through the window. I picked it up, I thought it would probably be useful. There was a silence. I did not guess at first that you had fainted. I thought that you had escaped. When I found out the truth it was too late for me to intervene. There were two men, both desperate, besides Miss Spencer – '

'Who was the other man?' asked Nella.

'I do not know. It was dark. They drove away with you to the harbour. Again I followed. I saw them carry you on board. Before the yacht weighed anchor I managed to climb unobserved into the dinghy. I lay down full length in it, and no one suspected that I was there. I think you know the rest.'

'Was the yacht all ready for sea?'

'The yacht was all ready for sea. The captain fellow was on the bridge, and steam was up.'

'Then they expected me! How could that be?'

'They expected some one. I do not think they expected you.'

'Did the second man go on board?'

'He helped to carry you along the gangway, but he came back again to the carriage. He was the driver.'

'And no one else saw the business?'

'The quay was deserted. You see, the last steamer had arrived for the night.'

There was a brief silence, and then Nella ejaculated, under her breath. 'Truly, it is a wonderful world!'

And it was a wonderful world for them, though scarcely perhaps, in the sense which Nella Racksole had intended. They had just emerged from a highly disconcerting experience. Among other minor inconveniences, they had had no breakfast. They were out in the sea in a tiny boat. Neither of them knew what the day might bring forth. The man, at least, had the most serious anxieties for the safety of his Royal nephew. And yet – and yet – neither of them wished that that voyage of the little boat on the summer tide should come to an end. Each, perhaps unconsciously, had a vague desire that it might last for ever, he lazily pulling, she directing his course at intervals by a movement of her distractingly pretty head. How was this condition of affairs to be explained? Well, they were both young; they both had superb health, and all the ardour of youth; and – they were together. The boat was very small indeed; her face was scarcely a yard from his. She, in his eyes, surrounded by the glamour of beauty and vast wealth; he, in her eyes, surrounded by the glamour of masculine intrepidity and the brilliance of a throne.

But all voyages come to an end, either at the shore or at the bottom of the sea, and at length the dinghy passed between the stone jetties of the harbour. The Prince rowed to the nearest steps, tied up the boat, and they landed. It was six o'clock in the morning, and a day of gorgeous sunlight had opened. Few people were about at that early hour.

'And now, what next?' said the Prince. 'I must take you to an hotel.'

'I am in your hands,' she acquiesced, with a smile which sent the blood racing through his veins. He perceived now that she was tired and overcome, suffering from a sudden and natural reaction.

At the Hôtel Wellington the Prince told the sleepy door-keeper that they had come by the early train from Bruges, and wanted breakfast at once. It was absurdly early, but a common English sovereign will work wonders in any Belgian hotel, and in a very brief time Nella and the Prince were breakfasting on the verandah of the hotel upon chocolate that had been specially and hastily brewed for them.

'I never tasted such excellent chocolate,' claimed the Prince.

The statement was wildly untrue, for the Hôtel Wellington is not celebrated for its chocolate. Nevertheless Nella replied enthusiastically, 'Nor I.' Then there was a silence, and Nella, feeling possibly that she had been too ecstatic, remarked in a very matter-of-fact tone: 'I must telegraph to Papa instantly.'

Thus it was that Theodore Racksole received the telegram which drew him away from Detective Marshall.

## Chapter Sixteen

# THE WOMAN WITH THE RED HAT

'THERE is one thing, Prince, that we have just got to settle straight off,' said Theodore Racksole.

They were all three seated – Racksole, his daughter, and Prince Aribert – round a dinner table in a private room at the Hôtel Wellington. Racksole had duly arrived by the afternoon boat, and had been met on the quay by the other two. They had dined early, and Racksole had heard the full story of the adventures by sea and land of Nella and the Prince. As to his own adventure of the previous night he said very little, merely explaining, with as little detail as possible, that Dimmock's body had come to light.

'What is that?' asked the Prince, in answer to Racksole's remark.

'We have got to settle whether we shall tell the police at once all that has occurred, or whether we shall proceed on our own responsibility. There can be no doubt as to which course we ought to pursue. Every consideration of prudence points to the advisability of taking the police into our confidence, and leaving the matter entirely in their hands.'

'Oh, Papa!' Nella burst out in her pouting, impulsive way. 'You surely can't think of such a thing. Why, the fun has only just begun.'

'Do you call last night fun?' questioned Racksole, gazing at her solemnly.

'Yes, I do,' she said promptly. 'Now.'

'Well, I don't,' was the millionaire's laconic response; but perhaps he was thinking of his own situation in the lift.

'Do you not think we might investigate a little further,' said the Prince judiciously, as he cracked a walnut, 'just a little further – and then, if we fail to accomplish anything, there would still be ample opportunity to consult the police?'

'How do you suggest we should begin?' asked Racksole.

'Well, there is the house which Miss Racksole so intrepidly entered last evening' – he gave her the homage of an admiring glance; 'you and I, Mr Racksole, might examine that abode in detail.'

'To-night?'

'Certainly. We might do something.'

'We might do too much.'

'For example?'

'We might shoot someone, or get ourselves mistaken for burglars. If we outstepped the law, it would be no excuse for us that we had been acting in a good cause.'

'True,' said the Prince. 'Nevertheless – ' He stopped.

'Nevertheless you have a distaste for bringing the police into the business. You want the hunt all to yourself. You are on fire with the ardour of the chase. Is not that it? Accept the advice of an older man, Prince, and sleep on this affair. I have little fancy for nocturnal escapades two nights together. As for you, Nella, off with you to bed. The Prince and I will have a yarn over such fluids as can be obtained in this hole.'

'Papa,' she said, 'you are perfectly horrid to-night.'

'Perhaps I am,' he said. 'Decidedly I am very cross with you for coming over here all alone. It was monstrous. If I didn't happen to be the most foolish of parents – There! Good-night. It's nine o'clock. The Prince, I am sure, will excuse you.'

If Nella had not really been very tired Prince Aribert might have been the witness of a good-natured but stubborn conflict between the millionaire and his spirited offspring. As it was, Nella departed with surprising docility, and the two men were left alone.

'Now,' said Racksole suddenly, changing his tone, 'I fancy that after all I'm your man for a little amateur investigation to-night. And, if I must speak the exact truth, I think that to sleep on this affair would be about the very worst thing we could do. But I was anxious to keep Nella out of harm's way at any rate till to-morrow. She is a very difficult creature to manage, Prince, and I may warn you,' he laughed grimly, 'that if we do succeed in doing anything to-night we shall catch it from her ladyship in the morning. Are you ready to take that risk?'

'I am,' the Prince smiled. 'But Miss Racksole is a young lady of quite remarkable nerve.'

'She is,' said Racksole drily. 'I wish sometimes she had less.'

'I have the highest admiration for Miss Racksole,' said the Prince, and he looked Miss Racksole's father full in the face.

'You honour us, Prince,' Racksole observed. 'Let us come to business. Am I right in assuming that you have a reason for keeping the police out of this business, if it can possibly be done?'

'Yes,' said the Prince, and his brow clouded. 'I am very much afraid that my poor nephew has involved himself in some scrape that he would wish not to be divulged.'

'Then you do not believe that he is the victim of foul play?'

'I do not.'

'And the reason, if I may ask it?'

'Mr Racksole, we speak in confidence – is it not so? Some years ago my foolish nephew had an affair – an affair with a feminine star of the Berlin stage. For anything I know, the lady may have been the very pattern of her sex, but where a reigning Prince is concerned scandal cannot be avoided in such a matter. I had thought that the affair was quite at an end, since my nephew's betrothal to Princess Anna of Eckstein-Schwartzburg is shortly to be announced. But yesterday I saw the lady to whom I have referred driving on the Digue. The coincidence of her presence here with my nephew's disappearance is too extraordinary to be disregarded.'

'But how does this theory square with the murder of Reginald Dimmock?'

'It does not square with it. My idea is that the murder of poor Dimmock and the disappearance of my nephew are entirely unconnected – unless, indeed, this Berlin actress is playing into the hands of the murderers. I had not thought of that.'

'Then what do you propose to do to-night?'

'I propose to enter the house which Miss Racksole entered last night and to find out something definite.'

'I concur,' said Racksole. 'I shall heartily enjoy it. But let me tell you, Prince, and pardon me for speaking bluntly, your surmise is incorrect. I would wager a hundred thousand dollars that Prince Eugen has been kidnapped.'

'What grounds have you for being so sure?'

'Ah! said Racksole, 'that is a long story. Let me begin by asking you this. Are you aware that your nephew, Prince Eugen, owes a million of money?'

'A million of money!' cried Prince Aribert astonished. 'It is impossible!'

'Nevertheless, he does,' said Racksole calmly. Then he told him all he had learnt from Mr Sampson Levi.

'What have you to say to that?' Racksole ended. Prince Aribert made no reply.

'What have you to say to that?' Racksole insisted.

'Merely that Eugen is ruined, even if he is alive.'

'Not at all,' Racksole returned with cheerfulness. 'Not at all. We shall see about that. The special thing that I want to know just now from you is this: Has any previous application ever been made for the hand of the Princess Anna?'

'Yes. Last year. The King of Bosnia sued for it, but his proposal was declined.'

'Why?'

'Because my nephew was considered to be a more suitable match for her.'

'Not because the personal character of his Majesty of Bosnia is scarcely of the brightest?'

'No. Unfortunately it is usually impossible to consider questions of personal character when a royal match is concerned.'

'Then, if for any reason the marriage of Princess Anna with your nephew was frustrated, the King of Bosnia would have a fair chance in that quarter?'

'He would. The political aspect of things would be perfectly satisfactory.'

'Thanks!' said Racksole. 'I will wager another hundred thousand dollars that someone in Bosnia – I don't accuse the King himself – is at the bottom of this business. The methods of Balkan politicians have always been half-Oriental. Let us go.'

'Where?'

'To this precious house of Nella's adventure.'

'But surely it is too early?'

'So it is,' said Racksole, 'and we shall want a few things, too. For instance, a dark lantern. I think I will go out and forage for a lantern.'

'And a revolver?' suggested Prince Aribert.

'Does it mean revolvers?' The millionaire laughed.

'It may come to that.'

'Here you are, then, my friend,' said Racksole, and he pulled one out of his hip pocket. 'And yours?'

'I,' said the Prince, 'I have your daughter's.'

'The deuce you have!' murmured Racksole to himself.

It was then half past nine. They decided that it would be impolitic to begin their operations till after midnight. There were three hours to spare.

'Let us go and see the gambling,' Racksole suggested. 'We might encounter the Berlin lady.'

The suggestion, in the first instance, was not made seriously, but it appeared to both men that they might do worse than spend the intervening time in the gorgeous saloon of the Kursaal, where, in the season, as much money is won and lost as at Monte Carlo. It was striking ten o'clock as they entered the rooms. There was a large company present – a company which included some of the most notorious persons in Europe. In that multifarious assemblage all were equal. The electric light shone coldly and impartially on the just and on the unjust, on the fool and the knave, on the European and the Asiatic. As usual, women monopolized the best places at the tables. The scene was familiar enough to Prince Aribert, who had witnessed it frequently at Monaco, but Theodore Racksole had never before entered any European gaming palace; he had only the haziest idea of the rules of play, and he was at once interested. For some time they watched the play at the table which happened to be nearest to them. Racksole never moved his lips. With his eyes glued on the table, and ears open for every remark, of the players and the croupier, he took his first lesson in roulette. He saw a mere youth win fifteen thousand francs, which were stolen in the most barefaced manner by a rouged girl scarcely older than the youth; he saw two old gamesters stake their coins, and lose, and walk quietly out of the place; he saw the bank win fifty thousand francs at a single turn.

'This is rather good fun,' he said at length, 'but the stakes are too small to make it really exciting. I'll try my luck, just for the experience. I'm bound to win.'

'Why?' asked the Prince.

'Because I always do, in games of chance,' Racksole answered with gay confidence. 'It is my fate. Then to-night, you must remember, I shall be a beginner, and you know the tyro's luck.'

In ten minutes the croupier of that table was obliged to suspend operations pending the arrival of a further supply of coin.

'What did I tell you?' said Racksole, leading the way to another table further up the room. A hundred curious glances went after him. One old woman, whose gay attire suggested a false youthfulness, begged him in French to stake a five-franc piece for her. She offered him the coin. He took it, and gave her a hundred-franc note in exchange. She clutched the crisp rustling paper, and with hysterical haste scuttled back to her own table.

At the second table there was a considerable air of excitement. In the forefront of the players was a woman in a low-cut evening dress of black silk and a large red picture hat. Her age appeared to be about twenty-eight; she had dark eyes, full lips, and a distinctly Jewish nose. She was handsome, but her beauty was of that forbidding, sinister order which is often called Junoesque. This woman was the centre of attraction. People said to each other that she had won a hundred and sixty thousand francs that day at the table.

'You were right,' Prince Aribert whispered to Theodore Racksole; 'that is the Berlin lady.'

'The deuce she is! Has she seen you? Will she know you?'

'She would probably know me, but she hasn't looked up yet.'

'Keep behind her, then. I propose to find her a little occupation.'

By dint of a carefully-exercised diplomacy, Racksole manoeuvred himself into a seat opposite to the lady in the red hat.

The fame of his success at the other table had followed him, and people regarded him as a serious and formidable player. In the first turn the lady put a thousand francs on double zero; Racksole put a hundred on number nineteen and a thousand on the odd numbers. Nineteen won. Racksole received four thousand four hundred francs. Nine times in succession Racksole backed number nineteen and the odd numbers; nine times the lady backed double zero. Nine times Racksole won and the lady lost. The other players, perceiving that the affair had resolved itself into a duel, stood back for the most part and watched those two. Prince Aribert never stirred from his position behind the great red hat. The game continued. Racksole lost trifles from time to time, but ninety-nine hundredths of the luck was with him. As an English spectator at the table remarked, 'he couldn't do wrong.' When midnight struck the lady in the red hat was reduced to a thousand francs. Then she fell into a winning vein for half an hour, but at one o'clock her resources were exhausted. Of the hundred and sixty thousand francs which she was reputed to have had early in the evening, Racksole held about ninety thousand, and the bank had the rest. It was a calamity for the Juno of the red hat. She jumped up, stamped her foot, and hurried from the room. At a discreet distance Racksole and the Prince pursued her.

'It might be well to ascertain her movements,' said Racksole.

Outside, in the glare of the great arc lights, and within sound of the surf which beats always at the very foot of the Kursaal, the Juno of the red hat summoned a fiacre and drove rapidly away. Racksole and the Prince took an open carriage and started in pursuit. They had not, however, travelled more than half a mile when Prince Aribert stopped the carriage, and, bidding Racksole get out, paid the driver and dismissed him.

'I feel sure I know where she is going,' he explained, 'and it will be better for us to follow on foot.'

'You mean she is making for the scene of last night's affair?' said Racksole.

'Exactly. We shall – what you call, kill two birds with one stone.'

Prince Aribert's guess was correct. The lady's carriage stopped in front of the house where Nella Racksole and Miss Spencer had had their interview on the previous evening, and the lady vanished into the building just as the two men appeared at the end of the street. Instead of proceeding along that street, the Prince led Racksole to the lane which gave on to the backs of the houses, and he counted the houses as they went up the lane. In a few minutes they had burglariously climbed over a wall, and crept, with infinite caution, up a long, narrow piece of ground – half garden, half paved yard, till they crouched under a window – a window which was shielded by curtains, but which had been left open a little.

'Listen,' said the Prince in his lightest whisper, 'they are talking.'

'Who?'

'The Berlin lady and Miss Spencer. I'm sure it's Miss Spencer's voice.'

Racksole boldly pushed the french window a little wider open, and put his ear to the aperture, through which came a beam of yellow light.

'Take my place,' he whispered to the Prince, 'they're talking German. You'll understand better.'

Silently they exchanged places under the window, and the Prince listened intently.

'Then you refuse?' Miss Spencer's visitor was saying.

There was no answer from Miss Spencer.

'Not even a thousand francs? I tell you I've lost the whole twenty-five thousand.'

Again no answer.

'Then I'll tell the whole story,' the lady went on, in an angry rush of words. 'I did what I promised to do. I enticed him here, and you've got him safe in your vile cellar, poor little man, and you won't give me a paltry thousand francs.'

'You have already had your price.' The words were Miss Spencer's. They fell cold and calm on the night air.

'I want another thousand.'

'I haven't it.'

'Then we'll see.'

Prince Aribert heard a rustle of flying skirts; then another movement – a door banged, and the beam of light through the aperture of the window suddenly disappeared. He pushed the window wide open. The room was in darkness, and apparently empty.

'Now for that lantern of yours,' he said eagerly to Theodore Racksole, after he had translated to him the conversation of the two women.

Racksole produced the dark lantern from the capacious pocket of his dust coat, and lighted it. The ray flashed about the ground.

'What is it?' exclaimed Prince Aribert with a swift cry, pointing to the ground. The lantern threw its light on a perpendicular grating at their feet, through which could be discerned a cellar. They both knelt down, and peered into the subterranean chamber. On a broken chair a young man sat listlessly with closed eyes, his head leaning heavily forward on his chest. In the feeble light of the lantern he had the livid and ghastly appearance of a corpse.

'Who can it be?' said Racksole.

'It is Eugen,' was the Prince's low answer.

## Chapter Seventeen

## THE RELEASE OF PRINCE EUGEN

'EUGEN,' Prince Arilbert called softly. At the sound of his own name the young man in the cellar feebly raised his head and stared up at the grating which separated him from his two rescuers. But his features showed no recognition. He gazed in an aimless, vague, silly manner for a few seconds, his eyes blinking under the glare of the lantern, and then his head slowly drooped again on to his chest. He was dressed in a dark tweed travelling suit, and Racksole observed that one sleeve – the left – was torn across the upper part of the cuff, and that there were stains of dirt on the left shoulder. A soiled linen collar, which had lost all its starch and was half unbuttoned, partially encircled the captive's neck; his brown boots were unlaced; a cap, a handkerchief, a portion of a watch-chain, and a few gold coins lay on the floor. Racksole flashed the lantern into the corners of the cellar, but he could discover no other furniture except the chair on which the Hereditary Prince of Posen sat and a small deal table on which were a plate and a cup.

'Eugen,' cried Prince Aribert once more, but this time his forlorn nephew made no response whatever, and then Aribert added in a low voice to Racksole: 'Perhaps he cannot see us clearly.'

'But he must surely recognize your voice,' said Racksole, in a hard, gloomy tone.

There was a pause, and the two men above ground looked at each other hesitatingly. Each knew that they must enter that cellar and get Prince Eugen out of it, and each was somehow afraid to take the next step.

'Thank God he is not dead!' said Aribert.

'He may be worse than dead!' Racksole replied.

'Worse than – What do you mean?'

'I mean – he may be mad.'

'Come,' Aribert almost shouted, with a sudden access of

energy – a wild impulse for action. And, snatching the lantern
from Racksole, he rushed into the dark room where they had
heard the conversation of Miss Spencer and the lady in the red
hat. For a moment Racksole did not stir from the threshold of
the window. 'Come,' Prince Aribert repeated, and there was an
imperious command in his utterance. 'What are you afraid of?'

'I don't know,' said Racksole, feeling stupid and queer; 'I
don't know.' Then he marched heavily after Prince Aribert into
the room. On the mantelpiece were a couple of candles which
had been blown out, and in a mechanical, unthinking way, Racksole lighted them, and the two men glanced round the room. It
presented no peculiar features: it was just an ordinary room,
rather small, rather mean, rather shabby, with an ugly wall-
paper and ugly pictures in ugly frames. Thrown over a chair was
a man's evening-dress jacket. The door was closed. Prince
Aribert turned the knob, but he could not open it.

'It's locked,' he said. 'Evidently they know we're here.'

'Nonsense,' said Racksole brusquely; 'how can they know?'
And, taking hold of the knob, he violently shook the door, and
it opened. 'I told you it wasn't locked,' he added, and this small
success of opening the door seemed to steady the man. It was a
curious psychological effect, this terrorizing (for it amounted to
that) of two courageous full-grown men by the mere apparition
of a helpless creature in a cellar. Gradually they both recovered
from it. The next moment they were out in the passage which
led to the front door of the house. The front door stood open.
They looked into the street, up and down, but there was not a
soul in sight. The street, lighted by three gas-lamps only, seemed
strangely sinister and mysterious.

'She has gone, that's clear,' said Racksole, meaning the woman
with the red hat.

'And Miss Spencer after her, do you think?' questioned Aribert.

'No. She would stay. She would never dare to leave. Let us
find the cellar steps.'

The cellar steps were happily not difficult to discover, for in
moving a pace backwards Prince Aribert had a narrow escape of
precipitating himself to the bottom of them. The lantern showed

that they were built on a curve. Silently Racksole resumed possession of the lantern and went first, the Prince close behind him. At the foot was a short passage, and in this passage crouched the figure of a woman. Her eyes threw back the rays of the lantern, shining like a cat's at midnight. Then, as the men went nearer, they saw that it was Miss Spencer who barred their way. She seemed half to kneel on the stone floor, and in one hand she held what at first appeared to be a dagger, but which proved to be nothing more romantic than a rather long bread-knife.

'I heard you, I heard you,' she exclaimed. 'Get back; you mustn't come here.'

There was a desperate and dangerous look on her face, and her form shook with scarcely controlled passionate energy.

'Now see here, Miss Spencer,' Racksole said calmly, 'I guess we've had enough of this fandango. You'd better get up and clear out, or we'll just have to drag you off.'

He went calmly up to her, the lantern in his hand. Without another word she struck the knife into his arm, and the lantern fell extinguished. Racksole gave a cry, rather of angry surprise than of pain, and retreated a few steps. In the darkness they could still perceive the glint of her eyes.

'I told you you mustn't come here,' the woman said. 'Now get back.'

Racksole positively laughed. It was a queer laugh, but he laughed, and he could not help it. The idea of this woman, this bureau clerk, stopping his progress and that of Prince Aribert by means of a bread-knife aroused his sense of humour. He struck a match, relighted the candle, and faced Miss Spencer once more.

'I'll do it again,' she said, with a note of hard resolve.

'Oh, no, you won't, my girl,' said Racksole; and he pulled out his revolver, cocked it, raised his hand.

'Put down that plaything of yours,' he said firmly.

'No,' she answered.

'I shall shoot.'

She pressed her lips together.

'I shall shoot,' he repeated. 'One – two – three.'

Bang, bang! He had fired twice, purposely missing her.

Miss Spencer never blenched. Racksole was tremendously surprised – and he would have been a thousandfold more surprised could he have contrasted her behaviour now with her abject terror on the previous evening when Nella had threatened her.

'You've got a bit of pluck,' he said, 'but it won't help you. Why won't you let us pass?'

As a matter of fact, pluck was just what she had not, really; she had merely subordinated one terror to another. She was desperately afraid of Racksole's revolver, but she was much more afraid of something else.

'Why won't you let us pass?'

'I daren't,' she said, with a plaintive tremor; 'Tom put me in charge.'

That was all. The men could see tears running down her poor wrinkled face. Theodore Racksole began to take off his light overcoat.

'I see I must take my coat off to you,' he said, and he almost smiled. Then, with a quick movement, he threw the coat over Miss Spencer's head and flew at her, seizing both her arms, while Prince Aribert assisted.

Her struggles ceased – she was beaten.

'That's all right,' said Racksole: 'I could never have used that revolver – to mean business with it, of course.'

They carried her, unresisting, upstairs and on to the upper floor, where they locked her in a bedroom. She lay in the bed as if exhausted.

'Now for my poor Eugen,' said Prince Aribert.

'Don't you think we'd better search the house first?' Racksole suggested; 'it will be safer to know just how we stand. We can't afford any ambushes or things of that kind, you know.'

The Prince agreed, and they searched the house from top to bottom, but found no one. Then, having locked the front door and the french window of the sitting-room, they proceeded again to the cellar.

Here a new obstacle confronted them. The cellar door was, of course, locked; there was no sign of a key, and it appeared to be a heavy door. They were compelled to return to the bedroom where Miss Spencer was incarcerated, in order to demand the key of the cellar from her. She still lay without movement on the bed.

'Tom's got it,' she replied, faintly, to their question: 'Tom's got it, I swear to you. He took it for safety.'

'Then how do you feed your prisoner?' Racksole asked sharply.

'Through the grating,' she answered.

Both men shuddered. They felt she was speaking the truth. For the third time they went to the cellar door. In vain Racksole thrust himself against it; he could do no more than shake it.

'Let's try both together,' said Prince Aribert. 'Now!' There was a crack. 'Again,' said Prince Aribert. There was another crack, and then the upper hinge gave way. The rest was easy. Over the wreck of the door they entered Prince Eugen's prison.

The captive still sat on his chair. The terrific noise and bustle of breaking down the door seemed not to have aroused him from his lethargy, but when Prince Aribert spoke to him in German he looked at his uncle.

'Will you not come with us, Eugen?' said Prince Aribert; 'you needn't stay here any longer, you know.'

'Leave me alone,' was the strange reply; 'leave me alone. What do you want?'

'We are here to get you out of this scrape,' said Aribert gently. Racksole stood aside.

'Who is that fellow?' said Eugen sharply.

'That is my friend Mr Racksole, an Englishman – or rather, I should say, an American – to whom we owe a great deal. Come and have supper, Eugen.'

'I won't,' answered Eugen doggedly. 'I'm waiting here for her. You didn't think anyone had kept me here, did you, against my will? I tell you I'm waiting for her. She said she'd come.'

'Who is she?' Aribert asked, humouring him.

'She! Why, you know! I forgot, of course, you don't know. You mustn't ask. Don't pry, Uncle Aribert. She was wearing a red hat.'

'I'll take you to her, my dear Eugen.' Prince Aribert put his hands on the other's shoulder, but Eugen shook him off violently, stood up, and then sat down again.

Aribert looked at Racksole, and they both looked at Prince Eugen. The latter's face was flushed, and Racksole observed that the left pupil was more dilated than the right. The man started, muttered odd, fragmentary scraps of sentences, now grumbling, now whining.

'His mind is unhinged,' Racksole whispered in English.

'Hush!' said Prince Aribert. 'He understands English.' But Prince Eugen took no notice of the brief colloquy.

'We had better get him upstairs, somehow,' said Racksole.

'Yes,' Aribert assented. 'Eugen, the lady with the red hat, the lady you are waiting for, is upstairs. She has sent us down to ask you to come up. Won't you come?'

'Himmel!' the poor fellow exclaimed, with a kind of weak anger. 'Why did you not say this before?'

He rose, staggered towards Aribert, and fell headlong on the floor. He had swooned. The two men raised him, carried him up the stone steps, and laid him with infinite care on a sofa. He lay, breathing queerly through the nostrils, his eyes closed, his fingers contracted; every now and then a convulsion ran through his frame.

'One of us must fetch a doctor,' said Prince Aribert.

'I will,' said Racksole. At that moment there was a quick, curt rap on the french window, and both Racksole and the Prince glanced round startled. A girl's face was pressed against the large window-pane. It was Nella's. Racksole unfastened the catch, and she entered.

'I have found you,' she said lightly; 'you might have told me. I couldn't sleep. I inquired from the hotel-folks if you had retired, and they said no; so I slipped out. I guessed where you were.' Racksole interrupted her with a question as to what she meant by this escapade, but she stopped him with a careless gesture. 'What's this?' She pointed to the form on the sofa.

'That is my nephew, Prince Eugen,' said Aribert.

'Hurt?' she inquired coldly. 'I hope not.'

'He is ill,' said Racksole, 'his brain is turned.'

Nella began to examine the unconscious Prince with the expert movements of a girl who had passed through the best hospital course to be obtained in New York.

'He has got brain fever,' she said. 'That is all, but it will be enough. Do you know if there is a bed anywhere in this remarkable house?'

## Chapter Eighteen

## IN THE NIGHT-TIME

'HE must on no account be moved,' said the dark little Belgian doctor, whose eyes seemed to peer so quizzically through his spectacles; and he said it with much positiveness.

That pronouncement rather settled their plans for them. It was certainly a professional triumph for Nella, who, previous to the doctor's arrival, had told them the very same thing. Considerable argument had passed before the doctor was sent for. Prince Aribert was for keeping the whole affair a deep secret among their three selves. Theodore Racksole agreed so far, but he suggested further that at no matter what risk they should transport the patient over to England at once. Racksole had an idea that he should feel safer in that hotel of his, and better able to deal with any situation that might arise. Nella scorned the idea. In her quality of an amateur nurse, she assured them that Prince Eugen was much more seriously ill than either of them suspected, and she urged that they should take absolute possession of the house, and keep possession till Prince Eugen was convalescent.

'But what about the Spencer female?' Racksole had said.

'Keep her where she is. Keep her a prisoner. And hold the house against all comers. If Jules should come back, simply defy him to enter – that is all. There are two of you, so you must keep an eye on the former occupiers, if they return, and on Miss Spencer, while I nurse the patient. But first, you must send for a doctor.'

'Doctor!' Prince Aribert had said, alarmed. 'Will it not be necessary to make some awkward explanation to the doctor?'

'Not at all!' she replied. 'Why should it be? In a place like Ostend doctors are far too discreet to ask questions; they see too much to retain their curiosity. Besides, do you want your nephew to die?'

Both the men were somewhat taken aback by the girl's sagacious grasp of the situation, and it came about that they began
to obey her like subordinates. She told her father to sally forth in
search of a doctor, and he went. She gave Prince Aribert certain
other orders, and he promptly executed them.

By the evening of the following day, everything was going
smoothly. The doctor came and departed several times, and sent
medicine, and seemed fairly optimistic as to the issue of the
illness. An old woman had been induced to come in and cook
and clean. Miss Spencer was kept out of sight on the attic floor,
pending some decision as to what to do with her. And no one
outside the house had asked any questions. The inhabitants of
that particular street must have been accustomed to strange
behaviour on the part of their neighbours, unaccountable appearances and disappearances, strange flittings and arrivals. This
strong-minded and active trio – Racksole, Nella, and Prince
Aribert – might have been the lawful and accustomed tenants
of the house, for any outward evidence to the contrary.

On the afternoon of the third day Prince Eugen was distinctly
and seriously worse. Nella had sat up with him the previous night
and throughout the day. Her father had spent the morning at the
hotel, and Prince Aribert had kept watch. The two men were
never absent from the house at the same time, and one of them
always did duty as sentinel at night. On this afternoon Prince
Aribert and Nella sat together in the patient's bedroom. The
doctor had just left. Theodore Racksole was downstairs reading
the *New York Herald*. The Prince and Nella were near the
window, which looked on to the back-garden. It was a queer
shabby little bedroom to shelter the august body of a European
personage like Prince Eugen of Posen. Curiously enough, both
Nella and her father, ardent democrats though they were, had
been somehow impressed by the royalty and importance of the
fever-stricken Prince – impressed as they had never been by
Aribert. They had both felt that here, under their care, was a
species of individuality quite new to them, and different from
anything they had previously encountered. Even the gestures and
tones of his delirium had an air of abrupt yet condescending

command – an imposing mixture of suavity and haughtiness. As for Nella, she had been first struck by the beautiful 'E' over a crown on the sleeves of his linen, and by the signet ring on his pale, emaciated hand. After all, these trifling outward signs are at least as effective as others of deeper but less obtrusive significance. The Racksoles, too, duly marked the attitude of Prince Aribert to his nephew: it was at once paternal and reverential; it disclosed clearly that Prince Aribert continued, in spite of everything, to regard his nephew as his sovereign lord and master, as a being surrounded by a natural and inevitable pomp and awe. This attitude, at the beginning, seemed false and unreal to the Americans; it seemed to them to be assumed; but gradually they came to perceive that they were mistaken, and that though America might have cast out 'the monarchial superstition', nevertheless that 'superstition' had vigorously survived in another part of the world.

'You and Mr Racksole have been extraordinarily kind to me,' said Prince Aribert very quietly, after the two had sat some time in silence.

'Why? How?' she asked unaffectedly. 'We are interested in this affair ourselves, you know. It began at our hotel – you mustn't forget that, Prince.'

'I don't,' he said. 'I forget nothing. But I cannot help feeling that I have led you into a strange entanglement. Why should you and Mr Racksole be here – you who are supposed to be on a holiday! – hiding in a strange house in a foreign country, subject to all sorts of annoyances and all sorts of risks, simply because I am anxious to avoid scandal, to avoid any sort of talk, in connection with my misguided nephew? It is nothing to you that the Hereditary Prince of Posen should be liable to a public disgrace. What will it matter to you if the throne of Posen becomes the laughing-stock of Europe?'

'I really don't know, Prince,' Nella smiled roguishly. 'But we Americans have a habit of going right through with anything we have begun.'

'Ah!' he said, 'who knows how this thing will end? All our trouble, our anxieties, our watchfulness, may come to nothing.

I tell you that when I see Eugen lying there, and think that we cannot learn his story until he recovers, I am ready to go mad. We might be arranging things, making matters smooth, preparing for the future, if only we knew – knew what he can tell us. I tell you that I am ready to go mad. If anything should happen to you, Miss Racksole, I would kill myself.'

'But why?' she questioned. 'Supposing, that is, that anything could happen to me – which it can't.'

'Because I have dragged you into this,' he replied, gazing at her. 'It is nothing to you. You are only being kind.'

'How do you know it is nothing to me, Prince?' she asked him quickly.

Just then the sick man made a convulsive movement, and Nella flew to the bed and soothed him. From the head of the bed she looked over at Prince Aribert, and he returned her bright, excited glance. She was in her travelling-frock, with a large white Belgian apron tied over it. Large dark circles of fatigue and sleeplessness surrounded her eyes, and to the Prince her cheek seemed hollow and thin; her hair lay thick over the temples, half covering the ears. Aribert gave no answer to her query – merely gazed at her with melancholy intensity.

'I think I will go and rest,' she said at last. 'You will know all about the medicine.'

'Sleep well,' he said, as he softly opened the door for her. And then he was alone with Eugen. It was his turn that night to watch, for they still half-expected some strange, sudden visit, or onslaught, or move of one kind or another from Jules. Racksole slept in the parlour on the ground floor. Nella had the front bedroom on the first floor; Miss Spencer was immured in the attic; the last-named lady had been singularly quiet and incurious, taking her food from Nella and asking no questions, the old woman went at nights to her own abode in the purlieus of the harbour. Hour after hour Aribert sat silent by his nephew's bedside, attending mechanically to his wants, and every now and then gazing hard into the vacant, anguished face, as if trying to extort from that mask the secrets which it held. Aribert was tortured by the idea that if he could have only half an hour's, only a quarter of an hour's, rational speech with Prince Eugen, all might be cleared up and put right, and by the fact that that rational talk was absolutely impossible on Eugen's part until the fever had run its course. As the minutes crept on to midnight the watcher, made nervous by the intense, electrical atmosphere which seems always to surround a person who is dangerously ill, grew more and more a prey to vague and terrible apprehensions. His mind dwelt hysterically on the most fatal possibilities. He wondered what would occur if by any ill-chance Eugen should die in that bed – how he would explain the affair to Posen and to the Emperor, how he would justify himself. He saw himself being tried for murder, sentenced (him – a Prince of the blood!), led to the scaffold . . . a scene unparalleled in Europe for over a century! . . . Then he gazed anew at the sick man, and thought he saw death in every drawn feature of that agonized face. He could have screamed aloud. His ears heard a peculiar resonant boom. He started – it was nothing but the city clock striking twelve. But there was another sound – a mysterious shuffle at the door. He listened; then jumped from his chair. Nothing now! Nothing! But still he felt drawn to the door, and after what seemed an interminable interval he went and opened it, his heart beating furiously. Nella lay in a heap on the door mat. She was fully dressed, but had apparently lost consciousness. He clutched at her slender body, picked her up, carried her to the chair by the fire-place, and laid her in it. He had forgotten all about Eugen.

'What is it, my angel?' he whispered, and then he kissed her – kissed her twice. He could only look at her; he did not know what to do to succour her.

At last she opened her eyes and sighed.

'Where am I?' she asked vaguely, in a tremulous tone. 'Ah!' as she recognized him. 'Is it you? Did I do anything silly? Did I faint?'

'What has happened? Were you ill?' he questioned anxiously. He was kneeling at her feet, holding her hand tight.

'I saw Jules by the side of my bed,' she murmured; 'I'm sure I saw him; he laughed at me. I had not undressed. I sprang up, frightened, but he had gone, and then I ran downstairs – to you.'

'You were dreaming,' he soothed her.

'Was I?'

'You must have been. I have not heard a sound. No one could have entered. But if you like I will wake Mr Racksole.'

'Perhaps I was dreaming,' she admitted. 'How foolish!'

'You were over-tired,' he said, still unconsciously holding her hand. They gazed at each other. She smiled at him.

'You kissed me,' she said suddenly, and he blushed red and stood up before her. 'Why did you kiss me?'

'Ah! Miss Racksole,' he murmured, hurrying the words out. 'Forgive me. It is unforgivable, but forgive me. I was overpowered by my feelings. I did not know what I was doing.'

'Why did you kiss me?' she repeated.

'Because – Nella! I love you. I have no right to say it.'

'Why have you no right to say it?'

'If Eugen dies, I shall owe a duty to Posen – I shall be its ruler.'

'Well!' she said calmly, with an adorable confidence. 'Papa is worth forty millions. Would you not abdicate?'

'Ah!' he gave a low cry. 'Will you force me to say these things? I could not shirk my duty to Posen, and the reigning Prince of Posen can only marry a Princess.'

'But Prince Eugen will live,' she said positively, 'and if he lives – '

'Then I shall be free. I would renounce all my rights to make you mine, if – if – '

'If what, Prince?'

'If you would deign to accept my hand.'

'Am I, then, rich enough?'

'Nella!' He bent down to her.

Then there was a crash of breaking glass. Aribert went to the window and opened it. In the starlit gloom he could see that a ladder had been raised against the back of the house. He thought he heard footsteps at the end of the garden.

'It was Jules,' he exclaimed to Nella, and without another word rushed upstairs to the attic. The attic was empty. Miss Spencer had mysteriously vanished.

*Chapter Nineteen*

## ROYALTY AT THE GRAND BABYLON

THE Royal apartments at the Grand Babylon are famous in the world of hotels, and indeed elsewhere, as being, in their own way, unsurpassed. Some of the palaces of Germany, and in particular those of the mad Ludwig of Bavaria, may possess rooms and saloons which outshine them in gorgeous luxury and the mere wild fairy-like extravagance of wealth; but there is nothing, anywhere, even on Eighth Avenue, New York, which can fairly be called more complete, more perfect, more enticing, or – not least important – more comfortable. The suite consists of six chambers – the ante-room, the saloon or audience chamber, the dining-room, the yellow drawing-room (where Royalty receives its friends), the library, and the State bedroom – to the last of which we have already been introduced. The most important and most impressive of these is, of course, the audience chamber, an apartment fifty feet long by forty feet broad, with a superb outlook over the Thames, the Shot Tower, and the higher signals of the South-Western Railway. The decoration of this room is mainly in the German taste, since four out of every six of its Royal occupants are of Teutonic blood; but its chief glory is its French ceiling, a masterpiece by Fragonard, taken bodily from a certain famous palace on the Loire. The walls are of panelled oak, with an eight-foot dado of Arras cloth imitated from unique Continental examples. The carpet, woven in one piece, is an antique specimen of the finest Turkish work, and it was obtained, a bargain, by Félix Babylon, from an impecunious Roumanian Prince. The silver candelabra, now fitted with electric light, came from the Rhine, and each had a separate history. The Royal chair – it is not etiquette to call it a throne, though it amounts to a throne – was looted by Napoleon from an Austrian city, and bought by Félix Babylon at the sale of a French collector. At each corner of the room stands a gigantic grotesque vase of German faïence of the sixteenth century. These were presented to Félix Babylon by William the First of Germany, upon the conclusion of his first incognito visit to London in connection with the French trouble of 1875. There is only one picture in the audience chamber. It is a portrait of the luckless but noble Dom Pedro, Emperor of the Brazils. Given to Félix Babylon by Dom Pedro himself, it hangs there solitary and sublime as a reminder to Kings and Princes that Empires may pass away and greatness fall. A certain Prince who was occupying the suite during the Jubilee of 1887 – when the Grand Babylon had seven persons of Royal blood under its roof – sent a curt message to Félix that the portrait must be removed. Félix respectfully declined to remove it, and the Prince left for another hotel, where he was robbed of two thousand pounds' worth of jewellery. The Royal audience chamber of the Grand Babylon, if people only knew it, is one of the sights of London, but it is never shown, and if you ask the hotel servants about its wonders they will tell you only foolish facts concerning it, as that the Turkey carpet costs fifty pounds to clean, and that one of the great vases is cracked across the pedestal, owing to the rough treatment accorded to it during a riotous game of Blind Man's Buff, played one night by four young Princesses, a Balkan King, and his aides-de-camp.

In one of the window recesses of this magnificent apartment, on a certain afternoon in late July, stood Prince Aribert of Posen. He was faultlessly dressed in the conventional frock-coat of English civilization, with a gardenia in his button-hole, and the indispensable crease down the front of the trousers. He seemed to be fairly amused, and also to expect someone, for at frequent intervals he looked rapidly over his shoulder in the direction of the door behind the Royal chair. At last a little wizened, stooping old man, with a distinctly German cast of countenance, appeared through the door, and laid some papers on a small table by the side of the chair.

'Ah, Hans, my old friend!' said Aribert, approaching the old man. 'I must have a little talk with you about one or two matters. How do you find His Royal Highness?'

The old man saluted, military fashion. 'Not very well, your

Highness,' he answered. 'I've been valet to your Highness's nephew since his majority, and I was valet to his Royal father before him, but I never saw – ' He stopped, and threw up his wrinkled hands deprecatingly.

'You never saw what?' Aribert smiled affectionately on the old fellow. You could perceive that these two, so sharply differentiated in rank, had been intimate in the past, and would be intimate again.

'Do you know, my Prince,' said the old man, 'that we are to receive the financier, Sampson Levi – is that his name? – in the audience chamber? Surely, if I may humbly suggest, the library would have been good enough for a financier?'

'One would have thought so,' agreed Prince Aribert, 'but perhaps your master has a special reason. Tell me,' he went on, changing the subject quickly, 'how came it that you left the Prince, my nephew, at Ostend, and returned to Posen?'

'His orders, Prince,' and old Hans, who had had a wide experience of Royal whims and knew half the secrets of the Courts of Europe, gave Aribert a look which might have meant anything. 'He sent me back on an – an errand, your Highness.'

'And you were to rejoin him here?'

'Just so, Highness. And I did rejoin him here, although, to tell the truth, I had begun to fear that I might never see my master again.'

'The Prince has been very ill in Ostend, Hans.'

'So I have gathered,' Hans responded drily, slowly rubbing his hands together. 'And his Highness is not yet perfectly recovered.'

'Not yet. We despaired of his life, Hans, at one time, but thanks to an excellent constitution, he came safely through the ordeal.'

'We must take care of him, your Highness.'

'Yes, indeed,' said Aribert solemnly, 'his life is very precious to Posen.'

At that moment, Eugen, Hereditary Prince of Posen, entered the audience chamber. He was pale and languid, and his uniform seemed to be a trouble to him. His hair had been slightly ruffled, and there was a look of uneasiness, almost of alarmed unrest, in his fine dark eyes. He was like a man who is afraid to look behind him lest he should see something there which ought not to be there. But at the same time, here beyond doubt was Royalty. Nothing could have been more striking than the contrast between Eugen, a sick man in the shabby house at Ostend, and this Prince Eugen in the Royal apartments of the Grand Babylon Hotel, surrounded by the luxury and pomp which modern civilization can offer to those born in high places. All the desperate episode of Ostend was now hidden, passed over. It was supposed never to have occurred. It existed only like a secret shame in the hearts of those who had witnessed it. Prince Eugen had recovered; at any rate, he was convalescent, and he had been removed to London, where he took up again the dropped thread of his princely life. The lady with the red hat, the incorruptible and savage Miss Spencer, the unscrupulous and brilliant Jules, the dark, damp cellar, the horrible little bedroom – these things were over. Thanks to Prince Aribert and the Racksoles, he had emerged from them in safety. He was able to resume his public and official career. The Emperor had been informed of his safe arrival in London, after an unavoidable delay in Ostend; his name once more figured in the Court chronicle of the newspapers. In short, everything was smothered over. Only – only Jules, Rocco, and Miss Spencer were still at large; and the body of Reginald Dimmock lay buried in the domestic mausoleum of the palace at Posen; and Prince Eugen had still to interview Mr Sampson Levi.

That various matters lay heavy on the mind of Prince Eugen was beyond question. He seemed to have withdrawn within himself. Despite the extraordinary experiences through which he had recently passed, events which called aloud for explanations and confidence between the nephew and the uncle, he would say scarcely a word to Prince Aribert. Any allusion, however direct, to the days at Ostend, was ignored by him with more or less ingenuity, and Prince Aribert was really no nearer a full solution of the mystery of Jules' plot than he had been on the night when he and Racksole visited the gaming tables at Ostend. Eugen was well aware that he had been kidnapped through the agency of the woman in the red hat, but, doubtless ashamed at having been her dupe, he would not proceed in any way with the clearing-up of the matter.

'You will receive in this room, Eugen?' Aribert questioned him.

'Yes,' was the answer, given pettishly. 'Why not? Even if I have no proper retinue here, surely that is no reason why I should not hold audience in a proper manner? . . . Hans, you can go.' The old valet promptly disappeared. 'Aribert,' the Hereditary Prince continued, when they were alone in the chamber, 'you think I am mad.'

'My dear Eugen,' said Prince Aribert, startled in spite of himself. 'Don't be absurd.'

'I say you think I am mad. You think that that attack of brain fever has left its permanent mark on me. Well, perhaps I am mad. Who can tell? God knows that I have been through enough lately to drive me mad.'

Aribert made no reply. As a matter of strict fact, the thought had crossed his mind that Eugen's brain had not yet recovered its normal tone and activity. This speech of his nephew's, however, had the effect of immediately restoring his belief in the latter's entire sanity. He felt convinced that if only he could regain his nephew's confidence, the old brotherly confidence which had existed between them since the years when they played together as boys, all might yet be well. But at present there appeared to be no sign that Eugen meant to give his confidence to anyone. The young Prince had come up out of the valley of the shadow of death, but some of the valley's shadow had clung to him, and it seemed he was unable to dissipate it.

'By the way,' said Eugen suddenly, 'I must reward these Racksoles, I suppose. I am indeed grateful to them. If I gave the girl a bracelet, and the father a thousand guineas – how would that meet the case?'

'My dear Eugen!' exclaimed Aribert aghast. 'A thousand guineas! Do you know that Theodore Racksole could buy up all Posen from end to end without making himself a pauper. A thousand guineas! You might as well offer him sixpence.'

'Then what must I offer?'

'Nothing, except your thanks. Anything else would be an insult. These are no ordinary hotel people.'

'Can't I give the little girl a bracelet?' Prince Eugen gave a sinister laugh.

Aribert looked at him steadily. 'No,' he said.

'Why did you kiss her – that night?' asked Prince Eugen carelessly.

'Kiss whom?' said Aribert, blushing and angry, despite his most determined efforts to keep calm and unconcerned.

'The Racksole girl.'

'When do you mean?'

'I mean,' said Prince Eugen, 'that night in Ostend when I was ill. You thought I was in a delirium. Perhaps I was. But somehow I remember that with extraordinary distinctness. I remember raising my head for a fraction of an instant, and just in that fraction of an instant you kissed her. Oh, Uncle Aribert!'

'Listen, Eugen, for God's sake. I love Nella Racksole. I shall marry her.'

'You!' There was a long pause, and then Eugen laughed. 'Ah!' he said. 'They all talk like that to start with. I have talked like that myself, dear uncle; it sounds nice, and it means nothing.'

'In this case it means everything, Eugen,' said Aribert quietly.

Some accent of determination in the latter's tone made Eugen rather more serious.

'You can't marry her,' he said. 'The Emperor won't permit a morganatic marriage.'

'The Emperor has nothing to do with the affair. I shall renounce my rights. I shall become a plain citizen.'

'In which case you will have no fortune to speak of.'

'But my wife will have a fortune. Knowing the sacrifices which I shall have made in order to marry her, she will not hesitate to place that fortune in my hands for our mutual use,' said Aribert stiffly.

'You will decidedly be rich,' mused Eugen, as his ideas dwelt on Theodore Racksole's reputed wealth. 'But have you thought of this,' he asked, and his mild eyes glowed again in a sort of madness. 'Have you thought that I am unmarried, and might die at any moment, and then the throne will descend to you — to you, Aribert?'

'The throne will never descend to me, Eugen,' said Aribert softly, 'for you will live. You are thoroughly convalescent. You have nothing to fear.'

'It is the next seven days that I fear,' said Eugen.

'The next seven days! Why?'

'I do not know. But I fear them. If I can survive them — '

'Mr Sampson Levi, sire,' Hans announced in a loud tone.

*Chapter Twenty*

# MR SAMPSON LEVI BIDS PRINCE EUGEN
## GOOD MORNING

PRINCE EUGEN started. 'I will see him,' he said, with a gesture to Hans as if to indicate that Mr Sampson Levi might enter at once.

'I beg one moment first,' said Aribert, laying a hand gently on his nephew's arm, and giving old Hans a glance which had the effect of precipitating that admirably trained servant through the doorway.

'What is it?' asked Prince Eugen crossly. 'Why this sudden seriousness? Don't forget that I have an appointment with Mr Sampson Levi, and must not keep him waiting. Someone said that punctuality is the politeness of princes.'

'Eugen,' said Aribert, 'I wish you to be as serious as I am. Why cannot we have faith in each other? I want to help you. I have helped you. You are my titular Sovereign; but on the other hand I have the honour to be your uncle: I have the honour to be the same age as you, and to have been your companion from youth up. Give me your confidence. I thought you had given it me years ago, but I have lately discovered that you had your secrets, even then. And now, since your illness, you are still more secretive.'

'What do you mean, Aribert?' said Eugen, in a tone which might have been either inimical or friendly. 'What do you want to say?'

'Well, in the first place, I want to say that you will not succeed with the estimable Mr Sampson Levi.'

'Shall I not?' said Eugen lightly. 'How do you know what my business is with him?'

'Suffice it to say that I know. You will never get that million pounds out of him.'

Prince Eugen gasped, and then swallowed his excitement. 'Who has been talking? What million?' His eyes wandered uneasily round the room. 'Ah!' he said, pretending to laugh. 'I see how it is. I have been chattering in my delirium. You mustn't take any notice of that, Aribert. When one has a fever one's ideas become grotesque and fanciful.'

'You never talked in your delirium,' Aribert replied; 'at least not about yourself. I knew about this projected loan before I saw you in Ostend.'

'Who told you?' demanded Eugen fiercely.

'Then you admit that you are trying to raise a loan?'

'I admit nothing. Who told you?'

'Theodore Racksole, the millionaire. These rich men have no secrets from each other. They form a coterie, closer than any coterie of ours. Eugen, and far more powerful. They talk, and in talking they rule the world, these millionaires. They are the real monarchs.'

'Curse them!' said Eugen.

'Yes, perhaps so. But let me return to your case. Imagine my shame, my disgust, when I found that Racksole could tell me more about your affairs than I knew myself. Happily, he is a good fellow; one can trust him; otherwise I should have been tempted to do something desperate when I discovered that all your private history was in his hands. Eugen, let us come to the point; why do you want that million? Is it actually true that you are so deeply in debt? I have no desire to improve the occasion. I merely ask.'

'And what if I do owe a million?' said Prince Eugen with assumed valour.

'Oh, nothing, my dear Eugen, nothing. Only it is rather a large sum to have scattered in ten years, is it not? How did you manage it?'

'Don't ask me, Aribert. I've been a fool. But I swear to you that the woman whom you call "the lady in the red hat" is the last of my follies. I am about to take a wife, and become a respectable Prince.'

'Then the engagement with Princess Anna is an accomplished fact?'

'Practically so. As soon as I have settled with Levi, all will be smooth. Aribert, I wouldn't lose Anna for the Imperial throne. She is a good and pure woman, and I love her as a man might love an angel.'

'And yet you would deceive her as to your debts, Eugen?'

'Not her, but her absurd parents, and perhaps the Emperor. They have heard rumours, and I must set those rumours at rest by presenting to them a clean sheet.'

'I am glad you have been frank with me, Eugen,' said Prince Aribert, 'but I will be plain with you. You will never marry the Princess Anna.'

'And why?' said Eugen, supercilious again.

'Because her parents will not permit it. Because you will not be able to present a clean sheet to them. Because this Sampson Levi will never lend you a million.'

'Explain yourself.'

'I propose to do so. You were kidnapped – it is a horrid word, but we must use it – in Ostend.'

'True.'

'Do you know why?'

'I suppose because that vile old red-hatted woman and her accomplices wanted to get some money out of me. Fortunately, thanks to you, they didn't.'

'Not at all,' said Aribert. 'They wanted no money from you. They knew well enough that you had no money. They knew you were the naughty schoolboy among European Princes, with no sense of responsibility or of duty towards your kingdom. Shall I tell you why they kidnapped you?'

'When you have done abusing me, my dear uncle.'

'They kidnapped you merely to keep you out of England for a few days, merely to compel you to fail in your appointment with Sampson Levi. And it appears to me that they succeeded. Assuming that you don't obtain the money from Levi, is there another financier in all Europe from whom you can get it – on such strange security as you have to offer?'

'Possibly there is not,' said Prince Eugen calmly. 'But, you see, I shall get it from Sampson Levi. Levi promised it, and I know from other sources that he is a man of his word. He said that the money, subject to certain formalities, would be available till –'

'Till?'

'Till the end of June.'

'And it is now the end of July.'

'Well, what is a month? He is only too glad to lend the money. He will get excellent interest. How on earth have you got into your sage old head this notion of a plot against me? The idea is ridiculous. A plot against me? What for?'

'Have you ever thought of Bosnia?' asked Aribert coldly.

'What of Bosnia?'

'I need not tell you that the King of Bosnia is naturally under obligations to Austria, to whom he owes his crown. Austria is anxious for him to make a good influential marriage.'

'Well, let him.'

'He is going to. He is going to marry the Princess Anna.'

'Not while I live. He made overtures there a year ago, and was rebuffed.'

'Yes; but he will make overtures again, and this time he will not be rebuffed. Oh, Eugen! can't you see that this plot against you is being engineered by some persons who know all about your affairs, and whose desire is to prevent your marriage with Princess Anna? Only one man in Europe can have any motive for wishing to prevent your marriage with Princess Anna, and that is the man who means to marry her himself.' Eugen went very pale.

'Then, Aribert, do you mean to convey to me that my detention in Ostend was contrived by the agents of the King of Bosnia?'

'I do.'

'With a view to stopping my negotiations with Sampson Levi, and so putting an end to the possibility of my marriage with Anna?'

Aribert nodded.

'You are a good friend to me, Aribert. You mean well. But you are mistaken. You have been worrying about nothing.'

'Have you forgotten about Reginald Dimmock?'

'I remember you said that he had died.'

'I said nothing of the sort. I said that he had been assassinated. That was part of it, my poor Eugen.'

'Pooh!' said Eugen. 'I don't believe he was assassinated. And as for Sampson Levi, I will bet you a thousand marks that he and I come to terms this morning, and that the million is in my hands before I leave London.' Aribert shook his head.

'You seem to be pretty sure of Mr Levi's character. Have you had much to do with him before?'

'Well,' Eugen hesitated a second, 'a little. What young man in my position hasn't had something to do with Mr Sampson Levi at one time or another?'

'I haven't,' said Aribert.

'You! You are a fossil.' He rang a silver bell. 'Hans! I will receive Mr Sampson Levi.'

Whereupon Aribert discreetly departed, and Prince Eugen sat down in the great velvet chair, and began to look at the papers which Hans had previously placed upon the table.

'Good morning, your Royal Highness,' said Sampson Levi, bowing as he entered. 'I trust your Royal Highness is well.'

'Moderately, thanks,' returned the Prince.

In spite of the fact that he had had as much to do with people of Royal blood as any plain man in Europe, Sampson Levi had never yet learned how to be at ease with these exalted individuals during the first few minutes of an interview. Afterwards, he resumed command of himself and his faculties, but at the beginning he was invariably flustered, scarlet of face, and inclined to perspiration.

'We will proceed to business at once,' said Prince Eugen. 'Will you take a seat, Mr Levi?'

'I thank your Royal Highness.'

'Now as to that loan which we had already practically arranged – a million, I think it was,' said the Prince airily.

'A million,' Levi acquiesced, toying with his enormous watch chain.

'Everything is now in order. Here are the papers and I should like to finish the matter up at once.'

'Exactly, your Highness, but –'

'But what? You months ago expressed the warmest satisfaction at the security, though I am quite prepared to admit that the security, is of rather an unusual nature. You also agreed to the rate of interest. It is not everyone, Mr Levi, who can lend out a million at 5½ per cent. And in ten years the whole amount will be paid back. I – er – I believe I informed you that the fortune of Princess Anna, who is about to accept my hand, will ultimately amount to something like fifty millions of marks, which is over two million pounds in your English money.' Prince Eugen stopped. He had no fancy for talking in this confidential manner to financiers, but he felt that circumstances demanded it.

'You see, it's like this, your Royal Highness,' began Mr Sampson Levi, in his homely English idiom. 'It's like this. I said I could keep that bit of money available till the end of June, and you were to give me an interview here before that date. Not having heard from your Highness, and not knowing your Highness's address, though my German agents made every inquiry, I concluded, that you had made other arrangements, money being so cheap this last few months.'

'I was unfortunately detained at Ostend,' said Prince Eugen, with as much haughtiness as he could assume, 'by – by important business. I have made no other arangements, and I shall have need of the million. If you will be so good as to pay it to my London bankers – '

'I'm very sorry,' said Mr Sampson Levi, with a tremendous and dazzling air of politeness, which surprised even himself, 'but my syndicate has now lent the money elsewhere. It's in South America – I don't mind telling your Highness that we've lent it to the Chilean Government.'

'Hang the Chilean Government, Mr Levi,' exclaimed the Prince, and he went white. 'I must have that million. It was an arrangement.'

'It was an arrangement, I admit,' said Mr Sampson Levi, 'but your Highness broke the arrangement.'

There was a long silence.

'Do you mean to say,' began the Prince with tense calmness, 'that you are not in a position to let me have that million?'

'I could let your Highness have a million in a couple of years' time.'

The Prince made a gesture of annoyance.

'Mr Levi,' he said, 'if you do not place the money in my hands to-morrow you will ruin one of the oldest of reigning families, and, incidentally, you will alter the map of Europe. You are not keeping faith, and I had relied on you.'

'Pardon me, your Highness,' said little Levi, rising in resentment, 'it is not I who have not kept faith. I beg to repeat that the money is no longer at my disposal, and to bid your Highness good morning.'

And Mr Sampson Levi left the audience chamber with an awkward, aggrieved bow.

It was a scene characteristic of the end of the nineteenth century – an overfed, commonplace, pursy little man who had been born in a Brixton semi-detached villa, and whose highest idea of pleasure was a Sunday up the river in an expensive electric launch, confronting and utterly routing, in a hotel belonging to an American millionaire, the representative of a race of men who had fingered every page of European history for centuries, and who still, in their native castles, were surrounded with every outward circumstance of pomp and power.

'Aribert,' said Prince Eugen, a little later, 'you were right. It is all over. I have only one refuge – '

'You don't mean – ' Aribert stopped, dumbfounded.

'Yes, I do,' he said quickly. 'I can manage it so that it will look like an accident.'

## Chapter Twenty-One

# THE RETURN OF FÉLIX BABYLON

ON the evening of Prince Eugen's fateful interview with Mr Sampson Levi, Theodore Racksole was wandering somewhat aimlessly and uneasily about the entrance hall and adjacent corridors of the Grand Babylon. He had returned from Ostend only a day or two previously, and had endeavoured with all his might to forget the affair which had carried him there – to regard it, in fact, as done with. But he found himself unable to do so. In vain he remarked, under his breath, that there were some things which were best left alone: if his experience as a manipulator of markets, a contriver of gigantic schemes in New York, had taught him anything at all, it should surely have taught him that. Yet he could not feel reconciled to such a position. The mere presence of the princes in his hotel roused the fighting instincts of this man, who had never in his whole career been beaten. He had, as it were, taken up arms on their side, and if the princes of Posen would not continue their own battle, nevertheless he, Theodore Racksole, wanted to continue it for them. To a certain extent, of course, the battle had been won, for Prince Eugen had been rescued from an extremely difficult and dangerous position, and the enemy – consisting of Jules, Rocco, Miss Spencer, and perhaps others – had been put to flight. But that, he conceived, was not enough; it was very far from being enough. That the criminals, for criminals they decidedly were, should still be at large, he regarded as an absurd anomaly. And there was another point: he had said nothing to the police of all that had occurred. He disdained the police, but he could scarcely fail to perceive that if the police should by accident gain a clue to the real state of the case he might be placed rather awkwardly, for the simple reason that in the eyes of the law it amounted to a misdemeanour to conceal as much as he had concealed. He asked himself, for the thousandth time, why he had adopted a policy of concealment from the police, why he had become in any way interested in the Posen matter, and why, at this present moment, he should be so anxious to prosecute it further? To the first two questions he replied, rather lamely, that he had been influenced by Nella, and also by a natural spirit of adventure; to the third he replied that he had always been in the habit of carrying things through, and was now actuated by a mere childish, obstinate desire to carry this one through. Moreover, he was spendidly conscious of his perfect ability to carry it through. One additional impulse he had, though he did not admit it to himself, being by nature adverse to big words, and that was an abstract love of justice, the Anglo-Saxon's deep-found instinct for helping the right side to conquer, even when grave risks must thereby be run, with no corresponding advantage.

He was turning these things over in his mind as he walked about the vast hotel on that evening of the last day in July. The Society papers had been stating for a week past that London was empty, but, in spite of the Society papers, London persisted in seeming to be just as full as ever. The Grand Babylon was certainly not as crowded as it had been a month earlier, but it was doing a very passable business. At the close of the season the gay butterflies of the social community have a habit of hovering for a day or two in the big hotels before they flutter away to castle and country-house, meadow and moor, lake and stream. The great basket-chairs in the portico were well filled by old and middle-aged gentlemen engaged in enjoying the varied delights of liqueurs, cigars, and the full moon which floated so serenely above the Thames. Here and there a pretty woman on the arm of a cavalier in immaculate attire swept her train as she turned to and fro in the promenade of the terrace. Waiters and uniformed commissionaires and gold-braided doorkeepers moved noiselessly about; at short intervals the chief of the doorkeepers blew his shrill whistle and hansoms drove up with tinkling bell to take away a pair of butterflies to some place of amusement or boredom; occasionally a private carriage drawn by expensive and self-conscious horses put the hansoms to shame by its mere outward glory. It was a hot night, a night for the summer woods, and save for the vehicles there was no rapid movement of any kind. It seemed as though the world – the world, that is to say, of the Grand Babylon – was fully engaged in the solemn processes of digestion and small-talk. Even the long row of the Embankment gas-lamps, stretching right and left, scarcely trembled in the still, warm, caressing air. The stars overhead looked down with many blinkings upon the enormous pile of the Grand Babylon, and the moon regarded it with bland and changeless face; what they thought of it and its inhabitants cannot, unfortunately, be recorded. What Theodore Racksole thought of the moon can be recorded: he thought it was a nuisance. It somehow fascinated his gaze with its silly stare, and so interfered with his complex meditations. He glanced round at the well-dressed and satisfied people – his guests, his customers. They appeared to ignore him absolutely. Probably only a very small percentage of them had the least idea that this tall spare man, with the iron-grey hair and the thin, firm, resolute face, who wore his American-cut evening clothes with such careless ease, was the sole proprietor of the Grand Babylon, and possibly the richest man in Europe. As has already been stated, Racksole was not a celebrity in England. The guests of the Grand Babylon saw merely a restless male person, whose restlessness was rather a disturber of their quietude, but with whom, to judge by his countenance, it would be inadvisable to remonstrate. Therefore Theodore Racksole continued his perambulations unchallenged, and kept saying to himself, 'I must do something.' But what? He could think of no course to pursue.

At last he walked straight through the hotel and out at the other entrance, and so up the little unassuming side street into the roaring torrent of the narrow and crowded Strand. He jumped on a Putney bus, and paid his fair to Putney, fivepence, and then, finding that the humble occupants of the vehicle stared at the spectacle of a man in evening dress but without a dustcoat, he jumped off again, oblivious of the fact that the conductor jerked a thumb towards him and winked at the passengers as who should say, 'There goes a lunatic.' He went into a tobacconist's shop and asked for a cigar. The shopman mildly inquired what price.

'What are the best you've got?' asked Theodore Racksole.

'Five shillings each, sir,' said the man promptly.

'Give me a penny one,' was Theodore Racksole's laconic request, and he walked out of the shop smoking the penny cigar. It was a new sensation for him.

He was inhaling the aromatic odours of Eugène Rimmel's establishment for the sale of scents when a gentleman, walking slowly in the opposite direction, accosted him with a quiet, 'Good evening, Mr Racksole.' The millionaire did not at first recognize his interlocutor, who wore a travelling overcoat, and was carrying a handbag. Then a slight, pleased smile passed over his features, and he held out his hand.

'Well, Mr Babylon,' he greeted the other, 'of all persons in the wide world you are the man I would most have wished to meet.'

'You flatter me,' said the little Anglicized Swiss.

'No, I don't,' answered Racksole; 'it isn't my custom, any more than it's yours. I wanted to have a real good long yarn with you, and lo! here you are! Where have you sprung from?'

'From Lausanne,' said Félix Babylon. 'I had finished my duties there, I had nothing else to do, and I felt homesick. I felt the nostalgia of London, and so I came over, just as you see,' and he raised the handbag for Racksole's notice. 'One toothbrush, one razor, two slippers, eh!' He laughed. 'I was wondering as I walked along where I should stay – me, Félix Babylon, homeless in London.'

'I should advise you to stay at the Grand Babylon,' Racksole laughed back. 'It is a good hotel, and I know the proprietor personally.'

'Rather expensive, is it not?' said Babylon.

'To you, sir,' answered Racksole, 'the inclusive terms will be exactly half a crown a week. Do you accept?'

'I accept,' said Babylon, and added, 'You are very good, Mr Racksole.'

They strolled together back to the hotel, saying nothing in particular, but feeling very content with each other's company.

'Many customers?' asked Félix Babylon.

'Very tolerable,' said Racksole, assuming as much of the air of the professional hotel proprietor as he could. 'I think I may say in the storekeeper's phrase, that if there is any business about I am doing it. To-night the people are all on the terrace in the portico – it's so confoundedly hot – and the consumption of ice is simply enormous – nearly as large as it would be in New York.'

'In that case,' said Babylon politely, 'let me offer you another cigar.'

'But I have not finished this one.'

'That is just why I wish to offer you another one. A cigar such as yours, my good friend, ought never to be smoked within the precincts of the Grand Babylon, not even by the proprietor of the Grand Babylon, and especially when all the guests are assembled in the portico. The fumes of it would ruin any hotel.'

Theodore Racksole laughingly lighted the Rothschild Havana which Babylon gave him, and they entered the hotel arm in arm. But no sooner had they mounted the steps than little Félix became the object of numberless greetings. It appeared that he had been highly popular among his quondam guests. At last they reached the managerial room, where Babylon was regaled on a chicken, and Racksole assisted him in the consumption of a bottle of Heidsieck Monopole, Carte d'Or.

'This chicken is almost perfectly grilled,' said Babylon at length. 'It is a credit to the house. But why, my dear Racksole, why in the name of Heaven did you quarrel with Rocco?'

'Then you have heard?'

'Heard! My dear friend, it was in every newspaper on the Continent. Some journals prophesied that the Grand Babylon would have to close its doors within half a year now that Rocco had deserted it. But of course I knew better. I knew that you must have a good reason for allowing Rocco to depart, and that you must have made arrangements in advance for a substitute.'

'As a matter of fact, I had not made arrangements in advance,' said Theodore Racksole, a little ruefully; 'but happily we have found in our second sous-chef an artist inferior only to Rocco himself. That, however, was mere good fortune.'

'Surely,' said Babylon, 'it was indiscreet to trust to mere good fortune in such a serious matter?'

'I didn't trust to mere good fortune. I didn't trust to anything except Rocco, and he deceived me.'

'But why did you quarrel with him?'

'I didn't quarrel with him. I found him embalming a corpse in the State bedroom one night – '

'You what?' Babylon almost screamed.

'I found him embalming a corpse in the State bedroom,' repeated Racksole in his quietest tones.

The two men gazed at each other, and then Racksole replenished Babylon's glass.

'Tell me,' said Babylon, settling himself deep in an easy chair and lighting a cigar.

And Racksole thereupon recounted to him the whole of the Posen episode, with every circumstantial detail so far as he knew it. It was a long and complicated recital, and occupied about an hour. During that time little Félix never spoke a word, scarcely moved a muscle; only his small eyes gazed through the bluish haze of smoke. The clock on the mantelpiece tinkled midnight.

'Time for whisky and soda,' said Racksole, and got up as if to ring the bell; but Babylon waved him back.

'You have told me that this Sampson Levi had an audience of Prince Eugen to-day, but you have not told me the result of that audience,' said Babylon.

'Because I do not yet know it. But I shall doubtless know to-morrow. In the meantime, I feel fairly sure that Levi declined to produce Prince Eugen's required million. I have reason to believe that the money was lent elsewhere.'

'H'm!' mused Babylon; and then, carelessly, 'I am not at all surprised at that arrangement for spying through the bathroom of the State apartments.'

'Why are you not surprised?'

'Oh!' said Babylon, 'it is such an obvious dodge – so easy to carry out. As for me, I took special care never to involve myself in these affairs. I knew they existed; I somehow felt that they existed. But I also felt that they lay outside my sphere. My business was to provide board and lodging of the most sumptuous kind to those who didn't mind paying for it; and I did my business. If anything else went on in the hotel, under the rose, I long determined to ignore it unless it should happen to be brought before my notice; and it never was brought before my notice. However, I admit that there is a certain pleasurable excitement in this kind of affair and doubtless you have experienced that.'

'I have,' said Racksole simply, 'though I believe you are laughing at me.'

'By no means,' Babylon replied. 'Now what, if I may ask the question, is going to be your next step?'

'That is just what I desire to know myself,' said Theodore Racksole.

'Well,' said Babylon, after a pause, 'let us begin. In the first place, it is possible you may be interested to hear that I happened to see Jules to-day.'

'You did!' Racksole remarked with much calmness. 'Where?'

'Well, it was early this morning, in Paris, just before I left there. The meeting was quite accidental, and Jules seemed rather surprised at meeting me. He respectfully inquired where I was going, and I said that I was going to Switzerland. At that moment I thought I was going to Switzerland. It had occurred to me that after all I should be happier there, and that I had better turn back and not see London any more. However, I changed my mind once again, and decided to come on to London, and accept the risks of being miserable there without my hotel. Then I asked Jules whither he was bound, and he told me that he was off to Constantinople, being interested in a new French hotel there. I wished him good luck, and we parted.'

'Constantinople, eh!' said Racksole. 'A highly suitable place for him, I should say.'

'But,' Babylon resumed, 'I caught sight of him again.'

'Where?'

'At Charing Cross, a few minutes before I had the pleasure of meeting you. Mr Jules had not gone to Constantinople after all. He did not see me, or I should have suggested to him that in going from Paris to Constantinople it is not usual to travel via London.'

'The cheek of the fellow!' exclaimed Theodore Racksole. 'The gorgeous and colossal cheek of the fellow!'

*Chapter Twenty-Two*

## IN THE WINE CELLARS OF THE
## GRAND BABYLON

'Do you know anything of the antecedents of this Jules,' asked Theodore Racksole, helping himself to whisky.

'Nothing whatever,' said Babylon. 'Until you told me, I don't think I was aware that his true name was Thomas Jackson, though of course I knew that it was not Jules. I certainly was not aware that Miss Spencer was his wife, but I had long suspected that their relations were somewhat more intimate than the nature of their respective duties in the hotel absolutely demanded. All that I do know of Jules – he will always be called Jules – is that he gradually, by some mysterious personal force, acquired a prominent position in the hotel. Decidedly he was the cleverest and most intellectual waiter I have ever known, and he was specially skilled in the difficult task of retaining his own dignity while not interfering with that of other people. I'm afraid this information is a little too vague to be of any practical assistance in the present difficulty.'

'What is the present difficulty?' Racksole queried, with a simple air.

'I should imagine that the present difficulty is to account for the man's presence in London.'

'That is easily accounted for,' said Racksole.

'How? Do you suppose he is anxious to give himself up to justice, or that the chains of habit bind him to the hotel?'

'Neither,' said Racksole. 'Jules is going to have another try – that's all.'

'Another try at what?'

'At Prince Eugen. Either at his life or his liberty. Most probably the former this time; almost certainly the former. He has guessed that we are somewhat handicapped by our anxiety to keep Prince Eugen's predicament quite quiet, and he is taking advantage of that fact. As he already is fairly rich, on his own admission, the reward which has been offered to him must be enormous, and he is absolutely determined to get it. He has several times recently proved himself to be a daring fellow; unless I am mistaken he will shortly prove himself to be still more daring.'

'But what can he do? Surely you don't suggest that he will attempt the life of Prince Eugen in this hotel?'

'Why not? If Reginald Dimmock fell on mere suspicion that he would turn out unfaithful to the conspiracy, why not Prince Eugen?'

'But it would be an unspeakable crime, and do infinite harm to the hotel!'

'True!' Racksole admitted, smiling. Little Félix Babylon seemed to brace himself for the grasping of his monstrous idea.

'How could it possibly be done?' he asked at length.

'Dimmock was poisoned.'

'Yes, but you had Rocco here then, and Rocco was in the plot. It is conceivable that Rocco could have managed it – barely conceivable. But without Rocco I cannot think it possible. I cannot even think that Jules would attempt it. You see, in a place like the Grand Babylon, as probably I needn't point out to you, food has to pass through so many hands that to poison one person without killing perhaps fifty would be a most delicate operation. Moreover, Prince Eugen, unless he has changed his habits, is always served by his own attendant, old Hans, and therefore any attempt to tamper with a cooked dish immediately before serving would be hazardous in the extreme.'

'Granted,' said Racksole. 'The wine, however, might be more easily got at. Had you thought of that?'

'I had not,' Babylon admitted. 'You are an ingenious theorist, but I happen to know that Prince Eugen always has his wine opened in his own presence. No doubt it would be opened by Hans. Therefore the wine theory is not tenable, my friend.'

'I do not see why,' said Racksole. 'I know nothing of wine as an expert, and I very seldom drink it, but it seems to me that a bottle of wine might be tampered with while it was still in the cellar, especially if there was an accomplice in the hotel.'

'You think, then, that you are not yet rid of all your conspirators?'

'I think that Jules might still have an accomplice within the building.'

'And that a bottle of wine could be opened and recorked without leaving any trace of the operation?' Babylon was a trifle sarcastic.

'I don't see the necessity of opening the bottle in order to poison the wine,' said Racksole. 'I have never tried to poison anybody by means of a bottle of wine, and I don't lay claim to any natural talent as a poisoner, but I think I could devise several ways of managing the trick. Of course, I admit I may be entirely mistaken as to Jules' intentions.'

'Ah!' said Félix Babylon. 'The wine cellars beneath us are one of the wonders of London. I hope you are aware, Mr Racksole, that when you bought the Grand Babylon you bought what is probably the finest stock of wines in England, if not in Europe. In the valuation I reckoned them at sixty thousand pounds. And I may say that I always took care that the cellars were properly guarded. Even Jules would experience a serious difficulty in breaking into the cellars without the connivance of the wine-clerk, and the wine-clerk is, or was, incorruptible.'

'I am ashamed to say that I have not yet inspected my wines,' smiled Racksole; 'I have never given them a thought. Once or twice I have taken the trouble to make a tour of the hotel, but I omitted the cellars in my excursions.'

'Impossible, my dear fellow!' said Babylon, amused at such a confession, to him – a great connoisseur and lover of fine wines – almost incredible. 'But really you must see them to-morrow. If I may, I will accompany you.'

'Why not to-night?' Racksole suggested, calmly.

'To-night! It is very late: Hubbard will have gone to bed.'

'And may I ask who is Hubbard? I remember the name but dimly.'

'Hubbard is the wine-clerk of the Grand Babylon,' said Félix, with a certain emphasis. 'A sedate man of forty. He has the keys of the cellars. He knows every bottle of every bin, its date, its qualities, its value. And he's a teetotaler. Hubbard is a curiosity. No wine can leave the cellars without his knowledge, and no person can enter the cellars without his knowledge. At least, that is how it was in my time,' Babylon added.

'We will wake him,' said Racksole.

'But it is one o'clock in the morning,' Babylon protested.

'Never mind – that is, if you consent to accompany me. A cellar is the same by night as by day. Therefore, why not now?'

Babylon shrugged his shoulders. 'As you wish,' he agreed, with his indestructible politeness.

'And now to find this Mr Hubbard, with his key of the cupboard,' said Racksole, as they walked out of the room together. Although the hour was so late, the hotel was not, of course, closed for the night. A few guests still remained about in the public rooms, and a few fatigued waiters were still in attendance. One of these latter was despatched in search of the singular Mr Hubbard, and it fortunately turned out that this gentleman had not actually retired, though he was on the point of doing so. He brought the keys to Mr Racksole in person, and after he had had a little chat with his former master, the proprietor and the ex-proprietor of the Grand Babylon Hotel proceeded on their way to the cellars.

These cellars extend over, or rather under, quite half the superficial areas of the whole hotel – the longitudinal half which lies next to the Strand. Owing to the fact that the ground slopes sharply from the Strand to the river, the Grand Babylon is, so to speak, deeper near the Strand than it is near the Thames. Towards the Thames there is, below the entrance level, a basement and a sub-basement. Towards the Strand there is basement, sub-basement, and the huge wine cellars beneath all. After descending the four flights of the service stairs, and traversing a long passage running parallel with the kitchen, the two found themselves opposite a door, which, on being unlocked, gave access to another flight of stairs. At the foot of this was the main entrance to the cellars. Outside the entrance was the wine-lift, for the ascension of delicious fluids to the upper floors, and, opposite, Mr Hubbard's little office. There was electric light everywhere. Babylon, who, as being most accustomed to them, held the bunch of keys, opened the great door, and then they were in the first cellar – the first of a suite of five. Racksole was struck not only by the icy coolness of the place, but also by its vastness. Babylon had seized a portable electric handlight, attached to a long wire, which lay handy, and, waving it about, disclosed the dimensions of the place. By that flashing illumination the subterranean chamber looked unutterably weird and mysterious, with its rows of numbered bins, stretching away into the distance till the radiance was reduced to the occasional far gleam of the light on the shoulder of a bottle. Then Babylon switched on the fixed electric lights, and Theodore Racksole entered upon a personally-conducted tour of what was quite the most interesting part of his own property.

To see the innocent enthusiasm of Félix Babylon for these stores of exhilarating liquid was what is called in the North 'a sight for sair een'. He displayed to Racksole's bewildered gaze, in their due order, all the wines of three continents – nay, of four, for the superb and luscious Constantia wine of Cape Colony was not wanting in that most catholic collection of vintages. Beginning with the unsurpassed products of Burgundy, he continued with the clarets of Médoc, Bordeaux, and Sauterne; then to the champagnes of Ay, Hautvilliers, and Pierry; then to the hocks and moselles of Germany, and the brilliant imitation champagnes of Main, Neckar, and Naumburg; then to the famous and adorable Tokay of Hungary, and all the Austrian varieties of French wines, including Carlowitz and Somlauer; then to the dry sherries of Spain, including purest Manzanilla, and Amontillado, and Vino de Pasto; then to the wines of Malaga, both sweet and dry, and all the 'Spanish reds' from Catalonia, including the dark 'Tent' so often used sacramentally; then to the renowned port of Oporto. Then he proceeded to the Italian cellar, and descanted upon the excellence of Barolo from Piedmont, of Chianti from Tuscany, of Orvieto from the Roman States, of the 'Tears of Christ' from Naples, and the commoner Marsala from Sicily. And so on, to an extent and with a fullness of detail which cannot be rendered here.

At the end of the suite of cellars there was a glazed door, which, as could be seen, gave access to a supplemental and smaller cellar, an apartment about fifteen or sixteen feet square.

'Anything special in there?' asked Racksole curiously, as they stood before the door, and looked within at the serried ends of bottles.

'Ah!' exclaimed Babylon, almost smacking his lips, 'therein lies the cream of all.'

'The best champagne, I suppose?' said Racksole.

'Yes,' said Babylon, 'the best champagne is there – a very special Sillery, as exquisite as you will find anywhere. But I see, my friend, that you fall into the common error of putting champagne first among wines. That distinction belongs to Burgundy. You have old Burgundy in that cellar, Mr Racksole, which cost me – how much do you think? – eighty pounds a bottle. Probably it will never be drunk,' he added with a sigh. 'It is too expensive even for princes and plutocrats.'

'Yes, it will,' said Racksole quickly. 'You and I will have a bottle up to-morrow.'

'Then,' continued Babylon, still riding his hobby-horse, 'there is a sample of the Rhine wine dated 1706 which caused such a sensation at the Vienna Exhibition of 1873. There is also a singularly glorious Persian wine from Shiraz, the like of which I have never seen elsewhere. Also there is an unrivalled vintage of Romanée-Conti, greatest of all modern Burgundies. If I remember right Prince Eugen invariably has a bottle when he comes to stay here. It is not on the hotel wine list, of course, and only a few customers know of it. We do not precisely hawk it about the dining-room.'

'Indeed!' said Racksole. 'Let us go inside.'

They entered the stone apartment, rendered almost sacred by the preciousness of its contents, and Racksole looked round with a strangely intent and curious air. At the far side was a grating, through which came a feeble light.

'What is that?' asked the millionaire sharply.

'That is merely a ventilation grating. Good ventilation is absolutely essential.'

'Looks broken, doesn't it?' Racksole suggested and then, putting a finger quickly on Babylon's shoulder, 'there's someone in the cellar. Can't you hear breathing, down there, behind that bin?'

The two men stood tense and silent for a while, listening, under the ray of the single electric light in the ceiling. Half the cellar was involved in gloom. At length Racksole walked firmly down the central passage-way between the bins and turned to the corner at the right.

'Come out, you villain!' he said in a low, well-nigh vicious tone, and dragged up a cowering figure.

He had expected to find a man, but it was his own daughter, Nella Racksole, upon whom he had laid angry hands.

## Chapter Twenty-Three

# FURTHER EVENTS IN THE CELLAR

'WELL, Father,' Nella greeted her astounded parent. 'You should make sure that you have got hold of the right person before you use all that terrible muscular force of yours. I do believe you have broken my shoulder bone.' She rubbed her shoulder with a comical expression of pain, and then stood up before the two men. The skirt of her dark grey dress was torn and dirty, and the usually trim Nella looked as though she had been shot down a. canvas fire-escape. Mechanically she smoothed her frock, and gave a straightening touch to her hair.

'Good evening, Miss Racksole,' said Félix Babylon, bowing formally. 'This is an unexpected pleasure.' Félix's drawing-room manners never deserted him upon any occasion whatever.

'May I inquire what you are doing in my wine cellar, Nella Racksole?' said the millionaire a little stiffly. He was certainly somewhat annoyed at having mistaken his daughter for a criminal; moreover, he hated to be surprised, and upon this occasion he had been surprised beyond any ordinary surprise; lastly, he was not at all pleased that Nella should be observed in that strange predicament by a stranger.

'I will tell you,' said Nella. 'I had been reading rather late in my room – the night was so close. I heard Big Ben strike half-past twelve, and then I put the book down, and went out on to the balcony of my window for a little fresh air before going to bed. I leaned over the balcony very quietly – you will remember that I am on the third floor now – and looked down below into the little sunk yard which separates the wall of the hotel from Salisbury Lane. I was rather astonished to see a figure creeping across the yard. I knew there was no entrance into the hotel from that yard, and besides, it is fifteen or twenty feet below the level of the street. So I watched. The figure went close up against the wall, and disappeared from my view. I leaned over the balcony as far as I dared, but I couldn't see him. I could hear him, however.'

'What could you hear?' questioned Racksole sharply.

'It sounded like a sawing noise,' said Nella; 'and it went on for quite a long time – nearly a quarter of an hour, I should think – a rasping sort of noise.'

'Why on earth didn't you come and warn me or someone else in the hotel?' asked Racksole.

'Oh, I don't know, Dad,' she replied sweetly. 'I had got interested in it, and I thought I would see it out myself. Well, as I was saying, Mr Babylon,' she continued, addressing her remarks to Félix, with a dazzling smile, 'that noise went on for quite a long time. At last it stopped, and the figure reappeared from under the wall, crossed the yard, climbed up the opposite wall by some means or other, and so over the railings into Salisbury Lane. I felt rather relieved then, because I knew he hadn't actually broken into the hotel. He walked down Salisbury Lane very slowly. A policeman was just coming up. "Goodnight, officer," I heard him say to the policeman, and he asked him for a match. The policeman supplied the match, and the other man lighted a cigarette, and proceeded further down the lane. By cricking your neck from my window, Mr Babylon, you can get a glimpse of the Embankment and the river. I saw the man cross the Embankment, and lean over the river wall, where he seemed to be talking to some one. He then walked along the Embankment to Westminster and that was the last I saw of him. I waited a minute or two for him to come back, but he didn't come back, and so I thought it was about time I began to make inquiries into the affair. I went downstairs instantly, and out of the hotel, through the quadrangle, into Salisbury Lane, and I looked over those railings. There was a ladder on the other side, by which it was perfectly easy – once you had got over the railings – to climb down into the yard. I was horribly afraid lest someone might walk up Salisbury Lane and catch me in the act of negotiating those railings, but no one did, and I surmounted them, with no worse damage than a torn skirt. I crossed the yard on tiptoe, and I found that in the wall, close to the ground and almost exactly under my window, there was an iron grating, about one foot by fourteen inches. I suspected, as there was no other ironwork near, that the mysterious visitor must have been sawing at this grating for private purposes of his own. I gave it a good shake, and I was not at all surprised that a good part of it came off in my hand, leaving just enough room for a person to creep through. I decided that I would creep through, and now wish I hadn't. I don't know, Mr Babylon, whether you have ever tried to creep through a small hole with a skirt on. Have you?'

'I have not had that pleasure,' said little Félix, bowing again, and absently taking up a bottle which lay to his hand.

'Well, you are fortunate,' the imperturbable Nella resumed. 'For quite three minutes I thought I should perish in that grating, Dad, with my shoulder inside and the rest of me outside. However, at last, by the most amazing and agonizing efforts, I pulled myself through and fell into this extraordinary cellar more dead than alive. Then I wondered what I should do next. Should I wait for the mysterious visitor to return, and stab him with my pocket scissors if he tried to enter, or should I raise an alarm? First of all I replaced the broken grating, then I struck a match, and I saw that I had got landed in a wilderness of bottles. The match went out, and I hadn't another one. So I sat down in the corner to think. I had just decided to wait and see if the visitor returned, when I heard footsteps, and then voices; and then you came in. I must say I was rather taken aback, especially as I recognized the voice of Mr Babylon. You see, I didn't want to frighten you. If I had bobbed up from behind the bottles and said "Booh!" you would have had a serious shock. I wanted to think of a way of breaking my presence gently to you. But you saved me the trouble, Dad. Was I really breathing so loudly that you could hear me?'

The girl ended her strange recital, and there was a moment's silence in the cellar. Racksole merely nodded an affirmative to her concluding question.

'Well, Nell, my girl,' said the millionaire at length, 'we are much obliged for your gymnastic efforts – very much obliged. But now, I think you had better go off to bed. There is going to be some serious trouble here, I'll lay my last dollar on that?'

'But if there is to be a burglary I should so like to see it, Dad,' Nella pleaded. 'I've never seen a burglar caught red-handed.'

'This isn't a burglary, my dear. I calculate it's something far worse than a burglary.'

'What?' she cried. 'Murder? Arson? Dynamite plot? How perfectly splendid!'

'Mr Babylon informs me that Jules is in London,' said Racksole quietly.

'Jules!' she exclaimed under her breath, and her tone changed instantly to the utmost seriousness. 'Switch off the light, quick!' Springing to the switch, she put the cellar in darkness.

'What's that for?' said her father.

'If he comes back he would see the light, and be frightened away,' said Nella. 'That wouldn't do at all.'

'It wouldn't, Miss Racksole,' said Babylon, and there was in his voice a note of admiration for the girl's sagacity which Racksole heard with high paternal pride.

'Listen, Nella,' said the latter, drawing his daughter to him in the profound gloom of the cellar. 'We fancy that Jules may be trying to tamper with a certain bottle of wine – a bottle which might possibly be drunk by Prince Eugen. Now do you think that the man you saw might have been Jules?'

'I hadn't previously thought of him as being Jules, but immediately you mentioned the name I somehow knew that he was. Yes, I am sure it was Jules.'

'Well, just hear what I have to say. There is no time to lose. If he is coming at all he will be here very soon – and you can help.' Racksole explained what he thought Jules' tactics might be. He proposed that if the man returned he should not be interfered with, but merely watched from the other side of the glass door.

'You want, as it were, to catch Mr Jules alive?' said Babylon, who seemed rather taken aback at this novel method of dealing with criminals. 'Surely,' he added, 'it would be simpler and easier to inform the police of your suspicion, and to leave everything to them.'

'My dear fellow,' said Racksole, 'we have already gone much too far without the police to make it advisable for us to call them in at this somewhat advanced stage of the proceedings. Besides, if you must know it, I have a particular desire to capture the scoundrel myself. I will leave you and Nella here, since Nella insists on seeing everything, and I will arrange things so that once he has entered the cellar Jules will not get out of it again – at any rate through the grating. You had better place yourselves on the other side of the glass door, in the big cellar; you will be in a position to observe from there, I will skip off at once. All you have to do is to take note of what the fellow does. If he has any accomplices within the hotel we shall probably be able by that means to discover who the accomplice is.'

Lighting a match and shading it with his hands, Racksole showed them both out of the little cellar. 'Now if you lock this glass door on the outside he can't escape this way: the panes of glass are too small, and the woodwork too stout. So, if he comes into the trap, you two will have the pleasure of actually seeing him frantically writhe therein, without any personal danger; but perhaps you'd better not show yourselves.'

In another moment Félix Babylon and Nella were left to themselves in the darkness of the cellar, listening to the receding footfalls of Theodore Racksole. But the sound of these footfalls had not died away before another sound greeted their ears – the grating of the small cellar was being removed.

'I hope your father will be in time,' whispered Félix.

'Hush!' the girl warned him, and they stooped side by side in tense silence.

A man cautiously but very neatly wormed his body through the aperture of the grating. The watchers could only see his form indistinctly in the darkness. Then, being fairly within the cellar, he walked without the least hesitation to the electric switch and turned on the light. It was unmistakably Jules, and he knew the geography of the cellar very well. Babylon could with difficulty repress a start as he saw this bold and unscrupulous ex-waiter moving with such an air of assurance and determination about the precious cellar. Jules went directly to a small bin which was numbered 17, and took therefrom the topmost bottle. 'The Romanée-Conti – Prince Eugen's wine!' Babylon exclaimed under his breath.

Jules neatly and quickly removed the seal with an instrument which he had clearly brought for the purpose. He then took a little flat box from his pocket, which seemed to contain a sort of black salve. Rubbing his finger in this, he smeared the top of the neck of the bottle with it, just where the cork came against the glass. In another instant he had deftly replaced the seal and restored the bottle to its position. He then turned off the light, and made for the aperture. When he was half-way through Nella exclaimed, 'He will escape, after all. Dad has not had time – we must stop him.'

But Babylon, that embodiment of caution, forcibly, but nevertheless politely, restrained this Yankee girl, whom he deemed so rash and imprudent, and before she could free herself the lithe form of Jules had disappeared.

## Chapter Twenty-Four

## THE BOTTLE OF WINE

As regards Theodore Racksole, who was to have caught his man from the outside of the cellar, he made his way as rapidly as possible from the wine-cellars, up to the ground floor, out of the hotel by the quadrangle, through the quadrangle, and out into the top of Salisbury Lane. Now, owing to the vastness of the structure of the Grand Babylon, the mere distance thus to be traversed amounted to a little short of a quarter of a mile, and, as it included a number of stairs, about two dozen turnings, and several passages which at that time of night were in darkness more or less complete, Racksole could not have been expected to accomplish the journey in less than five minutes. As a matter of fact, six minutes had elapsed before he reached the top of Salisbury Lane, because he had been delayed nearly a minute by some questions addressed to him by a muddled and whisky-laden guest who had got lost in the corridors. As everybody knows, there is a sharp short bend in Salisbury Lane near the top. Racksole ran round this at good racing speed, but he was unfortunate enough to run straight up against the very policeman who had not long before so courteously supplied Jules with a match. The policeman seemed to be scarcely in so pliant a mood just then.

'Hullo!' he said, his naturally suspicious nature being doubtless aroused by the spectacle of a bareheaded man in evening dress running violently down the lane. 'What's this? Where are you for in such a hurry?' and he forcibly detained Theodore Racksole for a moment and scrutinized his face.

'Now, officer,' said Racksole quietly, 'none of your larks, if you please. I've no time to lose.'

'Beg your pardon, sir,' the policeman remarked, though hesitatingly and not quite with good temper, and Racksole was allowed to proceed on his way. The millionaire's scheme for trapping Jules was to get down into the little sunk yard by means of the ladder, and then to secrete himself behind some convenient abutment of brickwork until Mr Tom Jackson should have got into the cellar. He therefore nimbly surmounted the railings – the railings of his own hotel – and was gingerly descending the ladder, when lo! a rough hand seized him by the coat-collar and with a ferocious jerk urged him backwards. The fact was, Theodore Racksole had counted without the policeman. That guardian of the peace, mistrusting Racksole's manner, had quietly followed him down the lane. The sight of the millionaire climbing the railings had put him on his mettle, and the result was the ignominious capture of Racksole. In vain Theodore expostulated, explained, anathematized. Only one thing would satisfy the stolid policeman – namely, that Racksole should return with him to the hotel and there establish his identity. If Racksole then proved to be Racksole, owner of the Grand Babylon, well and good – the policeman promised to apologize. So Theodore had no alternative but to accept the suggestion. To prove his identity was, of course, the work of only a few minutes, after which Racksole, annoyed, but cool as ever, returned to his railings, while the policeman went off to another part of his beat, where he would be likely to meet a comrade and have a chat.

In the meantime, our friend Jules, sublimely unconscious of the altercation going on outside, and of the special risk which he ran, was of course actually in the cellar, which he had reached before Racksole got to the railings for the first time. It was, indeed, a happy chance for Jules that his exit from the cellar coincided with the period during which Racksole was absent from the railings. As Racksole came down the lane for the second time, he saw a figure walking about fifty yards in front of him towards the Embankment. Instantly he divined that it was Jules, and that the policeman had thrown him just too late. He ran, and Jules, hearing the noise of pursuit, ran also. The ex-waiter was fleet; he made direct for a certain spot in the Embankment wall, and, to the intense astonishment of Racksole, jumped clean over the wall, as it seemed, into the river. 'Is he so desperate as to commit suicide?' Racksole exclaimed as he ran, but a second later the puff and snort of a steam launch told him that Jules was not quite driven to suicide. As the millionaire crossed the Embankment roadway he saw the funnel of the launch move out from under the river-wall. It swerved into midstream and headed towards London Bridge. There was a silent mist over the river. Racksole was helpless. . . .

Although Racksole had now been twice worsted in a contest of wits within the precincts of the Grand Babylon, once by Rocco and once by Jules, he could not fairly blame himself for the present miscarriage of his plans — a miscarriage due to the meddlesomeness of an extraneous person, combined with pure ill-fortune. He did not, therefore, permit the accident to interfere with his sleep that night.

On the following day he sought out Prince Aribert, between whom and himself there now existed a feeling of unmistakable, frank friendship, and disclosed to him the happenings of the previous night, and particularly the tampering with the bottle of Romanée-Conti.

'I believe you dined with Prince Eugen last night?'

'I did. And curiously enough we had a bottle of Romanée-Conti, an admirable wine, of which Eugen is passionately fond.'

'And you will dine with him to-night?'

'Most probably. To-day will, I fear, be our last day here. Eugen wishes to return to Posen early to-morrow.'

'Has it struck you, Prince,' said Racksole, 'that if Jules had succeeded in poisoning your nephew, he would probably have succeeded also in poisoning you?'

'I had not thought of it,' laughed Aribert, 'but it would seem so. It appears that so long as he brings down his particular quarry, Jules is careless of anything else that may be accidentally involved in the destruction. However, we need have no fear on that score now. You know the bottle, and you can destroy it at once.'

'But I do not propose to destroy it,' said Racksole calmly. 'If Prince Eugen asks for Romanée-Conti to be served to-night, as he probably will, I propose that that precise bottle shall be served to him – and to you.'

'Then you would poison us in spite of ourselves?'

'Scarcely,' Racksole smiled. 'My notion is to discover the accomplices within the hotel. I have already inquired as to the wine-clerk, Hubbard. Now does it not occur to you as extraordinary that on this particular day Mr Hubbard should be ill in bed? Hubbard, I am informed, is suffering from an attack of stomach poisoning, which has supervened during the night. He says that he does not know what can have caused it. His place in the wine cellars will be taken to-day by his assistant, a mere youth, but to all appearances a fairly smart youth. I need not say that we shall keep an eye on that youth.'

'One moment,' Prince Aribert interrupted. 'I do not quite understand how you think the poisoning was to have been effected.'

'The bottle is now under examination by an expert, who has instructions to remove as little as possible of the stuff which Jules put on the rim of the mouth of it. It will be secretly replaced in its bin during the day. My idea is that by the mere action of pouring out the wine takes up some of the poison, which I deem to be very strong, and thus becomes fatal as it enters the glass.'

'But surely the servant in attendance would wipe the mouth of the bottle?'

'Very carelessly, perhaps. And moreover he would be extremely unlikely to wipe off all the stuff: some of it has been ingeniously placed just on the inside edge of the rim. Besides, suppose he forgot to wipe the bottle?'

'Prince Eugen is always served at dinner by Hans. It is an honour which the faithful old fellow reserves for himself.'

'But suppose Hans – ' Racksole stopped.

'Hans an accomplice! My dear Racksole, the suggestion is wildly impossible.'

That night Prince Aribert dined with his august nephew in the superb dining-room of the Royal apartments. Hans served, the dishes being brought to the door by other servants. Aribert found his nephew despondent and taciturn. On the previous day, when, after the futile interview with Sampson Levi, Prince Eugen had despairingly threatened to commit suicide, in such

a manner as to make it 'look like an accident', Aribert had compelled him to give his word of honour not to do so.

'What wine will your Royal Highness take?' asked old Hans
in his soothing tones, when the soup was served.

'Sherry,' was Prince Eugen's curt order.

'And Romanée-Conti afterwards?' said Hans. Aribert looked
up quickly.

'No, not to-night. I'll try Sillery to-night,' said Prince Eugen.

'I think I'll have Romanée-Conti, Hans, after all,' he said. 'It
suits me better than champagne.'

The famous and unsurpassable Burgundy was served with the
roast. Old Hans brought it tenderly in its wicker cradle, inserted
the corkscrew with mathematical precision, and drew the cork,
which he offered for his master's inspection. Eugen nodded, and
told him to put it down. Aribert watched with intense interest.
He could not for an instant believe that Hans was not the very
soul of fidelity, and yet, despite himself, Racksole's words had
caused him a certain uneasiness. At that moment Prince Eugen
murmured across the table:

'Aribert, I withdraw my promise. Observe that, I withdraw it.'

Aribert shook his head emphatically, without removing his
gaze from Hans. The white-haired servant perfunctorily dusted
his napkin round the neck of the bottle of Romanée-Conti, and
poured out a glass. Aribert trembled from head to foot.

Eugen took up the glass and held it to the light.

'Don't drink it,' said Aribert very quietly. 'It is poisoned.'

'Poisoned!' exclaimed Prince Eugen.

'Poisoned, sire!' exclaimed old Hans, with an air of profound
amazement and concern, and he seized the glass. 'Impossible, sire.
I myself opened the bottle. No one else has touched it, and the
cork was perfect.'

'I tell you it is poisoned,' Aribert repeated.

'Your Highness will pardon an old man,' said Hans, 'but to
say that this wine is poison is to say that I am a murderer. I will
prove to you that it is not poisoned. I will drink it.'

And he raised the glass to his trembling lips. In that moment
Aribert saw that old Hans, at any rate, was not an accomplice of

Jules. Springing up from his seat, he knocked the glass from the aged servitor's hands, and the fragments of it fell with a light tinkling crash partly on the table and partly on the floor. The Prince and the servant gazed at one another in a distressing and terrible silence. There was a slight noise, and Aribert looked aside. He saw that Eugen's body had slipped forward limply over the left arm of his chair; the Prince's arms hung straight and lifeless; his eyes were closed; he was unconscious.

'Hans!' murmured Aribert. 'Hans! What is this?'

## Chapter Twenty-Five

## THE STEAM LAUNCH

MR TOM JACKSON'S notion of making good his escape from
the hotel by means of a steam launch was an excellent one, so
far as it went, but Theodore Racksole, for his part, did not consider that it went quite far enough. Theodore Racksole opined,
with peculiar glee, that he now had a tangible and definite clue
for the catching of the Grand Babylon's ex-waiter. He knew
nothing of the Port of London, but he happened to know a good
deal of the far more complicated, though somewhat smaller, Port
of New York, and he felt sure there ought to be no extraordinary
difficulty in getting hold of Jules' steam launch. To those who
are not thoroughly familiar with it the River Thames and its
docks, from London Bridge to Gravesend, seems a vast and
uncharted wilderness of craft – a wilderness in which it would be
perfectly easy to hide even a three-master successfully. To such
people the idea of looking for a steam launch on the river would
be about equivalent to the idea of looking for a needle in a bundle
of hay. But the fact is, there are hundreds of men between St
Katherine's Wharf and Blackwall who literally know the Thames
as the suburban householder knows his back-garden – who can
recognize thousands of ships and put a name to them at a distance
of half a mile, who are informed as to every movement of vessels
on the great stream, who know all the captains, all the engineers,
all the lightermen, all the pilots, all the licensed watermen, and all
the unlicensed scoundrels from the Tower to Gravesend, and a
lot further. By these experts of the Thames the slightest unusual
event on the water is noticed and discussed – a wherry cannot
change hands but they will guess shrewdly upon the price paid
and the intentions of the new owner with regard to it. They
have a habit of watching the river for the mere interest of the
sight, and they talk about everything like housewives gathered of
an evening round the cottage door. If the first mate of a Castle

Liner gets the sack they will be able to tell you what he said to the captain, what the old man said to him, and what both said to the Board, and having finished off that affair they will cheerfully turn to discussing whether Bill Stevens sank his barge outside the West Indian No. 2 by accident or on purpose.

Theodore Racksole had no satisfactory means of identifying the steam launch which carried away Mr Tom Jackson. The sky had clouded over soon after midnight, and there was also a slight mist, and he had only been able to make out that it was a low craft, about sixty feet long, probably painted black. He had personally kept a watch all through the night on vessels going upstream, and during the next morning he had a man to take his place who warned him whenever a steam launch went towards Westminster. At noon, after his conversation with Prince Aribert, he went down the river in a hired row-boat as far as the Custom House, and poked about everywhere in search of any vessel which could by any possibility be the one he was in search of. But he found nothing. He was, therefore, tolerably sure that the mysterious launch lay somewhere below the Custom House. At the Custom House stairs, he landed, and asked for a very high official – an official inferior only to a Commissioner – whom he had entertained once in New York, and who had met him in London on business at Lloyd's. In the large but dingy office of this great man a long conversation took place – a conversation in which Racksole had to exercise a certain amount of persuasive power, and which ultimately ended in the high official ringing his bell.

'Desire Mr Hazell – room No. 332 – to speak to me,' said the official to the boy who answered the summons, and then, turning to Racksole: 'I need hardly repeat, my dear Mr Racksole, that this is strictly unofficial.'

'Agreed, of course,' said Racksole.

Mr Hazell entered. He was a young man of about thirty, dressed in blue serge, with a pale, keen face, a brown moustache and a rather handsome brown beard.

'Mr Hazell,' said the high official, 'let me introduce you to Mr Theodore Racksole – you will doubtless be familiar with his name. Mr Hazell,' he went on to Racksole, 'is one of our outdoor staff – what we call an examining officer. Just now he is doing night duty. He has a boat on the river and a couple of men, and the right to board and examine any craft whatever. What Mr Hazell and his crew don't know about the Thames between here and Gravesend isn't knowledge.'

'Glad to meet you, sir,' said Racksole simply, and they shook hands. Racksole observed with satisfaction that Mr Hazell was entirely at his ease.

'Now, Hazell,' the high official continued, 'Mr Racksole wants you to help in a little private expedition on the river to-night. I will give you a night's leave. I sent for you partly because I thought you would enjoy the affair and partly because I think I can rely on you to regard it as entirely unofficial and not to talk about it. You understand? I dare say you will have no cause to regret having obliged Mr Racksole.'

'I think I grasp the situation,' said Hazell, with a slight smile.

'And, by the way,' added the high official, 'although the business is unofficial, it might be well if you wore your official overcoat. See?'

'Decidedly,' said Hazell; 'I should have done so in any case.'

'And now, Mr Hazell,' said Racksole, 'will you do me the pleasure of lunching with me? If you agree, I should like to lunch at the place you usually frequent.'

So it came to pass that Theodore Racksole and George Hazell, outdoor clerk in the Customs, lunched together at 'Thomas's Chop-House', in the city of London, upon mutton-chops and coffee. The millionaire soon discovered that he had got hold of a keen-witted man and a person of much insight.

'Tell me,' said Hazell, when they had reached the cigarette stage, 'are the magazine writers anything like correct?'

'What do you mean?' asked Racksole, mystified.

'Well, you're a millionaire – "one of the best", I believe. One often sees articles on and interviews with millionaires, which describe their private railroad cars, their steam yachts on the Hudson, their marble stables, and so on, and so on. Do you happen to have those things?'

'I have a private car on the New York Central, and I have a two thousand ton schooner-yacht – though it isn't on the Hudson. It happens just now to be on East River. And I am bound to admit that the stables of my uptown place are fitted with marble.' Racksole laughed.

'Ah!' said Hazell. 'Now I can believe that I am lunching with a millionaire. It's strange how facts like those – unimportant in themselves – appeal to the imagination. You seem to me a real millionaire now. You've given me some personal information; I'll give you some in return. I earn three hundred a year, and perhaps sixty pounds a year extra for overtime. I live by myself in two rooms in Muscovy Court. I've as much money as I need, and I always do exactly what I like outside office. As regards the office, I do as little work as I can, on principle – it's a fight between us and the Commissioners who shall get the best. They try to do us down, and we try to do them down – it's pretty even on the whole. All's fair in war, you know, and there ain't no ten commandments in a Government office.'

Racksole laughed. 'Can you get off this afternoon?' he asked.

'Certainly,' said Hazell; 'I'll get one of my pals to sign on for me, and then I shall be free.'

'Well,' said Racksole, 'I should like you to come down with me to the Grand Babylon. Then we can talk over my little affair at length. And may we go on your boat? I want to meet your crew.'

'That will be all right,' Hazell remarked. 'My two men are the idlest, most soul-less chaps you ever saw. They eat too much, and they have an enormous appetite for beer; but they know the river, and they know their business, and they will do anything within the fair game if they are paid for it, and aren't asked to hurry.'

That night, just after dark, Theodore Racksole embarked with his new friend George Hazell in one of the black-painted Customs wherries, manned by a crew of two men – both the later freemen of the river, a distinction which carries with it certain privileges unfamiliar to the mere landsman. It was a cloudy and oppressive evening, not a star showing to illumine the slow tide, now just past its flood. The vast forms of steamers at anchor – chiefly those of the General Steam Navigation and the Aberdeen Line – heaved themselves high out of the water, straining sluggishly at their mooring buoys. On either side the naked walls of warehouses rose like grey precipices from the stream, holding forth quaint arms of steam-cranes. To the west the Tower Bridge spanned the river with its formidable arch, and above that its suspended footpath – a hundred and fifty feet from earth. Down towards the east and the Pool of London a forest of funnels and masts was dimly outlined against the sinister sky. Huge barges, each steered by a single man at the end of a pair of giant oars, lumbered and swirled down-stream at all angles. Occasionally a tug snorted busily past, flashing its red and green signals and dragging an unwieldy tail of barges in its wake. Then a Margate passenger steamer, its electric lights gleaming from every porthole, swerved round to anchor, with its load of two thousand fatigued excursionists. Over everything brooded an air of mystery – a spirit and feeling of strangeness, remoteness, and the inexplicable. As the broad flat little boat bobbed its way under the shadow of enormous hulks, beneath stretched hawsers, and past buoys covered with green slime, Racksole could scarcely believe that he was in the very heart of London – the most prosaic city in the world. He had a queer idea that almost anything might happen in this seeming waste of waters at this weird hour of ten o'clock. It appeared incredible to him that only a mile or two away people were sitting in theatres applauding farces, and that at Cannon Street Station, a few yards off, other people were calmly taking the train to various highly respectable suburbs whose names he was gradually learning. He had the uplifting sensation of being in another world which comes to us sometimes amid surroundings violently different from our usual surroundings. The most ordinary noises – of men calling, of a chain running through a slot, of a distant siren – translated themselves to his ears into terrible and haunting sounds, full of portentous significance. He looked over the side of the boat into the brown water, and asked himself what frightful secrets lay hidden in its depth. Then he put his hand into his hip-pocket and touched the stock of his Colt revolver – that familiar substance comforted him.

The oarsmen had instructions to drop slowly down to the Pool, as the wide reach below the Tower is called. These two men had not been previously informed of the precise object of the expedition, but now that they were safely afloat Hazell judged it expedient to give them some notion of it. 'We expect to come across a rather suspicious steam launch,' he said. 'My friend here is very anxious to get a sight of her, and until he has seen her nothing definite can be done.'

'What sort of a craft is she, sir?' asked the stroke oar, a fat-faced man who seemed absolutely incapable of any serious exertion.

'I don't know,' Racksole replied; 'but as near as I can judge, she's about sixty feet in length, and painted black. I fancy I shall recognize her when I see her.'

'Not much to go by, that,' exclaimed the other man curtly. But he said no more. He, as well as his mate, had received from Theodore Racksole one English sovereign as a kind of prelimi-nary fee, and an English sovereign will do a lot towards silencing the natural sarcastic tendencies and free speech of a Thames waterman.

'There's one thing I noticed,' said Racksole suddenly, 'and I forgot to tell you of it, Mr Hazell. Her screw seemed to move with a rather irregular, lame sort of beat.'

Both watermen burst into a laugh.

'Oh,' said the fat rower, 'I know what you're after, sir – it's Jack Everett's launch, commonly called "Squirm". She's got a four-bladed propeller, and one blade is broken off short.'

'Ay, that's it, sure enough,' agreed the man in the bows. 'And if it's her you want, I seed her lying up against Cherry Gardens Pier this very morning.'

'Let us go to Cherry Gardens Pier by all means, as soon as possible,' Racksole said, and the boat swung across stream and then began to creep down by the right bank, feeling its way past wharves, many of which, even at that hour, were still busy with their cranes, that descended empty into the bellies of ships and came up full. As the two watermen gingerly manoeuvred the boat on the ebbing tide, Hazell explained to the millionaire that the 'Squirm' was one of the most notorious craft on the river. It appeared that when anyone had a nefarious or underhand scheme afoot which necessitated river work Everett's launch was always available for a suitable monetary consideration. The 'Squirm' had got itself into a thousand scrapes, and out of those scrapes again with safety, if not precisely with honour. The river police kept a watchful eye on it, and the chief marvel about the whole thing was that old Everett, the owner, had never yet been seriously compromised in any illegal escapade. Not once had the officer of the law been able to prove anything definite against the proprietor of the 'Squirm', though several of its quondam hirers were at that very moment in various of Her Majesty's prisons throughout the country. Latterly, however, the launch, with its damaged propeller, which Everett consistently refused to have repaired, had acquired an evil reputation, even among evil-doers, and this fraternity had gradually come to abandon it for less easily recognizable craft.

'Your friend, Mr Tom Jackson,' said Hazell to Racksole, 'committed an error of discretion when he hired the "Squirm". A scoundrel of his experience and calibre ought certainly to have known better than that. You cannot fail to get a clue now.'

By this time the boat was approaching Cherry Gardens Pier, but unfortunately a thin night-fog had swept over the river, and objects could not be discerned with any clearness beyond a distance of thirty yards. As the Customs boat scraped down past the pier all its occupants strained eyes for a glimpse of the mysterious launch, but nothing could be seen of it. The boat continued to float idly down-stream, the men resting on their oars. Then they narrowly escaped bumping a large Norwegian sailing vessel at anchor with her stem pointing down-stream. This ship they passed on the port side. Just as they got clear of her bowsprit the fat man cried out excitedly, 'There's her nose!' and he put the boat about and began to pull back against the tide.

And surely the missing 'Squirm' was comfortably anchored on the starboard quarter of the Norwegian ship, hidden neatly between the ship and the shore. The men pulled very quietly alongside.

## Chapter Twenty-Six

# THE NIGHT CHASE AND THE MUDLARK

'I'LL board her to start with,' said Hazell, whispering to Racksole. 'I'll make out that I suspect they've got dutiable goods on board, and that will give me a chance to have a good look at her.'

Dressed in his official overcoat and peaked cap, he stepped, rather jauntily as Racksole thought, on to the low deck of the launch. 'Anyone aboard?' Racksole heard him cry out, and a woman's voice answered. 'I'm a Customs examining officer, and I want to search the launch,' Hazell shouted, and then disappeared down into the little saloon amidships, and Racksole heard no more. It seemed to the millionaire that Hazell had been gone hours, but at length he returned.

'Can't find anything,' he said, as he jumped into the boat, and then privately to Racksole: 'There's a woman on board. Looks as if she might coincide with your description of Miss Spencer. Steam's up, but there's no engineer. I asked where the engineer was, and she inquired what business that was of mine, and requested me to get through with my own business and clear off. Seems rather a smart sort. I poked my nose into everything, but I saw no sign of any one else. Perhaps we'd better pull away and lie near for a bit, just to see if anything queer occurs.'

'You're quite sure he isn't on board?' Racksole asked.

'Quite,' said Hazell positively: 'I know how to search a vessel. See this,' and he handed to Racksole a sort of steel skewer, about two feet long, with a wooden handle. 'That,' he said, 'is one of the Customs' aids to searching.'

'I suppose it wouldn't do to go on board and carry off the lady?' Racksole suggested doubtfully.

'Well,' Hazell began, with equal doubtfulness, 'as for that – '

'Where's 'e orf?' It was the man in the bows who interrupted Hazell. Following the direction of the man's finger, both Hazell and Racksole saw with more or less distinctness a dinghy slip away from the forefoot of the Norwegian vessel and disappear downstream into the mist.

'It's Jules, I'll swear,' cried Racksole. 'After him, men. Ten pounds apiece if we overtake him!'

'Lay down to it now, boys!' said Hazell, and the heavy Customs boat shot out in pursuit.

'This is going to be a lark,' Racksole remarked.

'Depends on what you call a lark,' said Hazell; 'it's not much of a lark tearing down midstream like this in a fog. You never know when you mayn't be in kingdom come with all these barges knocking around. I expect that chap hid in the dinghy when he first caught sight of us, and then slipped his painter as soon as I'd gone.'

The boat was moving at a rapid pace with the tide. Steering was a matter of luck and instinct more than anything else. Every now and then Hazell, who held the lines, was obliged to jerk the boat's head sharply round to avoid a barge or an anchored vessel. It seemed to Racksole that vessels were anchored all over the stream. He looked about him anxiously, but for a long time he could see nothing but mist and vague nautical forms. Then suddenly he said, quietly enough, 'We're on the right road; I can see him ahead. We're gaining on him.' In another minute the dinghy was plainly visible, not twenty yards away, and the sculler – sculling frantically now – was unmistakably Jules – Jules in a light tweed suit and a bowler hat.

'You were right,' Hazell said; 'this is a lark. I believe I'm getting quite excited. It's more exciting than playing the trombone in an orchestra. I'll run him down, eh? – and then we can drag the chap in from the water.'

Racksole nodded, but at that moment a barge, with her red sails set, stood out of the fog clean across the bows of the Customs boat, which narrowly escaped instant destruction. When they got clear, and the usual interchange of calm, nonchalant swearing was over, the dinghy was barely to be discerned in the mist, and the fat man was breathing in such a manner that his sighs might almost have been heard on the banks. Racksole wanted violently to do something, but there was nothing to do;

he could only sit supine by Hazell's side in the stern-sheets. Gradually they began again to overtake the dinghy, whose one-man crew was evidently tiring. As they came up, hand over fist, the dinghy's nose swerved aside, and the tiny craft passed down a water-lane between two anchored mineral barges, which lay black and deserted about fifty yards from the Surrey shore. 'To starboard,' said Racksole. 'No, man!' Hazell replied; 'we can't get through there. He's bound to come out below; it's only a feint. I'll keep our nose straight ahead.'

And they went on, the fat man pounding away, with a face which glistened even in the thick gloom. It was an empty dinghy which emerged from between the two barges and went drifting and revolving down towards Greenwich.

The fat man gasped a word to his comrade, and the Customs boat stopped dead.

' 'E's all right,' said the man in the bows. 'If it's 'im you want, 'e's on one o' them barges, so you've only got to step on and take 'im orf.'

'That's all,' said a voice out of the depths of the nearest barge, and it was the voice of Jules, otherwise known as Mr Tom Jackson.

' 'Ear 'im?' said the fat man smiling. ' 'E's a good 'un, 'e is. But if I was you, Mr Hazell, or you, sir, I shouldn't step on to that barge so quick as all that.'

They backed the boat under the stern of the nearest barge and gazed upwards.

'It's all right,' said Racksole to Hazell; 'I've got a revolver. How can I clamber up there?'

'Yes, I dare say you've got a revolver all right,' Hazell replied sharply. 'But you mustn't use it. There mustn't be any noise. We should have the river police down on us in a twinkling if there was a revolver shot, and it would be the ruin of me. If an inquiry was held the Commissioners wouldn't take any official notice of the fact that my superior officer had put me on to this job, and I should be requested to leave the service.'

'Have no fear on that score,' said Racksole. 'I shall, of course, take all responsibility.'

'It wouldn't matter how much responsibility you took,' Hazell retorted; 'you wouldn't put me back into the service, and my career would be at an end.'

'But there are other careers,' said Racksole, who was really anxious to lame his ex-waiter by means of a judiciously–aimed bullet. 'There are other careers.'

'The Customs is my career,' said Hazell, 'so let's have no shooting. We'll wait about a bit; he can't escape. You can have my skewer if you like' – and he gave Racksole his searching instrument. 'And you can do what you please, provided you do it neatly and don't make a row over it.'

For a few moments the four men were passive in the boat, surrounded by swirling mist, with black water beneath them, and towering above them a half-loaded barge with a desperate and resourceful man on board. Suddenly the mist parted and shrivelled away in patches, as though before the breath of some monster. The sky was visible; it was a clear sky, and the moon was shining. The transformation was just one of those meteorological quick-changes which happen most frequently on a great river.

'That's a sight better,' said the fat man. At the same moment a head appeared over the edge of the barge. It was Jules' face – dark, sinister and leering.

'Is it Mr Racksole in that boat?' he inquired calmly; 'because if so, let Mr Racksole step up. Mr Racksole has caught me, and he can have me for the asking. Here I am.' He stood up to his full height on the barge, tall against the night sky, and all the occupants of the boat could see that he held firmly clasped in his right hand a short dagger. 'Now, Mr Racksole, you've been after me for a long time,' he continued; 'here I am. Why don't you step up? If you haven't got the pluck yourself, persuade someone else to step up in your place . . . the same fair treatment will be accorded to all.' And Jules laughed a low, penetrating laugh.

He was in the midst of this laugh when he lurched suddenly forward.

'What'r' you doing of aboard my barge? Off you goes!' It was a boy's small shrill voice that sounded in the night. A ragged boy's small form had appeared silently behind Jules, and two small arms with a vicious shove precipitated him into the water. He fell with a fine gurgling splash. It was at once obvious that swimming was not among Jules' accomplishments. He floundered wildly and sank. When he reappeared he was dragged into the Customs boat. Rope was produced, and in a minute or two the man lay ignominiously bound in the bottom of the boat. With the aid of a mudlark – a mere barge boy, who probably had no more right on the barge than Jules himself – Racksole had won his game. For the first time for several weeks the millionaire experienced a sensation of equanimity and satisfaction. He leaned over the prostrate form of Jules, Hazell's professional skewer in his hand.

'What are you going to do with him now?' asked Hazel.

'We'll row up to the landing steps in front of the Grand Babylon. He shall be well lodged at my hotel, I promise him.'

Jules spoke no word.

Before Racksole parted company with the Customs man that night Jules had been safely transported into the Grand Babylon Hotel and the two watermen had received their £10 apiece.

'You will sleep here?' said the millionaire to Mr George Hazell. 'It is late.'

'With pleasure,' said Hazell. The next morning he found a sumptuous breakfast awaiting him, and in his table-napkin was a Bank of England note for a hundred pounds. But, though he did not hear of them till much later, many things had happened before Hazell consumed that sumptuous breakfast.

## Chapter Twenty-Seven

# THE CONFESSION OF MR TOM JACKSON

IT happened that the small bedroom occupied by Jules during the years he was head-waiter at the Grand Babylon had remained empty since his sudden dismissal by Theodore Racksole. No other head-waiter had been formally appointed in his place; and, indeed, the absence of one man – even the unique Jules – could scarcely have been noticed in the enormous staff of a place like the Grand Babylon. The functions of a head-waiter are generally more ornamental, spectacular, and morally impressive than useful, and it was so at the great hotel on the Embankment. Racksole accordingly had the excellent idea of transporting his prisoner, with as much secrecy as possible, to this empty bedroom. There proved to be no difficulty in doing so; Jules showed himself perfectly amenable to a show of superior force. Racksole took upstairs with him an old commissionaire who had been attached to the outdoor service of the hotel for many years – a grey-haired man, wiry as a terrier and strong as a mastiff. Entering the bedroom with Jules, whose hands were bound, he told the commissionaire to remain outside the door. Jules' bedroom was quite an ordinary apartment, though perhaps slightly superior to the usual accommodation provided for servants in the caravanserais of the West End. It was about fourteen by twelve. It was furnished with a bedstead, a small wardrobe, a small washstand and dressing-table, and two chairs. There were two hooks behind the door, a strip of carpet by the bed, and some cheap ornaments on the iron mantelpiece. There was also one electric light. The window was a little square one, high up from the floor, and it looked on the inner quadrangle. The room was on the top storey – the eighth – and from it you had a view sheer to the ground. Twenty feet below ran a narrow cornice about a foot wide; three feet or so above the window another and wider cornice jutted out, and above that was the high steep roof of the hotel, though you could not see it from the window. As Racksole examined the window and the outlook, he said to himself that Jules could not escape by that exit, at any rate. He gave a glance up the chimney, and saw that the flue was far too small to admit a man's body.

Then he called in the commissionaire, and together they bound Jules firmly to the bedstead, allowing him, however, to lie down. All the while the captive never opened his mouth – merely smiled a smile of disdain. Finally Racksole removed the ornaments, the carpet, the chairs and the hooks, and wrenched away the switch of the electric light. Then he and the commissionaire left the room, and Racksole locked the door on the outside and put the key in his pocket.

'You will keep watch here,' he said to the commissionaire, 'through the night. You can sit on this chair. Don't go to sleep. If you hear the slightest noise in the room blow your cab-whistle; I will arrange to answer the signal. If there is no noise do nothing whatever. I don't want this talked about, you understand. I shall trust you; you can trust me.'

'But the servants will see me here when they get up tomorrow,' said the commissionaire, with a faint smile, 'and they will be pretty certain to ask what I'm doing of up here. What shall I say to 'em?'

'You've been a soldier, haven't you?' asked Racksole.

'I've seen three campaigns, sir,' was the reply, and, with a gesture of pardonable pride, the grey-haired fellow pointed to the medals on his breast.

'Well, supposing you were on sentry duty and some meddle-some person in camp asked you what you were doing – what should you say?'

'I should tell him to clear off or take the consequences, and pretty quick too.'

'Do that to-morrow morning, then, if necessary,' said Racksole, and departed.

It was then about one o'clock a.m. The millionaire retired to bed – not his own bed, but a bed on the seventh storey. He did not, however, sleep very long. Shortly after dawn he was wide awake, and thinking busily about Jules. He was, indeed, very curious to know Jules' story, and he determined, if the thing could be done at all, by persuasion or otherwise, to extract it from him. With a man of Theodore Racksole's temperament there is no time like the present, and at six o'clock, as the bright morning sun brought gaiety into the window, he dressed and went upstairs again to the eighth storey. The commissionaire sat stolid, but alert on his chair, and, at the sight of his master, rose and saluted.

'Anything happened?' Racksole asked.

'Nothing, sir.'

'Servants say anything?'

'Only a dozen or so of 'em are up yet, sir. One of 'em asked what I was playing at, and so I told her I was looking after a bull bitch and a litter of pups that you was very particular about, sir.'

'Good,' said Racksole, as he unlocked the door and entered the room. All was exactly as he had left it, except that Jules who had been lying on his back, had somehow turned over and was now lying on his face. He gazed silently, scowling at the millionaire. Racksole greeted him and ostentatiously took a revolver from his hip-pocket and laid it on the dressing-table. Then he seated himself on the dressing-table by the side of the revolver, his legs dangling an inch or two above the floor.

'I want to have a talk to you, Jackson,' he began.

'You can talk to me as much as you like,' said Jules. 'I shan't interfere, you may bet on that.'

'I should like you to answer some questions.'

'That's different,' said Jules. 'I'm not going to answer any questions while I'm tied up like this. You may bet on that, too.'

'It will pay you to be reasonable,' said Racksole.

'I'm not going to answer any questions while I'm tied up.'

'I'll unfasten your legs, if you like,' Racksole suggested politely, 'then you can sit up. It's no use you pretending you've been uncomfortable, because I know you haven't. I calculate you've been treated very handsomely, my son. There you are!' and he loosened the lower extremities of his prisoner from their bonds.

'Now I repeat you may as well be reasonable. You may as well admit that you've been fairly beaten in the game and act accordingly. I was determined to beat you, by myself, without the police, and I've done it.'

'You've done yourself,' retorted Jules. 'You've gone against the law. If you'd had any sense you wouldn't have meddled; you'd have left everything to the police. They'd have muddled about for a year or two, and then done nothing. Who's going to tell the police now? Are you? Are you going to give me up to 'em, and say, "Here, I've caught him for you". If you do they'll ask you to explain several things, and then you'll look foolish. One crime doesn't excuse another, and you'll find that out.'

With unerring insight, Jules had perceived exactly the difficulty of Racksole's position, and it was certainly a difficulty which Racksole did not attempt to minimize to himself. He knew well that it would have to be faced. He did not, however, allow Jules to guess his thoughts.

'Meanwhile,' he said calmly to the other, 'you're here and my prisoner. You've committed a variegated assortment of crimes, and among them is murder. You are due to be hung. You know that. There is no reason why I should call in the police at all. It will be perfectly easy for me to finish you off, as you deserve, myself. I shall only be carrying out justice, and robbing the hangman of his fee. Precisely as I brought you into the hotel, I can take you out again. A few days ago you borrowed or stole a steam yacht at Ostend. What you have done with it I don't know, nor do I care. But I strongly suspect that my daughter had a narrow escape of being murdered on your steam yacht. Now I have a steam yacht of my own. Suppose I use it as you used yours! Suppose I smuggle you on to it, steam out to sea, and then ask you to step off it into the ocean one night. Such things have been done. Such things will be done again. If I acted so, I should at least, have the satisfaction of knowing that I had relieved society from the incubus of a scoundrel.'

'But you won't,' Jules murmured.

'No,' said Racksole steadily, 'I won't – if you behave yourself this morning. But I swear to you that if you don't I will never rest till you are dead, police or no police. You don't know Theodore Racksole.'

'I believe you mean it,' Jules exclaimed, with an air of surprised interest, as though he had discovered something of importance.

'I believe I do,' Racksole resumed. 'Now listen. At the best, you will be given up to the police. At the worst, I shall deal with you myself. With the police you may have a chance – you may get off with twenty years' penal servitude, because, though it is absolutely certain that you murdered Reginald Dimmock, it would be a little difficult to prove the case against you. But with me you would have no chance whatever. I have a few questions to put to you, and it will depend on how you answer them whether I give you up to the police or take the law into my own hands. And let me tell you that the latter course would be much simpler for me. And I would take it, too, did I not feel that you were a very clever and exceptional man; did I not have a sort of sneaking admiration for your detestable skill and ingenuity.'

'You think, then, that I am clever?' said Jules. 'You are right. I am. I should have been much too clever for you if luck had not been against me. You owe your victory, not to skill, but to luck.'

'That is what the vanquished always say. Waterloo was a bit of pure luck for the English, no doubt, but it was Waterloo all the same.'

Jules yawned elaborately. 'What do you want to know?' he inquired, with politeness.

'First and foremost, I want to know the names of your accomplices inside this hotel.'

'I have no more,' said Jules. 'Rocco was the last.'

'Don't begin by lying to me. If you had no accomplice, how did you contrive that one particular bottle of Romanée-Conti should be served to his Highness Prince Eugen?'

'Then you discovered that in time, did you?' said Jules. 'I was afraid so. Let me explain that that needed no accomplice. The bottle was topmost in the bin, and naturally it would be taken. Moreover, I left it sticking out a little further than the rest.'

'You did not arrange, then, that Hubbard should be taken ill the night before last?'

'I had no idea,' said Jules, 'that the excellent Hubbard was not enjoying his accustomed health.'

'Tell me,' said Racksole, 'who or what is the origin of your vendetta against the life of Prince Eugen?'

'I had no vendetta against the life of Prince Eugen,' said Jules, 'at least, not to begin with. I merely undertook, for a consideration, to see that Prince Eugen did not have an interview with a certain Mr Sampson Levi in London before a certain date, that was all. It seemed simple enough. I had been engaged in far more complicated transactions before. I was convinced that I could manage it, with the help of Rocco and Em – and Miss Spencer.'

'Is that woman your wife?'

'She would like to be,' he sneered. 'Please don't interrupt. I had completed my arrangements, when you so inconsiderately bought the hotel. I don't mind admitting now that from the very moment when you came across me that night in the corridor I was secretly afraid of you, though I scarcely admitted the fact even to myself then. I thought it safer to shift the scene of our operations to Ostend. I had meant to deal with Prince Eugen in this hotel, but I decided, then, to intercept him on the Continent, and I despatched Miss Spencer with some instructions. Troubles never come singly, and it happened that just then that fool Dimmock, who had been in the swim with us, chose to prove refractory. The slightest hitch would have upset everything, and I was obliged to – to clear him off the scene. He wanted to back out – he had a bad attack of conscience, and violent measures were essential. I regret his untimely decease, but he brought it on himself. Well, everything was going serenely when you and your brilliant daughter, apparently determined to meddle, turned up again among us at Ostend. Only twenty-four hours, however, had to elapse before the date which had been mentioned to me by my employers. I kept poor little Eugen for the allotted time, and then you managed to get hold of him. I do not deny that you scored there, though, according to my original instructions, you scored too late. The time had passed, and so, so far as I knew, it didn't matter a pin whether Prince Eugen saw Mr Sampson Levi or not. But my employers were still uneasy. They were uneasy even after little Eugen had lain ill in Ostend for several weeks. It appears that they feared that even at that date an interview between Prince Eugen and Mr Sampson Levi might work harm to them. So they applied to me again. This time they wanted Prince Eugen to be – er – finished off entirely. They offered high terms.'

'What terms?'

'I had received fifty thousand pounds for the first job, of which Rocco had half. Rocco was also to be made a member of a certain famous European order, if things went right. That was what he coveted far more than the money – the vain fellow! For the second job I was offered a hundred thousand. A tolerably large sum. I regret that I have not been able to earn it.'

'Do you mean to tell me,' asked Racksole, horror-struck by this calm confession, in spite of his previous knowledge, 'that you were offered a hundred thousand pounds to poison Prince Eugen?'

'You put it rather crudely,' said Jules in reply. 'I prefer to say that I was offered a hundred thousand pounds if Prince Eugen should die within a reasonable time.'

'And who were your damnable employers?'

'That, honestly, I do not know.'

'You know, I suppose, who paid you the first fifty thousand pounds, and who promised you the hundred thousand.'

'Well,' said Jules, 'I know vaguely. I know that he came via Vienna from – er – Bosnia. My impression was that the affair had some bearing, direct or indirect, on the projected marriage of the King of Bosnia. He is a young monarch, scarcely out of political leading-strings, as it were, and doubtless his Ministers thought that they had better arrange his marriage for him. They tried last year, and failed because the Princess whom they had in mind had cast her sparkling eyes on another Prince. That Prince happened to be Prince Eugen of Posen. The Ministers of the King of Bosnia knew exactly the circumstances of Prince Eugen. They knew that he could not marry without liquidating his debts, and they knew that he could only liquidate his debts through this Jew, Sampson Levi. Unfortunately for me, they ultimately wanted to make too sure of Prince Eugen. They were afraid he might after all arrange his marriage without the aid of Mr Sampson Levi, and so – well, you know the rest. . . . It is a pity that the poor little innocent King of Bosnia can't have the Princess of his Ministers' choice.'

'Then you think that the King himself had no part in this abominable crime?'

'I think decidedly not.'

'I am glad of that,' said Racksole simply. 'And now, the name of your immediate employer.'

'He was merely an agent. He called himself Sleszak – S-l-e-s-z-a-k. But I imagine that that wasn't his real name. I don't know his real name. An old man, he often used to be found at the Hôtel Ritz, Paris.'

'Mr Sleszak and I will meet,' said Racksole.

'Not in this world,' said Jules quickly. 'He is dead. I heard only last night – just before our little tussle.'

There was a silence.

'It is well,' said Racksole at length. 'Prince Eugen lives, despite all plots. After all, justice is done.'

'Mr Racksole is here, but he can see no one, Miss.' The words came from behind the door, and the voice was the commissionaire's. Racksole started up, and went towards the door.

'Nonsense,' was the curt reply, in feminine tones. 'Move aside instantly.'

The door opened, and Nella entered. There were tears in her eyes.

'Oh! Dad,' she exclaimed, 'I've only just heard you were in the hotel. We looked for you everywhere. Come at once, Prince Eugen is dying – ' Then she saw the man sitting on the bed, and stopped.

Later, when Jules was alone again, he remarked to himself, 'I may get that hundred thousand.'

## Chapter Twenty-Eight

# THE STATE BEDROOM ONCE MORE

WHEN, immediately after the episode of the bottle of Romanée-Conti in the State dining-room, Prince Aribert and old Hans found that Prince Eugen had sunk in an unconscious heap over his chair, both the former thought, at the first instant, that Eugen must have already tasted the poisoned wine. But a moment's reflection showed that this was not possible. If the Hereditary Prince of Posen was dying or dead, his condition was due to some other agency than the Romanée-Conti. Aribert bent over him, and a powerful odour from the man's lips at once disclosed the cause of the disaster: it was the odour of laudanum. Indeed, the smell of that sinister drug seemed now to float heavily over the whole table. Across Aribert's mind there flashed then the true explanation. Prince Eugen, taking advantage of Aribert's attention being momentarily diverted, and yielding to a sudden impulse of despair, had decided to poison himself, and had carried out his intention on the spot. The laudanum must have been already in his pocket, and this fact went to prove that the unfortunate Prince had previously contemplated such a proceeding, even after his definite promise. Aribert remembered now with painful vividness his nephew's words: 'I withdraw my promise. Observe that – I withdraw it.' It must have been instantly after the utterance of that formal withdrawal that Eugen attempted to destroy himself.

'It's laudanum, Hans,' Aribert exclaimed, rather helplessly.

'Surely his Highness has not taken poison?' said Hans. 'It is impossible!'

'I fear it is only too possible,' said the other. 'It's laudanum. What are we to do? Quick, man!'

'His Highness must be roused, Prince. He must have an emetic. We had better carry him to the bedroom.'

They did, and laid him on the great bed; and then Aribert mixed an emetic of mustard and water, and administered it, but without any effect. The sufferer lay motionless, with every muscle relaxed. His skin was ice-cold to the touch, and the eyelids, half-drawn, showed that the pupils were painfully contracted.

'Go out, and send for a doctor, Hans. Say that Prince Eugen has been suddenly taken ill, but that it isn't serious. The truth must never be known.'

'He must be roused, sire,' Hans said again, as he hurried from the room.

Aribert lifted his nephew from the bed, shook him, pinched him, flicked him cruelly, shouted at him, dragged him about, but to no avail. At length he desisted, from mere physical fatigue, and laid the Prince back again on the bed. Every minute that elapsed seemed an hour. Alone with the unconscious organism in the silence of the great stately chamber, under the cold yellow glare of the electric lights, Aribert became a prey to the most despairing thoughts. The tragedy of his nephew's career forced itself upon him, and it occurred to him that an early and shameful death had all along been inevitable for this good-natured, weak-purposed, unhappy child of a historic throne. A little good fortune, and his character, so evenly balanced between right and wrong, might have followed the proper path, and Eugen might have figured at any rate with dignity on the European stage. But now it appeared that all was over, the last stroke played. And in this disaster Aribert saw the ruin of his own hopes. For Aribert would have to occupy his nephew's throne, and he felt instinctively that nature had not cut him out for a throne. By a natural impulse he inwardly rebelled against the prospect of monarchy. Monarchy meant so much for which he knew himself to be entirely unfitted. It meant a political marriage, which means a forced marriage, a union against inclination. And then what of Nella – Nella!

Hans returned. 'I have sent for the nearest doctor, and also for a specialist,' he said.

'Good,' said Aribert. 'I hope they will hurry.' Then he sat down and wrote a card. 'Take this yourself to Miss Racksole. If she is out of the hotel, ascertain where she is and follow her. Understand, it is of the first importance.'

Hans bowed, and departed for the second time, and Aribert was alone again. He gazed at Eugen, and made another frantic attempt to rouse him from the deadly stupor, but it was useless. He walked away to the window: through the opened casement he could hear the tinkle of passing hansoms on the Embankment below, whistles of door-keepers, and the hoot of steam tugs on the river. The world went on as usual, it appeared. It was an absurd world. He desired nothing better than to abandon his princely title, and live as a plain man, the husband of the finest woman on earth. . . . But now! . . . Pah! How selfish he was, to be thinking of himself when Eugen lay dying. Yet – Nella!

The door opened, and a man entered, who was obviously the doctor. A few curt questions, and he had grasped the essentials of the case. 'Oblige me by ringing the bell, Prince. I shall want some hot water, and an able-bodied man and a nurse.'

'Who wants a nurse?' said a voice, and Nella came quietly in. 'I am a nurse,' she added to the doctor, 'and at your orders.'

The next two hours were a struggle between life and death. The first doctor, a specialist who followed him, Nella, Prince Aribert, and old Hans formed, as it were, a league to save the dying man. None else in the hotel knew the real seriousness of the case. When a Prince falls ill, and especially by his own act, the precise truth is not issued broadcast to the universe. According to official intelligence, a Prince is never seriously ill until he is dead. Such is statecraft.

The worst feature of Prince Eugen's case was that emetics proved futile. Neither of the doctors could explain their failure, but it was only too apparent. The league was reduced to help-lessness. At last the great specialist from Manchester Square gave it out that there was no chance for Prince Eugen unless the natural vigour of his constitution should prove capable of throwing off the poison unaided by scientific assistance, as a drunkard can sleep off his potion. Everything had been tried, even to artificial respiration and the injection of hot coffee. Having emitted this pronouncement, the great specialist from Manchester Square left. It was one o'clock in the morning. By one of those strange and futile coincidences which sometimes startle us by their subtle significance, the specialist met Theodore Racksole and his captive as they were entering the hotel. Neither had the least suspicion of the other's business.

In the State bedroom the small group of watchers surrounded the bed. The slow minutes filed away in dreary procession. Another hour passed. Then the figure on the bed, hitherto so motionless, twitched and moved; the lips parted.

'There is hope,' said the doctor, and administered a stimulant which was handed to him by Nella.

In a quarter of an hour the patient had regained consciousness. For the ten thousandth time in the history of medicine a sound constitution had accomplished a miracle impossible to the accumulated medical skill of centuries.

In due course the doctor left, saying that Prince Eugen was 'on the high road to recovery,' and promising to come again within a few hours. Morning had dawned. Nella drew the great curtains, and let in a flood of sunlight. Old Hans, overcome by fatigue, dozed in a chair in a far corner of the room. The reaction had been too much for him. Nella and Prince Aribert looked at each other. They had not exchanged a word about themselves, yet each knew what the other had been thinking. They clasped hands with a perfect understanding. Their brief love-making had been of the silent kind, and it was silent now. No word was uttered. A shadow had passed from over them, but only their eyes expressed relief and joy.

'Aribert!' The faint call came from the bed. Aribert went to the bedside, while Nella remained near the window.

'What is it, Eugen?' he said. 'You are better now.'

'You think so?' murmured the other. 'I want you to forgive me for all this, Aribert. I must have caused you an intolerable trouble. I did it so clumsily; that is what annoys me. Laudanum was a feeble expedient; but I could think of nothing else, and I daren't ask anyone for advice. I was obliged to go out and buy the stuff for myself. It was all very awkward. But, thank goodness, it has not been ineffectual.'

'What do you mean, Eugen? You are better. In a day or so you will be perfectly recovered.'

'I am dying,' said Eugen quietly. 'Do not be deceived. I die because I wish to die. It is bound to be so. I know by the feel of my heart. In a few hours it will be over. The throne of Posen will be yours, Aribert. You will fill it more worthily than I have done. Don't let them know over there that I poisoned myself. Swear Hans to secrecy; swear the doctors to secrecy; and breathe no word yourself. I have been a fool, but I do not wish it to be known that I was also a coward. Perhaps it is not cowardice; perhaps it is courage, after all – courage to cut the knot. I could not have survived the disgrace of any revelations, Aribert, and revelations would have been sure to come. I have made a fool of myself, but I am ready to pay for it. We of Posen – we always pay – everything except our debts. Ah! those debts! Had it not been for those I could have faced her who was to have been my wife, to have shared my throne. I could have hidden my past, and begun again. With her help I really could have begun again. But Fate has been against me – always! always! By the way, what was that plot against me, Aribert? I forget, I forget.'

His eyes closed. There was a sudden noise. Old Hans had slipped from his chair to the floor. He picked himself up, dazed, and crept shamefacedly out of the room.

Aribert took his nephew's hand.

'Nonsense, Eugen! You are dreaming. You will be all right soon. Pull yourself together.'

'All because of a million,' the sick man moaned. 'One miserable million English pounds. The national debt of Posen is fifty millions, and I, the Prince of Posen, couldn't borrow one. If I could have got it, I might have held my head up again. Good-bye, Aribert. . . . Who is that girl?'

Aribert looked up. Nella was standing silent at the foot of the bed, her eyes moist. She came round to the bedside, and put her hand on the patient's heart. Scarcely could she feel its pulsation, and to Aribert her eyes expressed a sudden despair.

At that moment Hans re-entered the room and beckoned to her.

'I have heard that Herr Racksole has returned to the hotel,' he whispered, 'and that he has captured that man Jules, who they say is such a villain.'

Several times during the night Nella inquired for her father, but could gain no knowledge of his whereabouts. Now, at half-past six in the morning, a rumour had mysteriously spread among the servants of the hotel about the happenings of the night before. How it had originated no one could have determined, but it had originated.

'Where is my father?' Nella asked of Hans.

He shrugged his shoulders, and pointed upwards. 'Somewhere at the top, they say.'

Nella almost ran out of the room. Her interruption of the interview between Jules and Theodore Racksole has already been described. As she came downstairs with her father she said again, 'Prince Eugen is dying – but I think you can save him.'

'I?' exclaimed Theodore.

'Yes,' she repeated positively. 'I will tell you what I want you to do, and you must do it.'

## Chapter Twenty-Nine

## THEODORE IS CALLED TO THE RESCUE

As Nella passed downstairs from the top storey with her father – the lifts had not yet begun to work – she drew him into her own room, and closed the door.

'What's this all about?' he asked, somewhat mystified, and even alarmed by the extreme seriousness of her face.

'Dad,' the girl began, 'you are very rich, aren't you? very, very rich?' She smiled anxiously, timidly. He did not remember to have seen that expression on her face before. He wanted to make a facetious reply, but checked himself.

'Yes,' he said, 'I am. You ought to know that by this time.'

'How soon could you realize a million pounds?'

'A million – what?' he cried. Even he was staggered by her calm reference to this gigantic sum. 'What on earth are you driving at?'

'A million pounds, I said. That is to say, five million dollars. How soon could you realize as much as that?'

'Oh!' he answered, 'in about a month, if I went about it neatly enough. I could unload as much as that in a month without scaring Wall Street and other places. But it would want some arrangement.'

'Useless!' she exclaimed. 'Couldn't you do it quicker, if you really had to?'

'If I really had to, I could fix it in a week, but it would make things lively, and I should lose on the job.'

'Couldn't you,' she persisted, 'couldn't you go down this morning and raise a million, somehow, if it was a matter of life and death?'

He hesitated. 'Look here, Nella,' he said, 'what is it you've got up your sleeve?'

'Just answer my question, Dad, and try not to think that I'm a stark, staring lunatic.'

'I rather expect I could get a million this morning, even in

London. But it would cost pretty dear. It might cost me fifty thousand pounds, and there would be the dickens of an upset in New York – a sort of grand universal slump in my holdings.'

'Why should New York know anything about it?'

'Why should New York know anything about it!' he repeated. 'My girl, when anyone borrows a million sovereigns the whole world knows about it. Do you reckon that I can go up to the Governors of the Bank of England and say, "Look here, lend Theodore Racksole a million for a few weeks, and he'll give you an IOU and a covering note on stocks"?'

'But you could get it?' she asked again.

'If there's a million in London I guess I could handle it,' he replied.

'Well, Dad,' and she put her arms round his neck, 'you've just got to go out and fix it. See? It's for me. I've never asked you for anything really big before. But I do now. And I want it so badly.'

He stared at her. 'I award you the prize,' he said, at length. 'You deserve it for colossal and immense coolness. Now you can tell me the true inward meaning of all this rigmarole. What is it?'

'I want it for Prince Eugen,' she began, at first hesitatingly, with pauses. 'He's ruined unless he can get a million to pay off his debts. He's dreadfully in love with a Princess, and he can't marry her because of this. Her parents wouldn't allow it. He was to have got it from Sampson Levi, but he arrived too late – owing to Jules.'

'I know all about that – perhaps more than you do. But I don't see how it affects you or me.'

'The point is this, Dad,' Nella continued. 'He's tried to commit suicide – he's so hipped. Yes, real suicide. He took laudanum last night. It didn't kill him straight off – he's got over the first shock, but he's in a very weak state, and he means to die. And I truly believe he will die. Now, if you could let him have that million, Dad, you would save his life.'

Nella's item of news was a considerable and disconcerting surprise to Racksole, but he hid his feelings fairly well.

'I haven't the least desire to save his life, Nell. I don't over-much respect your Prince Eugen. I've done what I could for him – but only for the sake of seeing fair play, and because I object to conspiracies and secret murders. It's a different thing if he wants to kill himself. What I say is: Let him. Who is responsible for his being in debt to the tune of a million pounds? He's only got himself and his bad habits to thank for that. I suppose if he does happen to peg out, the throne of Posen will go to Prince Aribert. And a good thing, too! Aribert is worth twenty of his nephew.'

'That's just it, Dad,' she said, eagerly following up her chance. 'I want you to save Prince Eugen just because Aribert – Prince Aribert – doesn't wish to occupy the throne. He'd much prefer not to have it.'

'Much prefer not to have it! Don't talk nonsense. If he's honest with himself, he'll admit that he'll be jolly glad to have it. Thrones are in his blood, so to speak.'

'You are wrong, Father. And the reason is this: If Prince Aribert ascended the throne of Posen he would be compelled to marry a Princess.'

'Well! A Prince ought to marry a Princess.'

'But he doesn't want to. He wants to give up all his royal rights, and live as a subject. He wants to marry a woman who isn't a Princess.'

'Is she rich?'

'Her father is,' said the girl. 'Oh, Dad! can't you guess? He – he loves me.' Her head fell on Theodore's shoulder and she began to cry.

The millionaire whistled a very high note. 'Nell!' he said at length. 'And you? Do you sort of cling to him?'

'Dad,' she answered, 'you are stupid. Do you imagine I should worry myself like this if I didn't?' She smiled through her tears. She knew from her father's tone that she had accomplished a victory.

'It's a mighty queer arrangement,' Theodore remarked. 'But of course if you think it'll be of any use, you had better go down and tell your Prince Eugen that that million can be fixed up, if he really needs it. I expect there'll be decent security, or Sampson Levi wouldn't have mixed himself up in it.'

'Thanks, Dad. Don't come with me; I may manage better alone.'

She gave a formal little curtsey and disappeared. Racksole, who had the talent, so necessary to millionaires, of attending to several matters at once, the large with the small, went off to give orders about the breakfast and the remuneration of his assistant of the evening before, Mr George Hazell. He then sent an invitation to Mr Félix Babylon's room, asking that gentleman to take breakfast with him. After he had related to Babylon the history of Jules' capture, and had a long discussion with him upon several points of hotel management, and especially as to the guarding of wine-cellars, Racksole put on his hat, sallied forth into the Strand, hailed a hansom, and was driven to the City. The order and nature of his operations there were too complex and technical to be described here.

When Nella returned to the State bedroom both the doctor and the great specialist were again in attendance. The two physicians moved away from the bedside as she entered, and began to talk quietly together in the embrasure of the window.

'A curious case!' said the specialist.

'Yes. Of course, as you say, it's a neurotic temperament that's at the bottom of the trouble. When you've got that and a vigorous constitution working one against the other, the results are apt to be distinctly curious. Do you consider there is any hope, Sir Charles?'

'If I had seen him when he recovered consciousness I should have said there was hope. Frankly, when I left last night, or rather this morning, I didn't expect to see the Prince alive again – let alone conscious, and able to talk. According to all the rules of the game, he ought to get over the shock to the system with perfect ease and certainty. But I don't think he will. I don't think he wants to. And moreover, I think he is still under the influence of suicidal mania. If he had a razor he would cut his throat. You must keep his strength up. Inject, if necessary. I will come in this afternoon. I am due now at St James's Palace.' And the specialist hurried away, with an elaborate bow and a few hasty words of polite reassurances to Prince Aribert.

When he had gone Prince Aribert took the other doctor aside. 'Forget everything, doctor,' he said, 'except that I am one man and you are another, and tell me the truth. Shall you be able to save his Highness? Tell me the truth.'

'There is no truth,' was the doctor's reply. 'The future is not in our hands, Prince.'

'But you are hopeful? Yes or no.'

The doctor looked at Prince Aribert. 'No!' he said shortly. 'I am not. I am never hopeful when the patient is not on my side.'

'You mean – ?'

'I mean that his Royal Highness has no desire to live. You must have observed that.'

'Only too well,' said Aribert.

'And you are aware of the cause?'

Aribert nodded an affirmative.

'But cannot remove it?'

'No,' said Aribert. He felt a touch on his sleeve. It was Nella's finger. With a gesture she beckoned him towards the ante-room.

'If you choose,' she said, when they were alone, 'Prince Eugen can be saved. I have arranged it.'

'You have arranged it?' He bent over her, almost with an air of alarm.

'Go and tell him that the million pounds which is so necessary to his happiness will be forthcoming. Tell him that it will be forthcoming to-day, if that will be any satisfaction to him.'

'But what do you mean by this, Nella?'

'I mean what I say, Aribert,' and she sought his hand and took it in hers. 'Just what I say. If a million pounds will save Prince Eugen's life, it is at his disposal.'

'But how – how have you managed it? By what miracle?'

'My father,' she replied softly, 'will do anything that I ask him. Do not let us waste time. Go and tell Eugen it is arranged, that all will be well. Go!'

'But we cannot accept this – this enormous, this incredible favour. It is impossible.'

'Aribert,' she said quickly, 'remember you are not in Posen holding a Court reception. You are in England and you are talking to an American girl who has always been in the habit of having her own way.'

The Prince threw up his hands and went back in to the bedroom. The doctor was at a table writing out a prescription. Aribert approached the bedside, his heart beating furiously. Eugen greeted him with a faint, fatigued smile.

'Eugen,' he whispered, 'listen carefully to me. I have news. With the assistance of friends I have arranged to borrow that million for you. It is quite settled, and you may rely on it. But you must get better. Do you hear me?'

Eugen almost sat up in bed. 'Tell me I am not delirious,' he exclaimed.

'Of course you aren't,' Aribert replied. 'But you mustn't sit up. You must take care of yourself.'

'Who will lend the money?' Eugen asked in a feeble, happy whisper.

'Never mind. You shall hear later. Devote yourself now to getting better.'

The change in the patient's face was extraordinary. His mind seemed to have put on an entirely different aspect. The doctor was startled to hear him murmur a request for food. As for Aribert, he sat down, overcome by the turmoil of his own thoughts. Till that moment he felt that he had never appreciated the value and the marvellous power of mere money, of the lucre which philosophers pretend to despise and men sell their souls for. His heart almost burst in its admiration for that extraordinary Nella, who by mere personal force had raised two men out of the deepest slough of despair to the blissful heights of hope and happiness. 'These Anglo-Saxons,' he said to himself, 'what a race!'

By the afternoon Eugen was noticeably and distinctly better. The physicians, puzzled for the third time by the progress of the case, announced now that all danger was past. The tone of the announcement seemed to Aribert to imply that the fortunate issue was due wholly to unrivalled medical skill, but perhaps

Aribert was mistaken. Anyhow, he was in a most charitable mood, and prepared to forgive anything.

'Nella,' he said a little later, when they were by themselves again in the ante-chamber, 'what am I to say to you? How can I thank you? How can I thank your father?'

'You had better not thank my father,' she said. 'Dad will affect to regard the thing as a purely business transaction, as, of course, it is. As for me, you can – you can –'

'Well?'

'Kiss me,' she said. 'There! Are you sure you've formally proposed to me, *mon prince?*'

'Ah! Nell!' he exclaimed, putting his arms round her again. 'Be mine! That is all I want!'

'You'll find,' she said, 'that you'll want Dad's consent too!'

'Will he make difficulties? He could not, Nell – not with you!'

'Better ask him,' she said sweetly.

A moment later Racksole himself entered the room.

'Going on all right?' he enquired, pointing to the bedroom.

'Excellently,' the lovers answered together, and they both blushed.

'Ah!' said Racksole. 'Then, if that's so, and you can spare a minute, I've something to show you, Prince.'

*Chapter Thirty*

## CONCLUSION

'I've a great deal to tell you, Prince,' Racksole began, as soon as they were out of the room, 'and also, as I said, something to show you. Will you come to my room? We will talk there first. The whole hotel is humming with excitement.'

'With pleasure,' said Aribert.

'Glad his Highness Prince Eugen is recovering,' Racksole said, urged by considerations of politeness.

'Ah! As to that –' Aribert began.

'If you don't mind, we'll discuss that later, Prince,' Racksole interrupted him.

They were in the proprietor's private room.

'I want to tell you all about last night,' Racksole resumed, 'about my capture of Jules, and my examination of him this morning.' And he launched into a full acount of the whole thing, down to the least details. 'You see,' he concluded, 'that our suspicions as to Bosnia were tolerably correct. But as regards Bosnia, the more I think about it, the surer I feel that nothing can be done to bring their criminal politicians to justice.'

'And as to Jules, what do you propose to do?'

'Come this way,' said Racksole, and led Aribert to another room. A sofa in this room was covered with a linen cloth. Racksole lifted the cloth – he could never deny himself a dramatic moment – and disclosed the body of a dead man.

It was Jules, dead, but without a scratch or mark on him.

'I have sent for the police – not a street constable, but an official from Scotland Yard,' said Racksole.

'How did this happen?' Aribert asked, amazed and startled. 'I understood you to say that he was safely immured in the bedroom.'

'So he was,' Racksole replied. 'I went up there this afternoon, chiefly to take him some food. The commissionaire was on guard at the door. He had heard no noise, nothing unusual. Yet when

I entered the room Jules was gone. He had by some means or other loosened his fastenings; he had then managed to take the door off the wardrobe. He had moved the bed in front of the window, and by pushing the wardrobe door three parts out of the window and lodging the inside end of it under the rail at the head of the bed, he had provided himself with a sort of insecure platform outside the window. All this he did without making the least sound. He must then have got through the window, and stood on the little platform. With his fingers he would just be able to reach the outer edge of the wide cornice under the roof of the hotel. By main strength of arms he had swung himself on to this cornice, and so got on to the roof proper. He would then have the run of the whole roof. At the side of the building facing Salisbury Lane there is an iron fire-escape, which runs right down from the ridge of the roof into a little sunk yard level with the cellars. Jules must have thought that his escape was accomplished. But it unfortunately happened that one rung in the iron escape-ladder had rusted rotten through being badly painted. It gave way, and Jules, not expecting anything of the kind, fell to the ground. That was the end of all his cleverness and ingenuity.'

As Racksole ceased speaking he replaced the linen cloth with a gesture from which reverence was not wholly absent.

When the grave had closed over the dark and tempestuous career of Tom Jackson, once the pride of the Grand Babylon, there was little trouble for the people whose adventures we have described. Miss Spencer, that yellow-haired, faithful slave and attendant of a brilliant scoundrel, was never heard of again. Possibly to this day she survives, a mystery to her fellow-creatures, in the pension of some cheap foreign boarding-house. As for Rocco, he certainly was heard of again. Several years after the events set down, it came to the knowledge of Félix Babylon that the unrivalled Rocco had reached Buenos Aires, and by his culinary skill was there making the fortune of a new and splendid hotel. Babylon transmitted the information to Theodore Racksole, and Racksole might, had he chosen, have put the forces of the law in motion against him. But Racksole, seeing that everything pointed to the fact that Rocco was now pursuing his vocation honestly, decided to leave him alone. The one difficulty which Racksole experienced after the demise of Jules – and it was a difficulty which he had, of course, anticipated – was connected with the police. The police, very properly, wanted to know things. They desired to be informed what Racksole had been doing in the Dimmock affair, between his first visit to Ostend and his sending for them to take charge of Jules' dead body. And Racksole was by no means inclined to tell them everything. Beyond question he had transgressed the laws of England, and possibly also the laws of Belgium; and the moral excellence of his motives in doing so was, of course, in the eyes of legal justice, no excuse for such conduct. The inquest upon Jules aroused some bother; and about ninety-and-nine separate and distinct rumours. In the end, however, a compromise was arrived at. Racksole's first aim was to pacify the inspector whose clue, which by the way was a false one, he had so curtly declined to follow up. That done, the rest needed only tact and patience. He proved to the satisfaction of the authorities that he had acted in a perfectly honest spirit, though with a high hand, and that substantial justice had been done. Also, he subtly indicated that, if it came to the point, he should defy them to do their worst. Lastly, he was able, through the medium of the United States Ambassador, to bring certain soothing influences to bear upon the situation.

One afternoon, a fortnight after the recovery of the Hereditary Prince of Posen, Aribert, who was still staying at the Grand Babylon, expressed a wish to hold converse with the millionaire. Prince Eugen, accompanied by Hans and some Court officials whom he had sent for, had departed with immense *éclat*, armed with the comfortable million, to arrange formally for his betrothal. Touching the million, Eugen had given satisfactory personal security, and the money was to be paid off in fifteen years.

'You wish to talk to me, Prince,' said Racksole to Aribert, when they were seated together in the former's room.

'I wish to tell you,' replied Aribert, 'that it is my intention to renounce all my rights and titles as a Royal Prince of Posen, and to be known in future as Count Hartz – a rank to which I am entitled through my mother. Also that I have a private income of ten thousand pounds a year, and a château and a town house in Posen. I tell you this because I am here to ask the hand of your daughter in marriage. I love her, and I am vain enough to believe that she loves me. I have already asked her to be my wife, and she has consented. We await your approval.'

'You honour us, Prince,' said Racksole with a slight smile, 'and in more ways than one. May I ask your reason for renouncing your princely titles?'

'Simply because the idea of a morganatic marriage would be as repugnant to me as it would be to yourself and to Nella.'

'That is good.'

The Prince laughed.

'I suppose it has occurred to you that ten thousand pounds per annum, for a man in your position, is a somewhat small income. Nella is frightfully extravagant. I have known her to spend sixty thousand dollars in a single year, and have nothing to show for it at the end. Why! she would ruin you in twelve months.'

'Nella must reform her ways,' Aribert said.

'If she is content to do so,' Racksole went on, 'well and good! I consent.'

'In her name and my own, I thank you,' said Aribert gravely.

'And,' the millionaire continued, 'so that she may not have to reform too fiercely, I shall settle on her absolutely, with reversion to your children, if you have any, a lump sum of fifty million dollars, that is to say, ten million pounds, in sound, selected railway stock. I reckon that is about half my fortune. Nella and I have always shared equally.'

Aribert made no reply. The two men shook hands in silence, and then it happened that Nella entered the room.

That night, after dinner, Racksole and his friend Félix Babylon were walking together on the terrace of the Grand Babylon Hotel.

Félix had begun the conversation.

'I suppose, Racksole,' he had said, 'you aren't getting tired of the Grand Babylon?'

'Why do you ask?'

'Because I am getting tired of doing without it. A thousand times since I sold it to you I have wished I could undo the bargain. I can't bear idleness. Will you sell?'

'I might,' said Racksole, 'I might be induced to sell.'

'What will you take, my friend?' asked Félix.

'What I gave,' was the quick answer.

'Eh!' Félix exclaimed. 'I sell you my hotel with Jules, with Rocco, with Miss Spencer. You go and lose all those three inestimable servants, and then offer me the hotel without them at the same price! It is monstrous.' The little man laughed heartily at his own wit. 'Nevertheless,' he added, 'we will not quarrel about the price. I accept your terms.'

And so was brought to a close the complex chain of events which had begun when Theodore Racksole ordered a steak and a bottle of Bass at the table d'hôte of the Grand Babylon Hotel.

# MORE ABOUT PENGUINS, PELICANS
# AND PUFFINS

For further information about books available from Penguins please write to Dept EP, Penguin Books Ltd, Harmondsworth, Middlesex UB7 0DA.

*In the U.S.A.*: For a complete list of books available from Penguins in the United States write to Dept DG, Penguin Books, 299 Murray Hill Parkway, East Rutherford, New Jersey 07073.

*In Canada*: For a complete list of books available from Penguins in Canada write to Penguin Books Canada Ltd, 2801 John Street, Markham, Ontario L3R 1B4.

*In Australia*: For a complete list of books available from Penguins in Australia write to the Marketing Department, Penguin Books Australia Ltd, P.O. Box 257, Ringwood, Victoria 3134.

*In New Zealand*: For a complete list of books available from Penguins in New Zealand write to the Marketing Department, Penguin Books (N.Z.) Ltd, Private Bag, Takapuna, Auckland 9.

*In India*: For a complete list of books available from Penguins in India write to Penguin Overseas Ltd, 706 Eros Apartments, 56 Nehru Place, New Delhi 110019.

*Penguin Modern Classics*

# ARNOLD BENNETT

### CLAYHANGER

Arnold Bennett's careful evocation of a boy growing to manhood during the last quarter of the nineteenth century, with its superb portrait of an autocratic father, stands on a literary level with *The Old Wives' Tale*. Set, like its successful predecessor, in the Five Towns, *Clayhanger* was destined to be the first novel in a trilogy.

Of the book and its hero Walter Allen has written in *The English Novel* : 'He is one of the most attractive heroes in twentieth-century fiction.' Bennett, who believed inordinately in the 'interestingness' of ordinary things and ordinary people, was never more successful in revealing the 'interestingness' of an apparently ordinary man than in Edwin Clayhanger.

### THE GRIM SMILE OF THE FIVE TOWNS

In the short stories which make up *The Grim Smile of the Five Towns*, Arnold Bennett caught some of the manner of Maupassant, one of the French writers on whom he modelled his writing. The redolent tale of the coffin and the cheese, 'In a New Bottle', and 'The Silent Brothers' (who have not addressed one another for ten years) possess the true ring.

The pride, pretensions and provincial snobbery of the Potteries are handled by Arnold Bennett with amused tolerance. Most of his stories, like the four linked adventures of Vera Cheswardine, set the home life of middle-class manufacturers of earthenware and porcelain against a 'singular scenery of coaldust, potsherds, flame and steam'. But Bennett never ignores the less successful members of families in a region where 'clogs to clogs is only three generations'.

*Also Published in Penguins*

HILDA LESSWAYS
THESE TWAIN

# HENRY JAMES

### THE WINGS OF THE DOVE

Milly Theale, the 'dove' of the title, knows when she visits
Europe that she is shortly to die which lends urgency to her
eager search for happiness.

### WHAT MAISIE KNEW

'One of the most remarkable technical achievements in fiction.
We are shown corruption through the eyes of innocence that
will not be corrupted' – Walter Allen in *The English Novel*

### THE AWKWARD AGE

Thrust suddenly into the immoral circle gathered round her
mother, Nanda Brookenham finds herself in competition with
Mrs Brookenham for the affection of a man she admires.

### THE SPOILS OF POYNTON

Here both the characters and the setting are English. The
novel opens with some of the triviality of drawing-room
comedy and deepens into a perceptive study of good and evil.

### THE TURN OF THE SCREW AND OTHER STORIES

For James the whole world of Americans, Cockneys, upper-
class snobs, writers, dilettanti and intriguers allowed him to
indulge his greatest obsession: observation.

### THE AMBASSADORS

One of his last three great novels and the story of successive
'embassies' despatched from America to Paris to bring back
the scion of a wealthy manufacturing family.

*and*

### THE GOLDEN BOWL